# Pretty Mrs. Gaston,

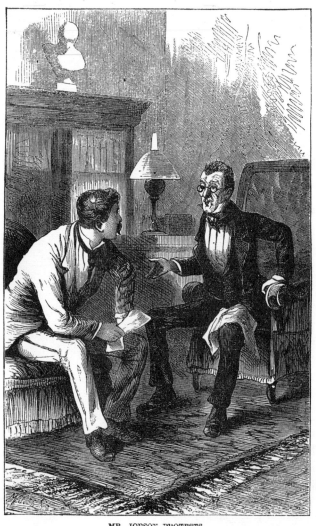

MR. JOBSON PROTESTS.

*(Frontispiece. See page 24.)*

# Pretty Mrs. Gaston,

## AND OTHER STORIES.

BY

JOHN ESTEN COOKE

ILLUSTRATED.

Short Story Index Reprint Series

**BOOKS FOR LIBRARIES PRESS**
FREEPORT, NEW YORK

First Published 1874
Reprinted 1969

PS.
1382
P7
1969

STANDARD BOOK NUMBER:
8369-3092-4

LIBRARY OF CONGRESS CATALOG CARD NUMBER:
74-94713

MANUFACTURED BY
HALLMARK LITHOGRAPHERS, INC.
IN THE U.S.A.

TO THE CRITICS

(*radiant in ribbons and roses*)

who sat under the evergreens and read this history,

"*PRETTY MRS. GASTON*"

is respectfully dedicated.

# CONTENTS.

—•◇•—

## PRETTY MRS. GASTON.

PAGE.

CHAPTER 1.—Love and Beggary... ..................................... 9

CHAPTER 2.—An Eccentric............................................ 13

CHAPTER 3.—Mr. and Mrs. Ormby............. .... .................... 20

CHAPTER 4.—Mr. Jobson Protests........................ . ............ 24

CHAPTER 5.—A Fox-Hunt and What Followed It......................... 27

CHAPTER 6.—The Crisis in A Young Man's Life.................... ...... 35

CHAPTER 7.—Mr. Jobson Consults with Dr. Harrington ........ ... ...... 41

CHAPTER 8.—A Nest of Doves..................... ..................... 45

CHAPTER 9.—Harrington Feels His Way ......... ...................... 54

CHAPTER 10.—George Cleave and His "Little Sister"....... ............. 59

CHAPTER 11.—The Result of Breaking One's Leg.......................... 68

CHAPTER 12.—Mr. Brown....... .......................... ............... 74

CHAPTER 13.—Which Brings Up the Narrative.........................,, 79

CHAPTER 14.—Mr. Daintrees Makes an Elaborate Toilette and Visits The
Hollies...................... ................................ 83

CHAPTER 15.—In the Swamp.... ................... ................ .. 88

CHAPTER 16.—Beside the Fire in the Swamp................ . ........... 91

CHAPTER 17.—The Physician in Spite of Himself.................... ...... 97

CHAPTER 18.—Harrington Announces His Intention to Leave Waterford...104

CHAPTER 19.—The Woes of Daintrees... ... ........ ..... .................109

CHAPTER 20.—How Harrington Declared that He Had Grown Ten Years
Younger... ...... .......................... ...... ....114

CHAPTER 21.—Allan Gartrell, Esq...........................................119

CHAPTER 22.—What Money-Trouble Brings Some Men To....... .........123

CHAPTER 23.—Mr. Gartrell and His Friend Mr. Brown.... ............ ....128

CHAPTER 24.—Jack Daintrees Entertains Some Friends......... ...........135

CHAPTER 25.—The Lawyer and the Lumber Agent ........................140

CHAPTER 26.—What Occurred at The Hollies on a Summer Night..........146

CHAPTER 27.—What Occurred at Bay View............... ............... 155

CHAPTER 28.—Mr. Brown Pronounces Sentence .. .........................161

CHAPTER 29.—Skirmishing at The Hollies......... .. ..................... 165

CHAPTER 30.—A General Engagement... ............... ... ............. 170

CHAPTER 31.—The Cypress Leaf—and the Sunshine.......................173

CHAPTER 32.—Mr. Brown Departs............................. .... ....183

CHAPTER 33.—Which Treats of the Mysterious Movements of Mr. Jobson...189

CHAPTER 34.—Waiting... .. .................... ..........................195

CHAPTER 35.—In Conclave ................. .............................198

**8** CONTENTS.

CHAPTER 36.—Mr. Brown Begins............................................202
CHAPTER 37.—Mr. Brown Continues...............  .......................205
CHAPTER 38.—Mr. Brown Concludes His Explanation ......................210
CHAPTER 39.—And the Curtain Falls upon the Comedy...................221

## ANNIE AT THE CORNER.

                                                                PAGE.
CHAPTER 1.—From a Window ..............   ...........................224
CHAPTER 2.—A School Girl.............   ....  ......  ...............232
CHAPTER 3.—Two Rivals .................................................238
CHAPTER 4.—Parting... .................   .........  .........  243
CHAPTER 5.—The Return...........   ...................  .........  247
CHAPTER 6.—A Woman.. ...............................................252
CHAPTER 7.—The Old House..............   ............  .........  258
CHAPTER 8.—At the Corner.......   ....................  .........  264
CHAPTER 9.—Conclusion.....................   .......................270

THE WEDDING AT DULUTH...........  ...................  ....273

# ILLUSTRATIONS.

Mr. Jobson Protests.... ...........................................*Frontispiece.*
"I Am a Beggar, Marian—a Beggar!"...........  ...........  ....... 11
Annie Bell Stopped and Turned Round—a Statue of Surprise........... .. 50
"Oh! Mr. Daintrees!"... ..........  ...............  ............... 91
"Good Morning, Sir!" Said Marian Rising.... ......................... 125
"His Health!".............................................  ...  ......131
"No Offence is Meant by Either Gentleman, I Am Sure."... ............137
Cries Were Heard One or Two Hundred Yards in Front of The Hollies......153
"Your Father, Miss ——?"......................................................158
The Prying Moon—What It Lingered upon Now ..........................176
The Individual Resembling a Bull-dog Had Listened .......................219

# PRETTY MRS. GASTON.

## CHAPTER I.

### LOVE AND BEGGARY.

O N an autumn afternoon, some years ago, a young girl
was standing before her mirror in an upper chamber of Bayview, an old house on the western bank of the
Chesapeake, making her toilet, evidently for a ride on
horseback.

She was about seventeen, had very large blue eyes full
of candor and sweetness, a delicate complexion, lips that
seemed always smiling, and a figure slender, supple, and
undulating.  You might have called her a beauty as she
stood before her mirror with her graceful arms raised,
and the small hands balancing the brown felt riding-hat
on her braids.

Having arranged her hat to her satisfaction, she took a
riding whip with an ivory handle and a pair of buff

gauntlets from the table, and went down stairs supporting her long skirt on her left arm.    In front of the portico a groom was holding two horses, one with a lady's
side-saddle.    At the door a young gentleman was waiting
for her.

The character of some human beings is read at a glance
without trouble.    The person who had come to ride out
with Miss Marian Ormby might have been described as
the "average young man."    He was well-shaped, well-
dressed, had a handsome, if not very intellectual face,
and *smiled naturally*, which is a distinct gift.

The greeting exchanged between the two young persons, and the manner in which the gentleman assisted
the lady to mount her horse, indicated relations of an
intimate character.    It required, in fact, but a very small
amount of perspicacity to understand that they were
engaged—since there was not only fondness, but confidence and tranquillity.

The countenance of the young gentleman had glowed
suddenly as the girl came out ; but as they rode down
the hill and into the fields beyond the great gate enclos-
ing the grounds this glow disappeared, and the face
became gloomy.

Thereupon followed this dialogue :

"What is the matter, George ?"

"The matter, Marian ?"

"You seem to be troubled, and are actually pale."

"Well, I *have* something to trouble me——"

He stopped, sighing.    The young lady looked at him
more attentively.

"I never saw you so dispirited. Is anything the matter? Tell me, George!"

"Marian—I am—it is hard to tell you."

"I AM A BEGGAR, MARIAN—A BEGGAR!"

"I have the right to share your troubles if you have any."

The gentle and caressing voice touched him. He said with a deeper sigh than before:

"Do you know whom you are engaged to?"

"I believe I do!"

It was pleasant to hear the little laugh and to see the faint blush.

"I supposed at least that the name of the gentleman was—Mr. George Cleave, of Cleaveland."

"Cleaveland is not mine."

"Not your own?"

"I am a beggar, Marian—a beggar! I only found it out last night, and have come to tell you all about it, and—and—ask you for some advice and—comfort, Marian."

Now as Mr. George Cleave was at this time aware of only a part of the circumstances leading to the critical change in his worldly affairs, we shall supply the omissions, and narrate fully if briefly what had happened, going back to a chamber in the great mansion of Cleaveland three or four years before the date of this history.

# CHAPTER II.

### AN ECCENTRIC.

HAMILTON CLEAVE, Esq., possessor of Cleaveland, one of the amplest estates in that part of Virginia, returned home one evening through a heavy rain after a ride over his property, and on the next day took to his bed and sent for his family physician.

The physician did not make his appearance until evening, when the disease—pneumonia—had made gigantic strides.

"Well, Doctor? What do you think?" said Mr. Cleave.

The doctor looked dispirited, and made an evasive reply. He remained all night, and in the evening of the next day Mr. Cleave asked again, this time in a much weaker voice:

"What do you think now, Doctor?"

"I regret to say that you are very ill, Mr. Cleave."

"I know that. I wish you to speak plainly. I am going to die, am I not?"

The doctor hesitated.

"Speak plainly."

"I am sorry to say, Mr. Cleave, that your condition is critical—very critical indeed."

"Is there a chance for my recovery?"

The doctor made no reply; whereupon Mr. Cleave moved his head feebly and said:

"I know what I wanted to know now. Oblige me by sending a servant to Mr. Marks, my legal adviser."

Having uttered these words with entire nonchalance, the sick man closed his eyes and seemed to be reflecting.

Mr. Marks promptly made his appearance, and the old planter requested him to take his seat at the table and write his will.

"I will state briefly my wishes in reference to the disposal of my property, Mr. Marks. There are three persons only who have any claims upon me—my nephew, George Cleave, who is at college; a second nephew, Allan Gartrell, now in Paris, I believe; and Annie Bell, the daughter of an old friend, adopted by me."

"Yes, Mr. Cleave."

"I wish the Cleaveland property here, with all the personal estate, to go to George Cleave, who has nothing, and my 'Free Hill' farm to go to Annie Bell, with all the personal effects, as in the first instance."

"And Mr. Gartrell, sir?"

"No part of my real estate. He is well provided for— his father left him an ample property. I give him, however, as a mark of my regard, the certificates of railway and other stock, which you will find in the drawer of that desk in the corner."

"Any further directions, Mr. Cleave?"

" None, sir."

" The Cleaveland property, real and personal, to your nephew, Mr. George Cleave; the Free Hill estate and personalty to Miss Annie Bell; the railway and other certificates of stock to Mr. Allan Gartrell?"

Mr. Cleave nodded and closed his eyes. Half an hour afterwards Mr. Marks said:

" I have finished. Shall I read the paper, Mr. Cleave?"

" If you please."

The lawyer read it slowly.

" Correct," was the sole comment of the sick man.

" I have left a blank for the name of your executor."

" I will add it later."

On the next day the will was executed, two friends who came to see Mr. Cleave officiating as witnesses. In the evening they were gone, and the doctor only was present.

" Doctor," said Mr. Cleave feebly, " where is Annie?"

" Down-stairs, sir."

" Poor thing! she will be alone now. And George—I wish George would come!"

" He has been sent for, Mr. Cleave, and will arrive, I hope, to-night."

" As soon as he comes, say I wish to see him, and—stop, Doctor; I have executed my will, but——"

The voice ceased for an instant.

" She will have no home," he went on in a faint, dreamy voice. " If I could only bring about——"

He stopped again.

" Doctor," he said in a moment, " you are a friend,

and have often visited me here. Have you observed
George and Annie ?"

"I have frequently seen them, Mr. Cleave."

"Do you think them fond of each other ?"

"I think I have observed that they were quite fond."

The dying man seemed much gratified by these words.

"If George would only come," he said; "all depends
on that now——"

He lay for an hour after this without moving or speaking; his eyes closed, his breathing faint and irregular.
Then he opened his eyes and said :

"I wish you—to tell me, Doctor—how long I have to
live ! It is important that you should speak plainly."

It was evident that the dying man had some fixed
design, and the physician knew that he would insist
upon a response.

"I regret to say, Mr. Cleave," he replied, "that you
are sinking steadily. Before midnight, I fear."

"That is enough. Do me the favor to go to the window, Doctor, and listen if you hear George coming.
The noise of the carriage wheels may be heard."

The physician went and listened. The wind was sobbing without, but no other sound disturbed the silence.

"I hear nothing, Mr. Cleave."

"Then no time is to be lost. Do me the kindness to
seat yourself, Doctor, and write from my dictation a
codicil to my will."

The old physician was accustomed to obey Mr. Cleave,
who always insisted on things. He sat down, drew a
sheet of paper to him, and dipped the pen in the ink.

What Mr. Cleave dictated in the clearest, briefest, but most definite manner was a codicil to his will to the effect that the estate of "Cleaveland," with all pertaining to it, should go to his nephew George Cleave only on condition that he should marry Annie Bell *before he was twenty-five years of age.* This condition failing, the estate was to go to Allan Gartrell—but the said George Cleave was meanwhile to have possession.

The physician listened with some astonishment, but mechanically wrote what the patient dictated.

"Read it, Doctor."

The codicil was read.

"Accurate.  Give me the paper and a pen."

He affixed his name, and had just done so, when his head fell, and he dropped the pen.

"Mr. Cleave!"

The paper escaped from the dying man's hand and fell to the floor.

The physician called loudly for the sick man's nurse, an old house-keeper, who ran at the call.  When she reached the chamber Mr. Cleave was dead.

An hour afterwards the physician set out to ride home, his mind so oppressed by the death of one whom he had greatly esteemed that he had entirely lost sight of the codicil to the will.  A singular event followed.  A heavy rain storm had arisen, accompanied by thunder and lightning—the aged doctor was exposed to it during his long ride, and an acute attack of fever followed, which resulted ten days afterwards in his death.  In his last hours when he was nearly speechless, he seemed desirous

of making some communication—probably to speak of
the codicil—but his broken words were not understood,
and he died without making any statement.

A fatality indeed seemed connected with this singular
document.   The aged house-keeper of Mr. Cleave had
proceeded after his death to "set the room to rights"
her eyes blinded by tears, and seeing on the floor what
appeared to be a piece of waste paper, had picked it up,
folded it neatly, and placed it in a book, which she had
afterwards consigned to the book-case in the library.   It
was thus effectually lost—to be discovered only three
years afterwards by George Cleave, who had arrived an
hour after his uncle's death.

He had been sitting in the library at twilight smoking
and his cigar had gone out.   Looking for a piece of
waste paper to relight it, he had seen what appeared to
be a book-mark in a volume in the book-case, drawn it
out, lit one corner of the paper in the fire, and was about
to apply his cigar to the flame when some writing on the
paper attracted his attention, and he extinguished it.
He then obtained a light, read the paper—he must
marry Annie Bell, then residing with a Mrs. Gaston in
the neighborhood, or surrender Cleaveland.

This was the discovery which George Cleave announced
to Miss Marian Ormby, to whom he was engaged to be
married, as they rode out together on this autumn evening.

It is unnecessary to repeat their conversation.   It was
gloomy enough.   Cleave lamented bitterly his idle and
luxurious life since taking possession of Cleaveland—he

might have established himself in his profession of the law—he had been criminally indolent—he could not drag down Marian, even if Mr. Ormby consented, and it was certain that he would never consent! So the youth went on, refusing comfort.

But the "weaker vessel" consoled the other. He had nothing? He was alone and poor? No, he had *herself*, and what did *she* care for wealth? She would live with him in a cabin! the brave girl said with flushed cheeks, and eyes glowing through tears. And her father would consent—George must tell him all—they could wait if necessary until he established himself in his profession, *she* would wait for *him* just as long as he wished, and all would be well—unless—unless——

The young lady laughed.

"Unless you would rather marry Miss Annie Bell!"

It is unnecessary to repeat the reply of George Cleave to these words, or describe his proceeding. A little gleam of joy broke through the gloom—they rode back— and Cleave returned to his own house to concoct a statement of affairs for the eyes of Ormby *père*.

Alas! two young and throbbing hearts, strong only in love and faith were matching themselves against that horny and ossified something passing for a heart beneath the ruffles of Mr. J. Ormby.

## CHAPTER III.

### MR. AND MRS. ORMBY.

TOWARD noon on the day after the ride, Mr. Ormby, a portly gentleman of about sixty, came out of his library at Bayview, took his gold-headed cane from its corner, put on his hat, and descending to the smooth gravel walk in front of the house, began walking slowly to and fro.

Mr. Ormby's walk was peculiar, as indeed was the whole carriage of his person. He held his chin aloft, with his gold-headed cane beneath his left arm, and seemed to take the surrounding landscape under his protection. From time to time he turned his head slowly from side to side, bestowed a glance of seignorial complacence upon the fertile fields before him, and cleared his throat in a grave and dignified manner, indicative of landed proprietorship and self-esteem. He might have been described indeed as overpowering the face of nature, as he overpowered his company.

Having walked slowly to and fro in front of the house for a quarter of an hour, Mr. Ormby paused, cleared his throat, and was about to reënter the mansion, when a servant rode up the hill and respectfully delivered a letter.

"Eh? Eh?" said Mr. Ormby. A note? And from my young friend at Cleaveland."

With dignified deliberation he opened the letter, placed upon his venerable nose a pair of gold spectacles, and began the perusal of the document. No sooner, however, had he read two or three lines, than he lost his air of composure, glared at the paper, and turning very red in the face, hastened—actually hastened—into the house.

In the hall he stopped, fixing his eyes again upon the paper. Then he crumpled it in his hand, and went hurriedly to announce its contents to Mrs. Ormby.

This lady was seated in her chamber—a mild and rather feeble looking personage in a black alpaca dress, a lace cap, spectacles, and apparently about the age of Mr. Ormby. She was slowly netting some article of worsted work, and raised her eyes, with an air of disquiet, as Mr. Ormby entered.

"Here's a pretty business, Mrs. Ormby! a pretty business!" exclaimed Mr. Ormby; "I am astounded, madam —fairly astounded!"

"Yes, my dear," said Mrs. Ormby with gentle acquiescence.

"You always say, 'Yes, my dear,' madam!" said Mr. Ormby, now very red in the face, "and never wait to hear what is said to you! As I have observed, madam, this is a pretty business! Here is a letter from young Cleave—he has found a new will of his uncle's—he is to marry Miss Bell, the young woman residing with her cousin, Mrs. Gaston, at The Hollies, or the fine estate of Cleaveland goes to Gartell, the other nephew!"

"Yes, my ——," began Mrs. Ormby, looking startled. Then she stopped, gazing in a feeble way at Mr. Ormby.

"The young man—I refer to Mr. George Cleave," said Mr. Ormby, walking about in an excited manner, "writes to inform me of the discovery of the new will— a codicil—he makes no concealment—acts honorably in the affair—and it is due to *him* that I should be equally candid, Mrs. Ormby!"

"Yes, my dear," said Mrs. Ormby, except that the "dear" was inaudible. She gazed at him in a vague and helpless way, not having the remotest idea of what Mr. Ormby meant by being "equally candid."

"I shall be plain I say, madam; and much as I regret it, inform young Cleave that his engagement with Marian can not—hem!—under the circumstances—hem!—continue!"

"Oh Mr. Ormby!"

It was the most original observation made for many months by the excellent lady.

"Eh! Eh!" exclaimed the now irate gentleman, "you object then! You oppose me! You wish your daughter to marry a beggar!"

Mrs. Ormby subsided meekly to netting.

"*Of course*, madam," continued Mr. Ormby with extreme dignity, "Miss Ormby, of Bayview, can not be expected to unite herself with a young person who has no estate and no means of marrying. It is only necessary to state the fact, madam—ahem! It is painful, extremely painful—but it is my duty—I owe it to my daughter!"

"Poor George!" muttered Mrs. Ormby.

"What's that, madam?"

"Yes, my dear."

Mr. Ormby raised his head with dignity.

"I am pleased to see that you agree with me, Mrs. Ormby! I shall therefore write to young Cleave the result of this conversation. His obvious course is to follow the wishes of his uncle, and pay his addresses at once to Miss Bell. I will therefore proceed to write, madam."

And Mr. Ormby, far more agitated than he appeared, left the room to go to his library, Mrs. Ormby subsiding feebly in her chair, the netting-needles resting on her lap.

# CHAPTER IV.

## MR.  JOBSON  PROTESTS.

GEORGE CLEAVE was engaged in conversation at
Cleaveland with Mr. Jobson, attorney-at-law from
the neighboring town of Waterford.

Mr. Jobson was a thin and wiry old gentleman, with
short hair, a piercing pair of eyes behind huge spectacles,
a reticent expression—and had the habit of looking at
the person to whom he was speaking out of the upper
portion of his eyes, above his glasses.  He wore a suit of
rusty black, and seemed to carry about with him the
odor of law-books bound in calf, and dusty papers tied
with pink tape, with which was mingled the perfume of
the old-fashioned Scotch snuff spilt upon his coat-sleeves.

Mr. Jobson had been engaged for fully half an hour
in a silent examination of the codicil to Mr. Hamilton
Cleave's will, and now quietly laid the document on the
table, helping himself thereafter to a large pinch of snuff
out of a black box.

"I understand you to ask my professional opinion of
this paper, Mr. Cleave, and whether it is valid and binding in law?"

" Yes, sir."

" It is of no force or effect whatever, and I hope you have taken no steps of any sort consequent upon its discovery."

" Of no force ?  Explain yourself, Mr. Jobson !"

" Look at it.   In whose handwriting is it ?"

" It seems to be dictated—that is to say, is not in my uncle's writing ; but the signature is his own."

" I do not know that, but grant so much.   His signature is the only one."

" The only one ?"

" There are no witnesses."

" Is that necessary ?"

" Absolutely necessary.   If written throughout by your uncle's hand the paper would be valid without witnesses. Written by the hand of another, witnesses signing in his presence and in the presence of each other, are indispensable."

George Cleave took up the paper, and scanned it thoughtfully.

" That is beyond all doubt my uncle's signature," he said.

" I think it more than probable."

" And he must have designed this paper to be binding, else he would not have signed it."

" Granted, if you choose."

" Then, Mr. Jobson, I consider myself bound as a gentleman not to contest it."

" Not contest it !" exclaimed Mr. Jobson.

" Certainly not, sir."

"Not contest a paper of no earthly validity! Surrender the finest property in the county under a paper like this, not worth the ink it was written with!"

Cleave shook his head.

"I know you are my friend, Mr. Jobson, but your advice is bad. You acknowledge that the only flaw in this paper is the omission of a legal formality; it is plain, nevertheless, that my uncle *intended* to execute the codicil—I have nothing to do with his motives, and I will carry out his intentions."

"Give up the property?"

"Yes, sir. I can not offer myself to Miss Bell, and I know she has not the least wish to marry *me*. The only thing, therefore, is to write to my cousin Allan Gartrell— I will give you the address of his banker in Liverpool. I wish you would do so, and say that I am ready to surrender this estate to him."

Mr. Jobson burst forth into exclamations and remonstrances, but the young man insisted.

"Well," said the old lawyer at length, "your father was my best friend, and here his son is about to ruin himself. Give me a few days to think of it—something may turn up—there ought to be a compromise at the very least, if there is to be no contest."

Mr. Jobson groaned.

"My young friend," he added with pathetic solemnity, "if business was conducted in the way *you* conduct it the world would not go on for a day!"

And with this last protest Mr. Jobson went away— groaning.

## CHAPTER V.

### A FOX-HUNT AND WHAT FOLLOWED IT.

A FEW miles from Bayview toward the interior, stood "The Lodge," the bachelor stronghold of one of the most popular gentlemen of the county. The name of this gentleman was Mr. John, or "Jack," Daintrees, and, perhaps, the adjective "bachelor" applied to his residence was a little inappropriate. Mr. Daintrees was a widower of some years' standing; but then he was childless, extremely jovial in his tastes, and led the life of a rollicking bachelor and fox-hunter, keeping open house at The Lodge, where everybody was welcome.

The Lodge was what is called a "hip-roofed" house, of moderate size, built of wood, overshadowed by tall elms, and extremely bright-looking and comfortable. It was perfectly plain at the first glance that no ladies lived at The Lodge, which had a free and careless bachelor-look about it; but Mr. Daintrees was an excellent manager, was well to do, and surrounded by every comfort; and his bachelor entertainments, thanks to accomplished servants, were the talk of the county.

The tastes of Mr. Daintrees were soon seen. About the lawn extending in front of the house ran twenty or thirty tawny fox-hounds, dragging their blocks, and hastening to caress their master whenever he appeared ; and the stables, which were kept in perfect order by an old gray-headed negro groom with an army of young Africans under him, boasted quite a number of thorough-bred horses, upon which Mr. Daintrees was accustomed to follow the hounds.

The interior of the mansion was old-fashioned and well appointed. The walls, covered with a light, gray paper, were hung round with hunting scenes and pictures of English race-horses in plain walnut frames. The fire-places were large, and for half the year roared with great hickory logs, making the apartments of The Lodge a pleasant sight to behold—especially the dining-room, when Mr. Daintrees assembled around his mahogany table, dark with age, and decorated with decanters, his bachelor friends. In the hall a spreading pair of deer's antlers did duty as a coat and hat rack ; and behind the front-door hung a hunting-horn, the spoil of some mighty ox, the small end carved to set well to the lips of the blower, and around the larger end a silver band, on which was carved, "John Daintrees, The Lodge."

Mr. Jack Daintrees was about forty, with rather a full figure, a ruddy and smiling face, a fine forehead, fine eyes, and dressed rather jauntily. He was the perfection of good-humor and hospitality, gay in his address, and universally popular with ladies of all ages. He did not affect youth, and, indeed, was accustomed to speak of himself as an old fellow who had done with the vanities of life; but in spite of these disclaimers he was welcomed everywhere by the youngest of the young ladies, who laughed delightedly at his gay jests, and with marked attention by those of more advanced age, with pretensions still—under favorable circumstances—to matrimony.

On the morning when we visit The Lodge, Mr. Jack Daintrees rose at daybreak, and descended to his breakfast-room dressed in full hunting-costume—short coat, top boots, and jockey cap; for on this day Mr. Daintrees proposed to follow the hounds in company with several of his friends who had spent the night with him. The breakfast-table was set, a cheerful fire blazing, and Dan, his old black groom, was waiting to report.

A rapid consultation took place on the subject of the horses, Dan went out and Mr. Daintrees proceeded to ring a huge bell, which brought down-stairs his half-dozen guests, fresh and full of ardor for the hunt.

Mr. Jack Daintrees had a jest for everybody, and mixed with an experienced hand a jorum of peach brandy and honey, which was passed around. Then a hearty breakfast was dispatched; the horses were led out; Mr. Daintrees blew a resounding blast upon his horn, swung around his shoulder by its green cord; and the gay party set out after the hounds toward a neighboring copse, where a gray fox had been seen on the preceding day.

Fifteen minutes afterwards the hounds were in full cry, and the chase had opened under the most favorable auspices.

Three hours passed. The fox, evidently old and gray, had taken straight across the country, and now the gay companions of the morning were dispersed. One of them had rolled in a ditch, the horses of nearly all the rest had given out or fallen behind, and only Mr. Jack Daintrees and one other had kept up. The personage in question was Dr. Ralph Harrington, a young physician, who had settled down a year or two before at Waterford, and who combined out-door amusements with his professional pursuits in the most harmonious manner.

Dr. Ralph Harrington impressed you at the first glance. He was about twenty-eight, tall, very erect, with a face full of intellect, a somewhat satirical expression of the lips, dark eyes, which looked calmly into your own, and carried himself generally with an air of lazy good-nature. A shrinking want of confidence in himself did not strike strangers as a very marked characteristic of Dr. Ralph Harrington; but he was popular, nevertheless; was justly regarded as an able physician, and had already secured an excellent practice.

During the fox-hunt, Dr. Harrington had kept up with the foremost, and now found himself far ahead of all but his friend Jack Daintrees. They were riding neck and neck. The fox had gone on in a straight course for nearly ten miles, had then doubled and came back by Cleaveland, and was passing between The Lodge and The Hollies, the home of a fair neighbor of Mr. Daintrees, when the hunters saw emerge from a woodland road a small sorrel ridden by a young lady. The gay little animal had evidently been inspired by the cry of the hounds, and was going at full speed now upon their track—a proceeding which seemed to afford intense delight to his mistress. She was a young girl of about eighteen, with a complexion all roses, red lips which seemed made for smiling, and dancing eyes across which some brown ringlets were driven by the rapid motion. Eyes, lips, ringlets, all were indicative of gayety and enjoyment.

In three bounds the small animal bore the young lady to the side of Mr. Daintrees, who cried:

"Miss Annie! Take care!"

"No, no, don't stop Brownie!" was the quick protest. "He is running away!"

"No, indeed, Mr. Daintrees! He is only—following the hounds!"

"A heroine!" cried Mr. Daintrees, "and I see you have command of him, Miss Annie. Let me introduce my friend, Dr. Harrington—Miss Bell!"

Dr. Harrington and Miss Bell exchanged a polite salutation with their heads while going at full gallop; and then, as if between sportsmen there was no time for ceremony, they went on at high speed as before. Dr. Harrington was evidently much impressed by his new acquaintance. It was very plain that Miss Annie Bell was an excellent rider, and she cleared two or three fences in a way which filled her companions with admiration. Unluckily her good fortune deserted her at the fourth obstacle. Her small steed descended into one of those ditches which are common in the tide-water region; did not recover himself, and Miss Annie Bell would inevitably have rolled beneath the animal had not Dr. Ralph Harrington, who cleared the obstacle at the same moment, passed his arm around her and saved her from falling.

Mr. Daintrees had shot ahead, and as this scene took place, his horn was heard sounding the death. A few minutes afterwards he galloped back, holding up the tail. Suddenly he stopped. He saw before him a graceful but unexpected tableau—Dr. Ralph Harrington standing by his horse, and supporting the young lady of the ringlets in his arms.

"My *dear* Miss Annie!" exclaimed Mr. Daintrees.

"Don't be uneasy! I'm not hurt in the least, sir!"

And the ringlets quickly receded from Dr. Ralph Harrington—their owner uttering a laugh.

"Well!" said Mr. Jack Daintrees. "Here's an adventure for you! A fox-hunt, a lady come to grief, and a rescue! But—oh! what will Mrs. Gaston say, my *dear* Miss Annie?"

"She shall not scold you, Mr. Daintrees, you have had nothing to do with it; and besides it is nothing, I have only sprained my ankle."

"Only sprained your ankle! that is too bad. What on earth are we to do?"

There was but one thing to do. The Lodge was seen across the field, not more than a quarter of a mile away, and to The Lodge the young lady was slowly conducted, her companions gallantly supporting her as she limped along, and leading their horses. It was quite encouraging to see what a jest she made of her accident, with what grace and agility she got over a fence which interposed,

and when she drew near the mansion of Mr. Daintrees
she exclaimed with a delighted laugh :

" I knew I should be at The Lodge some day.  What
a fearful bachelor den it is !"

" Well, walk into the parlor, Miss Annie," said Mr.
Daintrees.  "I am not a spider and you are not a fly,
and you will come out safe and sound.  Now to write to
Mrs. Gaston.  I am in deadly terror of her, but it must
be done."

" She is an awful person indeed !" said Miss Annie
Bell, subsiding into a chair.  And then Mr. Daintrees,
who owing to his preference for the saddle had no species
of carriage whatever, wrote and dispatched a note to
The Hollies, sending back the young lady's pony by the
bearer.

An hour afterwards a family carriage rolled quickly up
to the door of The Lodge, and a lady's voice exclaimed :

" Where is Annie ?"

" She is quite well, madam," said Mr. Daintrees hastening forth to receive his guest.  " A slight sprain only, a
mere nothing."

And Mr. Daintrees gallantly supported the lady as she
issued from her carriage.  Mrs. Gaston might have
aroused the gallantry of a less susceptible person than
Mr. Jack Daintrees.  She was a lady of about thirty-five,
with a plump and most graceful figure, blue eyes, brown
hair in braids, and a neck so round and white that the
bow of pink ribbon holding the delicate lace collar resembled a rose on a snow-drift.  There were red roses
too, in the pretty Mrs. Gaston's cheeks—for this lady

had an unconquerable habit of blushing—and a little shrinking, timid smile never left her.

In half an hour Mrs. Gaston had observed all the ceremonies peculiar to ladies upon such occasions; that is to say, she had clasped Annie in her arms, kissed her with animation, examined the sprained ankle, and scolded the victim mildly for her imprudence. Mrs. Gaston then gently rose, said with her shrinking smile that she must go, and with the assistance of the two gentlemen, Miss Annie Bell, limping and laughing, was conducted to the carriage.

"After all your den is not such a fearful place, Mr. Daintrees," said Miss Annie as she got into the carriage. "You must come and see us, and return our visit at The Hollies."

Mrs. Gaston said in her turn that they would be very glad to see Mr. Daintrees and Dr. Harrington, and then the carriage rolled away.

Dr. Ralph Harrington stood gazing after it, and then turned with his air of satire mingled with lazy good-nature to Mr. Jack Daintrees.

"Daintrees, my dear fellow," he said, "this looks something like an adventure."

"Most romantic—and delightful, my dear Harrington!"

"Well, improve it," said his friend.

"Improve it?"

"Court the widow, Jack! She'll suit you exactly!"

# CHAPTER VI.

### THE CRISIS IN A YOUNG MAN'S LIFE.

THE worthy Mr. Ormby had retired to his library after paralyzing Mrs. Ormby in the manner which we have described, and seating himself at his writing-table of carved walnut with a green cloth top, had essayed to answer George Cleave's letter.

Having commenced three several epistles, he finished by tearing up all, and leaning back in his large arm-chair with a blank and dissatisfied expression, began to reflect. His position was truly embarrassing. It was impossible to write and say to a young gentleman whose pretensions to his daughter's hand he had tacitly recognized, "Sir, you have lost your property, and as you are now poor, your engagement to my daughter must terminate;" and yet with Mr. Ormby's views, it was impossible, however he might word his reply, to say in reality anything else. He had firmly resolved ten minutes after receiving Cleave's letter that the engagement should end. *How* he was to bring it to an end, now, was the puzzle.

For a long time the worthy Mr. Ormby reflected with

knit brows, looking a little ashamed. At last he resolutely took up his pen, selected another sheet, and concocted the following note :

"Sir—I have the honor to acknowledge the receipt of
your communication of to-day on the subject of the late
Mr. Cleave's testamentary disposition of his estate, and
to express my regret that the discovery of the wishes of
the deceased in connection with Miss Bell should have
taken place after so long a period of time. As the friend
of the late Mr. Cleave, and if you will permit me to add,
as the friend of yourself, I would suggest, as your most
advisable course under all the circumstances, a prompt
compliance with the terms of the instrument referred
to. Miss Bell is, I am informed, a young lady of amiable disposition and great personal attractions, and I have
no doubt would readily be brought to see the propriety
of the arrangement in question.

"In reference to that portion of your communication
which relates to a prolongation of the engagement—of
which I am now distinctly informed for the first time—
with my daughter, I regret to be compelled from a sense
of duty to say that I am wholly unable to comply with
your request. I refrain from entering at large upon my
views upon the subject, and shall only say that Miss
Ormby is still much too young to assume responsibilities
so serious as those which are imposed by matrimony. In
regard to the desire expressed on your part that the
engagement of which you inform me may continue indefi-
nitely, I am reluctantly obliged to say that in my opinion
it would only result in unhappiness, and to inform you,

frankly and distinctly, that it can not continue.    This, I beg to add, is my fixed and irrevocable decision.

" Regretting the unpleasant character of this communication, which a sense of parental duty renders unavoidable,

"I am, sir, your ob't, humble serv't,

J. ORMBY."

Having dispatched this letter, Mr. Ormby rang and directed the servant who came at the summons to inform Miss Ormby that he wished to see her in the library.    It was not without emotion that he awaited her appearance. He was a wilful and imperious person, this Mr. Ormby, but not a cold or really harsh man ; and now said to himself that he was acting for his daughter's good—that her marriage with an impoverished young man could result in nothing but suffering, and that it was his duty to prevent their union at whatever expense of feeling.

Marian came in and took the seat which Mr. Ormby pointed out.    She was trembling a little, and the color had faded from her cheeks.    Mr. Ormby cleared his throat elaborately, and entered directly upon the subject, announcing in plain terms that the engagement with George Cleave must be broken off.

At this abrupt announcement, Marian trembled visibly, and in broken words protested.    Thereat Mr. Ormby grew hard and stern.    It was then her purpose, he said, to resist the will of her own parents—to oppose her caprice to their authority.    She had no such desire, the poor girl replied, but—but—she could not—could not— give up George !

At these words Mr. Ormby knit his brows, and directed an imperious look at his daughter. So it had come to this! he said. He was to be defied by his own child, when he was actuated only by an anxiety to secure her welfare! He, an old and gray-haired man, was to yield his judgment to a girl's!

It was possible, as she thus opposed him, that she designed to wed Mr. George Cleave with or without the consent of her parents! Was that her design?

"Oh no, sir; I will never do so," faltered the young lady. "I can assure you of that much; but do not ask me to give up George—it would break his heart—and my own too."

At the end of an hour Mr. Ormby had proceeded no further than this. The young lady declared that she would never marry without the approval of her parents, but again and again—she could not give up George! The interview then terminated, and she went to her chamber, from which she was summoned an hour afterwards by the intelligence that George Cleave had called to see Mr. Ormby, but finding that he had ridden out, had asked for her.

Marian went down, and they remained for two hours shut up in the drawing-room. When she came out her eyes were red with weeping, and as she went up the staircase she uttered a sob. She had told the young man of the promise made her father, that she would never marry without his consent; and as he was, now at least, bitterly opposed to their union, it would be better, Marian said, that he, George, should cease his visits for some time, and thus avoid inflaming still further Mr. Ormby's displeasure.

Thereat George Cleave had grown indignant, and intimated that she too was about to desert him. A few sobs and tears only replied to this cruel charge—the young lady seemed to regard it as unworthy of further notice. Then George Cleave rose, permitted his wrath and wretchedness to get the better of him, and terminated the interview—returning to Cleaveland full of indignation and despair.

He held out for three days, and then went again to Bayview and asked for Marian. The reply was that the young lady was too unwell to see him. He then stayed away two days, when he repeated his visit. Marian had had another wretched interview with her father—had been driven step by step to make the cruel promise that she would simply decline seeing him if he came again— and did so.

A week afterwards George Cleave came once more. He was so thin and pale now that he was scarcely recognizable. Was Miss Ormby at home? She was confined to her chamber, and Mrs. Ormby was also unwell. Mr. Ormby? He had ridden out, but left a letter for Mr. Cleave. The young man took it, and read :

" Mr. Ormby presents his respects to Mr. Cleave, and begs that he will discontinue his visits to Miss Ormby, as they are disagreeable both to Miss Ormby and to her family."

When George Cleave read this note his head grew dizzy and his pulse throbbed. He looked from the letter to the servant, and then again at the letter. Then his pale face slowly filled with blood, and his eyes habitually so frank and kindly grew cold and stern.

" So be it !" he muttered.

He then slowly mounted his horse, and rode back to Cleaveland, where he sat down, gazing at the floor in a sort of stupor of wrath and despair. He was still plunged in this apathy, when the door opened, a firm step advanced toward him, and a cheery voice exclaimed :

" How are you. George !"

# CHAPTER VII.

## MR. JOBSON CONSULTS WITH DR. HARRINGTON.

A WEEK or two after the fox-hunt and dinner at The Lodge Dr. Ralph Harrington was seated about dusk in a cane-bottomed chair, in his office, on the main street of Waterford, smoking a cigar and musing.

His surroundings were commonplace and prosaic. In one corner of the room stood an old set of shelves containing an array of dusty bottles; on the mantel-piece was a skull which, owing to the fact that some visitor had thrust a cigar into its mouth, presented rather a jocose than a tragic appearance; and on a table in the centre of the office lay piles of medical books and journals. The floor was covered with a rag carpet, intended evidently for use instead of ornament; the iron fender was very old and rusty; and a pair of tongs—the legs dislocated and crossed with a bacchanalian air—leaned rakishly in one corner of the fire-place, where burned a cheerful fire.

Dr. Harrington puffed lazily at his cigar, looking around him as he did so.

"This is homeless enough," he muttered, "and I miss the old folks at home—and the young folks too. Even Daintrees is better off. I am glad I went on that fox-hunt and met with that small sort of adventure. Annie Bell? Well, Miss Annie Bell came near being a beauty ——"

He had left the door open a little. A voice behind him said :

"Then you have heard about that paper, Doctor?"

Harrington turned round and saw Mr. Jobson, who came in and sat down.

"Glad to see you, Mr. Jobson. What paper?" said Harrington.

"You have not heard of it then. I thought as you mentioned Miss Bell—but I will tell you all about it. You are a friend of George Cleave's, and something must be done in his affairs. I think you can help."

"If I can do anything for George I'll certainly do it," said Harrington ; "I went to college with him—he's as fine a fellow as I know. Tell me about this, Mr. Jobson."

Mr. Jobson proceeded to inform his companion of the discovery of the codicil, and of George Cleave's resolution.

"He is resolved not to contest the paper," he added, "and will not hear of paying his addresses to Miss Bell, which results, I suppose, from his engagement, which I have heard spoken of, with Miss Ormby."

Harrington shook his head.

"His engagement in that quarter is broken off. I heard the news this morning, and now I know the reason.  Ormby Senior has found out that poor George is or will be penniless—was there ever such a strange incident as the discovery of that paper!—and George is shown to the door."

Mr. Jobson nodded.

"Then he may be induced to think of Miss Bell."

Harrington reflected for a moment, and then said :

"I'm afraid not.  George Cleave is not that sort of person.  As long as Miss Ormby is not to blame and remains faithful to him he would not look at another woman.  Do you know anything about that?"

"Nothing," returned Mr. Jobson.

Harrington rose, and standing with his back to the fire, puffed thoughtfully at his cigar.

"I'll tell you what I'll do, Mr. Jobson," he said at length, "I'll go and see George and talk the matter over with him.  Perhaps we can devise some way of getting him out of this ugly scrape.  I don't know how it is in your profession, but in mine a patient's condition is often more favorable than it appears at the first glance. What must that queer old gentleman, Mr. Cleave, think of this eccentric arrangement I wonder?—hum! hum! hum!"

Mr. Jobson rose.

"You have struck out the right course, Doctor, and just the proceeding I meant to suggest.  George Cleave instructed me to write to Gartrell to say that the estate would be surrendered to him immediately, but I don't mean to be in any hurry about it.  The thing is absurd. A compromise is the least, but I am even against that."

"You are for fighting it out in a chancery suit, Mr. Jobson?" said Harrington laughing.

"I am," said Mr. Jobson emphatically, "to the death."

"To the *death?* A bad programme for a doctor to assist in, Mr. Jobson! but I intend to assist, and to make my diagnosis of the case to-morrow morning!"

With which understanding they parted.

## CHAPTER VIII.

### A NEST OF DOVES.

WHILE engaged in the operation of shaving, on the following morning, Ralph Harrington made the affairs of George Cleave the subject of his reflections, and, after full consideration of everything, determined to open his campaign by a reconnoissance first in the direction of The Hollies.

"I know the state of things with Cleave," he said half aloud, as he carefully wiped his razor; "but I would like to discover, if I can, the strength and position of the enemy. Yes, I'll go to The Hollies."

Having decided upon this course, Dr. Ralph Harrington proceeded to breakfast at the village inn where he took his meals—his sleeping apartment being in the same building with his office—and then mounting his horse, with his professional saddlebags behind him, set out for The Hollies, which he reached about noon.

As he entered the handsome grounds of Mrs. Gaston's residence, the lazy, satirical smile habitual with him came to the face of Dr. Ralph Harrington; for there, affixed to a drooping bough, was the favorite steed of Mr. Daintrees.

"My friend Jack don't mean to let the grass grow under his feet," he muttered; "he has come to visit the fair chatelaine of this castle, and I think he shows his taste!"

The Hollies was in fact a charming place—a veritable nest of doves, all flowers, grass, and verdure. All about the locality was fresh, bright, and attractive. The house was a species of cottage, but a cottage of very considerable size, and stood in the midst of beautiful grounds. Along three sides of the building stretched a graceful veranda, edged with ornamental scroll-work above, and supported by slender, white pillars; and from this veranda two or three flights of steps descended to the sward as smooth as velvet; a number of cedars, ash-trees, and two or three great holly trees were scattered here and there, with fantastic "rustic seats" beneath them; and on every side were seen capriciously-shaped beds of autumn flowers; lattice-work trellises covered with creeping plants in bloom, and ornamental baskets running over with moss, ferns, and variegated asters; a gravel carriage-way, as white and smooth as a walk, ran around the green circle; a neat coach-house and numerous outbuildings were in rear; a grove served as a background, with an old garden next to it. The Hollies, you could see, was the residence of a lady, and a lady exceedingly "well to do!"

The surroundings, indeed, of the fair Mrs. Gaston accurately represented her "circumstances" and her tastes. She was the widow of a gentleman who had resided in a neighboring city, and on his death, finding town-life

distasteful to her, she had purchased The Hollies, made
great improvements in it, and lived in the utmost comfort upon her investments. She had shrunk at first from
the idea of living alone, and had nearly given up her
project, when Mr. Cleave's death had left Annie Bell
homeless. Then Mrs. Gaston saw the means of extricating herself from her embarrassment. Annie's mother
had been a distant relation of her own, and having come
to look at The Hollies just as Mr. Cleave died, Mrs.
Gaston had ordered her carriage driven over to Cleaveland, and brought Annie back with her to live at The
Hollies. This event had taken place three or four years
before, when Annie was fourteen or fifteen, and from
that moment the two became inseparable. Annie
promptly developed into a young lady of unbounded
gayety, whose entrance into a room was like the sudden
gleam of sunshine; and she ran about, laughed, teased
"Auntie," as she called Mrs. Gaston, from morning to
night, and took command of The Hollies in the most
arbitrary manner. Everything, indeed, was subjected to
Miss Annie Bell's sway. The servants smiled when she
appeared, and did not cease smiling when she scolded
them. The old gardener deferred to her, groaning his
protests against the new "book" way of doing things,
but submitting. The dogmatic old coachman actually
permitted her to lecture him upon the subject of horses;
and as to Mrs. Gaston, that mild, gentle, and affectionate
creature had yielded without a struggle to her fate.
Annie teased her, lectured her, scolded her, informed her
that she was the most ridiculous little auntie that ever

lived ; and then putting her arm around the waist of the pretty Mrs. Gaston, would drag her forth to look at the flowers—sole passion in the tranquil lives of these two attractive specimens of feminine humanity.

Dr. Ralph Hàrrington dismounted just inside the grounds, and was approaching the house over a neat gravel walk when Miss Annie Bell came out with a watering-pot in her hand and a sun-bonnet on her head. She stopped suddenly as her eyes fell upon the visitor, but came forward at once, limping a little as she walked.

"I am very glad to see you, Doctor!"

She held out her hand as she spoke, and added smiling:

"And Auntie will be as much pleased as myself."

Dr. Ralph Harrington took the small hand and bowed over it.

"Will somebody else be disposed to welcome me as cordially, Miss Bell ? If I am not mistaken I recognize the horse of one of my most esteemed friends, Mr. Daintrees, of that bachelor den, The Lodge."

Harrington spoke in a tone of lazy amusement which seemed to agreeably impress Miss Bell. She burst into a frank fit of laughter, and then assuming an extremely demure expression of countenance, said :

"Mr. Daintrees has called, I believe, on business, and I have come out to water my flowers. I hope you will excuse my toilet——"

"No excuses, I beg, Miss Bell. I am flattered at being received as a friend. No bad effects from your accident, I trust ? Do you know that I am much morti- fied at not having been called in as your physician ?

Surely you need the services of an old and experienced gentleman like myself even yet?"

Miss Bell began to laugh anew.

"No indeed, sir," she replied. "I am getting well without medicine. I am very glad I did not break my neck, for which I am indebted to you."

Harrington bowed.

"You exaggerate my heroic services, Miss Bell. Permit me to relieve you of that watering-pot."

He took the watering-pot from her hands, and directed by Miss Annie Bell, who seemed in no degree averse to the interview, thus *tête-à-tête* under the trees, proceeded to water the asters. At the end of a quarter of an hour they had become extremely sociable, and Dr. Harrington said casually :

"This is sad news about my friend George Cleave— I think you know him—he has been jilted by Miss Ormby."

Annie Bell stopped training a creeping plant on one of the trellises, and turned round—a statue of surprise.

"George! Jilted by Marian Ormby !"

Harrington, watching his companion closely out of the corners of his eyes, said quietly :

"I do not know what you young ladies mean when you employ the term *jilted*, but men mean by it that a gentleman who has been engaged to a lady and is then discarded is jilted."

"George jilted by Marian Ormby !" repeated Miss Annie Bell, too much astonished apparently to discuss the etymological or social significance of the term.

"Yes," said Dr. Ralph Harrington quietly. "He was engaged to be married to Miss Marian, and Miss Marian is not going to marry him. I believe the reason is that there has been some discovery of another will or something of Mr. Cleave, Sr., giving his property to a Mr. Gartrell. So you see there's no chance for poor George."

ANNIE BELL STOPPED AND TURNED ROUND—A STATUE OF SURPRISE.

Annie Bell stood perfectly silent and motionless, looking at her companion.

"Is it possible you heard nothing of all this?" said Harrington.

"Not one word."

"I thought news flew faster in a country neighborhood! Yes, George is jilted, and what is worse—or at least very bad—he is ruined. I am sorry to see, Miss Bell, that you seem to take it so much to heart."

"Take it to heart? Oh! Dr. Harrington! Poor George! You do not know how much I love him! Oh! oh! I do not care about Marian Ormby. I always said she was not worthy of him. He is the noblest fellow! I was brought up with him, and I love him like a sister; and now he is jilted and ruined!"

Annie Bell completely lost sight of her companion, and burst into an honest flood of tears, which, unlike the result of crying generally, made her look extremely pretty.

"He shall have Tree Hill," she suddenly added. "I will go and tell him so this very day. He is better entitled to it than I am. Dr. Harrington, I *hate* this Marian Ormby who has *presumed* to jilt my brother George!"

A somewhat singular circumstance followed this outburst. The quiet, easy, jocose, self-possessed Dr. Ralph Harrington suddenly colored. Something had plainly made his heart beat.

"I am as much attached to George Cleave as you are, Miss Bell," he said. "He was the closest and best friend I had at college. I am going to see him this very day, and will carry any message you may desire to send him."

Annie Bell looked into her companion's face with the open, frank, ardent glance of a true-hearted woman, and said impulsively:

"Tell him that he shall not be ruined as long as I

have anything in the world, that he shall have every
foot of Tree Hill; and tell him that I love him a thousand times more in his trouble than I ever loved him in
his prosperity."

Before Annie Bell was aware of his intention, Dr.
Ralph Harrington seized one of her small hands and
pressed it closely to his lips.

"Pardon me!" he said in hurried tones, very different
from his ordinary manner, "it is not often that I meet
persons like yourself, Miss Bell. Mr. Cleave is fortunate. I am going now to tell him that in his disappoint-
ment and misfortune he has something which is better
than what the world calls good fortune—that he has
*your* heart."

Mr. Jack Daintrees came out of the house a moment
after these words were uttered, and Dr. Ralph Harrington grew suddenly commonplace.

"Please present my compliments to Mrs. Gaston, Miss
Bell. I am truly rejoiced to find that you have sustained
no ill effects from your accident. Why, good-day, my
dear Daintrees! I thought I knew your horse. You are
going? So am I, and we will ride together."

And after bowing low to Annie, Harrington went and
mounted his horse, in which proceeding he was imitated
by Mr. Daintrees.

As they rode out of the grounds together, Harrington
turned to his companion, and, surveying him with rather
satirical glances and a wicked smile, said:

"I thought something would come of your interview
at The Lodge with the fair madam, my dear Daintrees!"

"Ah! bother!" said Mr. Daintrees, "what an idea!"

"Such things will happen," said Ralph Harrington philosophically, with his lazy smile; "but beware, my dear Daintrees. You are both young and impressible. Now to the news of the moment. This is a bad business of poor Cleave's, which it seems Miss Bell had not heard —his discardal. Suppose we take the youth in hand and heal his wounds. Have you a fox-hunt in perspective? Nothing like life and movement for a lacerated bosom."

"The very thing!" said Daintrees. "I am going out with the hounds on the day after to-morrow. Come yourself and bring George—my favorite of all the youngsters. Remember—on the night before."

"I will; if not, we will be with you before sunrise."

They had reached the forks of the road where they were to separate.

"A last word, my dear Daintrees," said Harrington. "I am in a match-making humor to-day, I believe. I am about to turn completely around. Why not court the fair widow?"

But Mr. Daintrees shook his head.

"I am not a marrying man, and——"

"There, my dear Daintrees, that is enough. It will take place in six months. Invite me—I will be your first groomsman!"

And Dr. Ralph Harrington rode on, laughing.

## CHAPTER IX.

### HARRINGTON FEELS HIS WAY.

AS Harrington rode up the long avenue stretching from the tall gateway to the imposing front of the great Cleaveland house, he looked at the façade of the mansion, bright in the mild sunshine of the autumn afternoon, and muttered:

"It will never do for George to be turned out of these excellent headquarters, if he can help it, and I think he can. He is right, I suppose—at least it's just like him— not to contest a paper expressing plainly, if not legally, his uncle's wishes in the disposition of the property; but why should he not marry this pretty little rose-bud of The Hollies? That would suit exactly; and Mr. Gartrell would find himself disinherited in his turn. Well, I am on a strange errand. I am going to try to marry off Miss Annie Bell, when, if I consulted my own sentiments, I would—pshaw! what folly! I am like Jack Daintrees— or unlike him—not a marrying man!"

He dismounted, knocked with the butt of his riding-whip on the finely carved door, entered without waiting, and called out, as he opened the drawing-room door:

"How are you, George?"

Cleave rose.

"My dear Harrington, I am very glad to see you. The fact is, I was moping."

If Cleave had said *raging internally*, he would have come nearer the truth. His brow was lowering and his lips set. Indignation at his treatment at Bayview had quite supplanted his first sentiment of despair.

"A moment, my dear George," said Harrington, after shaking hands and sitting down. "How long since have you learned to use my surname instead of my Christian name? At college I was *Ralph*, as you were *George*."

"Well, Ralph, pardon me, my dear friend; the fact is I am out of sorts."

"And I am not surprised."

"You?"

"I never criticise the proceedings of the ladies," said Harrington, "but I must say that your treatment by—— shall I go on?"

"Speak plainly and frankly."

"Well, your treatment by Miss Ormby is strange—to say the least. She's charming, I acknowledge that, but I am your friend and will say that she has behaved most singularly—has she not?"

Cleave's face darkened.

"She has thrown me away like a worthless kid glove."

"Meaning that the little hand that wore the glove is not for you, George, any longer, eh? Well, believe me, old fellow, it won't hurt long or amount to much, and I have come in good time to bind up your wounds. Tell me all about it."

Cleave asked nothing better.  His indignation required some outlet.  He related everything, and finished by saying :

"So you see the whole affair is over, and I am perfectly willing that it should be !"

Harrington looked at the flushed face, the disdainful lip, and the sparkling eyes of his friend.

"Now is the time," he said to himself; "there's nothing like taking the ball at the rebound.  *Pique* is the trump card !"

"Well, George," he said with an easy smile, "your treatment has been precisely such as everybody says it has been—the whole neighborhood is talking about it and pitying you, old fellow.  I confess I should not like, myself, to be *pitied;* but then nobody blames you.  That must be some consolation to you."

Cleave became suddenly irate.  All the pride of his nature was outraged.

"No one *shall* pity me !" he said.

"Spoken like a man ! and there is an adage that as good fish swim in the sea as were ever caught out of it.  You have missed your mark this time, George ; feather your shaft and shoot in some other direction."

Cleave shook his head.

"No, I thank you," he said still irate ; "I've enough of the sex for the present."

"And you won't marry ?  Well, I think you are right, old fellow.  Nothing like the life of a bachelor, as I had the presumption to say to a little beauty I saw to-day.  I mean Miss Bell at The Hollies, and by the by I was enough of a gossip to allude to this confounded discovery of Mr. Cleave's new will and your bad luck with Miss Ormby. You should have heard Miss Bell thereupon, my dear fellow. She burst into tears, exclaimed: *'Dear George!'* and protested that Miss Ormby was 'a goose' or something of that sort for discarding you; it was either 'goose' or 'mercenary.' Miss Bell then added that you were the only brother she had, and that you should never want as long as she had anything."

Cleave's face colored a little.

"Annie is the best girl I know," he said; "and I will go and thank her. I have not been there for a month."

Harrington had reached his aim with less difficulty than he had anticipated.

"Well, you could not do a more appropriate thing, George," he said rising, "and I have never seen anybody whose sympathy and affection would console *me* more than Miss Bell's. She is a treasure of beauty, goodness, and sweetness. You see even cynical Ralph Harrington can be earnest sometimes! and now I must go, old fellow; no, thank you, I can't stay."

Harrington shook hands, drew on his gloves, and moved toward the door.

"By the by, George, Daintrees invites you to a fox-hunt at The Lodge day after to-morrow. I am going and took the liberty of saying that you would come. Don't decline. We'll have a good run and a jolly dinner."

Cleave refused and then accepted. It was arranged that Harrington should call by Cleaveland early on the morning fixed, and they should proceed together to The Lodge; after which the visitor took his departure.

Harrington rode on slowly for about a mile in profound thought. Then a singular smile came to his lips —a smile, half lazy, half satirical, and not without a tinge of melancholy.

"Well," he muttered, "it is hard to account for the actions of the human species. Here I am trying to bring about a match between Cleave and a young lady, which young lady, if I am not mistaken, I am beginning to fall in love with myself!"

# CHAPTER X.

### GEORGE CLEAVE AND HIS "LITTLE SISTER."

AFTER the departure of Ralph Harrington George Cleave fell back into his mood of anger and melancholy—weary of himself, of life, of his past, present, and future. The sight of the familiar objects around him was quite hateful to him, and he muttered:

"How am I to get through this stupid, wretched, dragging day! I'll go to The Hollies, I believe. I want a little sympathy, and am certain to find it there! At least the ride will divert me from this eternal brooding, and the only thing for me now is to forget."

He ordered his riding horse, and slowly mounted with a weary air, very different from his habitual vivacity. Once in the saddle, however, he went on at full gallop, and about sunset reached The Hollies. Let us precede him.

Annie Bell having bestowed a little nod of amicable farewell upon Dr. Harrington and Mr. Daintrees—which movement caused her ringlets to momentarily obscure her vision—had hastened into The Hollies, and met Mrs. Gaston at the door.

"Oh! my dear little auntie!" she exclaimed. "I have a good joke to tease you about at last! Mr. Daintrees! Who would have imagined such a thing! He's going to be my 'Uncle Jack,' I hope!"

"What a goose you are, Annie!" replied Mrs. Gaston, with a faint little blush which made her look extremely pretty. "You know very well Mr. Daintrees came to inquire about your sprain!"

"And never looked at me! Besides, he said he came on *business*—business!"

"I had quite forgotten—there was a message from Mr. Jobson about the small tract I wish to purchase."

"And so Mr. Daintrees is not going to become my Uncle Jack after all!" said the small witch, pretending to sigh and look disconsolate.

"What an idea! I should be much more rational if I were to ask if Dr. Harrington came with the view of proposing to become *my nephew*."

"Dr. Harrington!"

"Why not?"

"Propose for *me!*"

Mrs. Gaston smiled and said:

"You forget your romantic adventure, and that he saved your life, Annie. You have only to read love romances, my dear, to find that these incidents generally lead to—catastrophes."

"You are certainly dreaming—yes, dreaming and talking in your sleep!" exclaimed Miss Bell; "and of all the absurd little aunties that ever lived——"

"Why, you really are blushing, Annie!"

"Fiddle-dedee!" exclaimed the girl, pirouetting upon the point of her slipper, and carrying the smiling Mrs. Gaston with her in her rotary motion by means of the arm around the fair widow's waist. "I am not blushing in the least, having the best conscience in the world, madam, and nothing to blush for. Dr. Harrington!"

"You were talking *very* confidentially with him, my dear. I saw you through the window."

"It was all about George! Oh! the dreadful news, Auntie! Come and sit down, I must tell you all about it. Marian Ormby—hateful thing—has jilted him, and a new will is found giving Cleaveland to Allan Gartrell!"

"Is it possible?"

"Yes, indeed; Dr. Harrington told me. Oh! poor, poor George! To think, Auntie! he is all alone by himself at Cleaveland—jilted and ruined! Marian Ormby! —presume to jilt *George!*—I wish he would ask *me.* I would marry him in a minute, whether Cleaveland was his or not!"

Thereupon Annie burst into tears and ran up-stairs, forgetting her sprained foot. When she came down to dinner her eyes were swollen, and it was not until about sunset that she resumed her cheerfulness in some degree, and went out to look again at her dear flowers.

Mrs. Gaston joined her, and the setting sun bathed the attractive figures in its mild light—Annie, a slender, graceful little sprite, with rosy cheeks and glossy brown ringlets; her companion, pink, plump, with a bow of ribbon half hiding her pretty neck, and on her lips the modest, shrinking smile which they habitually wore.

George Cleave and his misfortunes again became the topic of conversation, and Annie had just exclaimed impetuously, with tears in her eyes, "*Any* girl might be proud to marry my dear George!" when the dear George in question rode into the grounds, and dismounting came to meet his cousin—for such was Mrs. Gaston, as we have said—and his adopted sister. The young man was received by both with an affectionate kiss—his habit in boyhood—and was struck, in spite of himself, by the beauty and emotion of Annie.

"I see, Cousin," he said gloomily, although he attempted to utter a light laugh, "that you and Annie have heard of my misfortunes! Well, I am not going to marry—anybody; and I am quite ruined. You see, I have come *home* for comfort."

"And you shall have it, George!" Mrs. Gaston said with impulsive affection. "We have heard of everything, and it made our hearts bleed for you, my dear."

George shook his head, and said proudly:

"You must not take it so seriously, Cousin. I am not as much distressed as you may think. And now come and let us sit down on the porch. I will tell you and my little sister everything."

Half an hour afterwards Cleave had narrated all, not omitting, as Harrington had done, the singular condition in the codicil.

"You see, I am to marry *you*, Annie," he said laughing, "or give up Cleaveland!"

Annie colored a little, but suddenly laughed in her turn, and exclaimed:

" Well, then, sir—why not keep Cleaveland ?"

" Annie !" exclaimed Mrs. Gaston.

" What, Auntie ?" said Miss Annie demurely.

" You must remember, my dear, that although you call George your brother, he is not related to you, and that he may accept your liberal proposal !"

General laughter followed this speech, and the slight cloud of embarrassment which had succeeded the young lady's audacious speech was dissipated.

"You are two very ridiculous young people," said pretty Mrs. Gaston, smiling and blushing ; " and now come in to tea."

Cleave remained until eleven o'clock, and then was easily persuaded that The Hollies was a much more cheerful place than Cleaveland whereat to spend the night. The hours passed in the society of these two charming persons had indeed proved an inexpressible comfort to him. This young man was not of that stern and resolute stuff of which novelists construct their " heroes." He was warm-hearted, honest, impulsive, and easily impressed. He was unhappy, and the faces full of affectionate sympathy were a balm to him.

He and Annie had indulged indeed in something like a *tête-à-tête*, Mrs. Gaston pretending to have her house-keeping to attend to. She accordingly remained for some time in the adjoining apartment, rattling spoons and ranging the silver service with unusual deliberation on the polished mahogany sideboard. From time to time she glanced through the half-open door at George and Annie, seated side by side upon a sofa, in confidential conversation ; and the pair brought to the pretty face of Mrs. Gaston a covert smile.

Had the fair widow suddenly conceived a domestic plot—arranged the scenes of a little comedy in which George and Annie should perform the chief parts, with a marriage for the denouement ? Match-making is said to be a weakness of all good women past thirty; and here seemed to be suddenly presented to Mrs. Gaston an opportunity to indulge this darling propensity. There was in her eyes absolutely no objection whatever to such a match, and everything to recommend it. She loved George sincerely ; and by marrying Annie he would preserve his estate. It was true that she, Mrs. Gaston, would lose her little companion—but the widow was a most unselfish person. She had often reflected with anxiety upon Annie's future, in case of her own death ; had resolved not to oppose any suitable match which offered itself—and here was the opportunity of securing the happiness of her dear Annie. That such was the plan of Mrs. Gaston, subsequent events seemed to indicate.

George fell asleep that night at The Hollies, surprised to find that he had actually passed a happy evening. Annie had certainly grown a beauty, suddenly—what a tender and sympathetic smile she had ! what a luxury it was to have a *little sister* who looked at him with those large, soft, beautiful eyes, weighed down by tears as she spoke of his troubles !—— and (with the eyes, which were fast shut in the next room, still looking at him) George fell asleep.

He remained at The Hollies on the next day until

noon; and then promising to repeat his visit, took his leave. Instead of going back to Cleaveland, however, he rode to Waterford, and entered Ralph Harrington's office just as that gentleman was compounding a prescription.

"Why, what is the matter, my dear fellow?" said Harrington; "if I were called upon to express a physiological opinion I should say that you had grown about five years younger since I saw you yesterday."

"I have been riding, and that gives color and good spirits, you know, Ralph!"

Cleave laughed almost gaily. Harrington looked at him.

"You have been to The Hollies," he said.

"How do you know that?"

"From your face; and the angels there have consoled you."

This was said rather ruefully, but Harrington quickly resumed his lazy smile and said:

"Well, why don't you pay your addresses to Miss Bell?"

"*I* court *Annie?*"

"Why not?"

"We are like brother and sister."

"Without, however, being in the least related. Well, what of that? All the better. Why shouldn't you court her? To speak by the card, old fellow, she is the finest girl in the county; you will make her a present of Cleaveland on the day of your marriage; she will marry you, I think, and perhaps the Ormbys will then realize the fact that they have been a little hard on you."

Cleave's cheek flushed red.

"No," he said, "the thing would be disgraceful, Ralph. To offer myself to Annie to retain possession of this property! I would rather starve!"

"Come," said Harrington, "don't act on sublimated grounds. Or if you are a shrinking, sensitive, timid young person, fearing the gossip of shallowpates more than a good conscience, surrender Cleaveland to Gartrell. But that need not prevent you from asking the little beauty of The Hollies to become Mrs. Cleave."

"What do you mean, Ralph?"

"I mean that you are a full-grown man in perfect health, have your profession, and have as perfect a right to propose for the hand of Miss Annie Bell, as if you were the possessor of a quarter of a mile of buildings in the heart of Broadway."

Cleave did not reply.

"Look at the affair in a business point of view," continued Harrington: "Miss Bell has the estate of 'Free Hill,' and whether you are rich or poor can want nothing, which is something in this ticklish matter of matrimony, George! It will not be an unfair offer—your income against Miss Bell's. Go and court her. It will make the Ormbys furious; and you will be happy in spite of them."

The pride and pique of the young man were touched, and responded. His face flushed; and Annie's smile came to his mind.

"Well," he said, "I am going to make a foolish speech. I will think of what you say, and if I give up Cleaveland no one can say I was mercenary."

" Certainly not."

"We will talk over this again, Ralph."

"All right. Think of it and try your luck. And, stop !—if you fail I think I'll try myself !"

"Are you in earnest, Ralph ? It is not possible that *you*——"

"Are jesting for my private amusement here among my gallipots ? Certainly I am ! Do you think if I cared anything for the fair one that I would be giving you all this good advice ?"

Harrington laughed heartily ; lit a cigar in the laziest manner ; and it was not until the door had closed on Cleave that his face grew a little gloomy, and he muttered :

"This goes a little harder against the grain than I supposed !"

## CHAPTER XI.

### THE RESULT OF BREAKING ONE'S LEG.

A SOMEWHAT curious but perfectly natural revul-
sion now took place in the feelings of Dr. Ralph
Harrington, and he became convinced that he was proceeding in a very absurd manner in thus endeavoring to
persuade his friend Cleave to change his fealty, and
transfer his affections from Miss Marian Ormby to Miss
Annie Bell. Was it not highly discreditable in himself
to thus coöperate in an affair which must reflect so little
honor upon his friend? Could he justify his conduct,
even as a friend of Miss Bell, whom he sought thus to
push into what must be, in substance, a mercenary
match?

In other words, Dr. Ralph Harrington had, in the
most rapid and unexpected manner, fallen in love with
the young beauty of The Hollies; and it was with rather
rueful feelings that he set out early on the appointed
morning to accompany Cleave to the fox-hunt. He fore-
saw that the subject of Miss Annie Bell would be dwelt
upon, and he was not mistaken. He found George
Cleave ready, and they rode on toward The Lodge.

"After all, Ralph," said the young man, who had
again become rather gloomy; "I don't see if I fancy

Annie, and she fancies me, why—if I surrender Cleaveland——" There he stopped.

"No reason," was the brief reply of Harrington, in a
somewhat curt tone of voice.

"I need something to divert my mind—I am wretched
enough. Yes, I'll take your advice, I think, and 'try.'"

At that moment Ralph Harrington experienced very
unchristian sentiments toward his companion. "To
divert his mind!"

"Well—try!" he grunted.

George Cleave was too busy with his own thoughts to
observe the tone of his friend.

"There will at least be no deception or false profes-
sions in the matter," Cleave added.

And as they were now in sight of The Lodge, the conversation ceased.

An extremely gay company had assembled, and Mr.
Jack Daintrees did the honors of his breakfast-table in
the most cordial and jovial manner. Then there was a
great tramping of feet, jingling of spurs, and blowing of
horns, to which the hoarse bay of the hounds came as an
echo. The fox-hunters mounted; the dogs were un-
leashed; even the game was started from a copse near at
hand; and the chase opened with ardor.

Four hours afterwards a light country wagon moved
slowly and carefully through the gateway of The Hollies,
and this wagon contained the nearly inanimate form of
George Cleave. In attempting to clear a wide ravine not
far from The Hollies, his jaded horse had fallen short of
the opposite bank, clung to the edge a moment with his

fore feet, and ended by falling back, rolling over his rider, and kicking him so severely as to produce a serious and most painful fracture of the bone of one of his legs. Dr. Ralph Harrington had been at some distance from the spot, riding with a reckless spur, as he had been observed to do throughout the entire hunt. Seeing his friend fall, he had stopped suddenly, however, hastened to his aid, and extricating him from his dangerous position, had promptly rendered him professional assistance. A light wagon was passing, and this had been engaged to convey the young man to The Hollies, not a mile distant, which the vehicle soon reached, escorted by Dr. Harrington.

The ladies duly went through all the forms of exclamation, agitation, sympathy, and George was taken to bed. Dr. Harrington then proceeded to set the limb, to apply the bandages, and administer an anodyne. George Cleave, who had opened his eyes during the bandaging process, now closed them again, and under the effect of the anodyne fell into uneasy slumber.

Harrington then went down-stairs, and found himself subjected to an agitated cross-examination upon the incident and the extent of the danger.

"There is no serious danger, my dear madam," said the young physician, "if proper care is taken, and the case be treated with attention. As Mr. Cleave is my intimate friend I shall spare no efforts to effect a speedy cure. The only danger is in the event of amputation which—to be frank—may become necessary."

This was sad comfort; and Mrs. Gaston and Annie re-

ceived the announcement with some silent tears. Then
the doctor took his leave, promising to call again at
night.

George slept until sunset, and then opened his eyes.
Mrs. Gaston and Annie were in the room. It was a
cordial to him to see their faces full of love and sympathy,
and the smile of his friend Ralph was soon added.

"You had a bad fall, George," said Ralph Harrington
cheerily, "but you are doing excellently. Your leg is
fractured, but not a compound fracture. You see I tell
you the worst, and think I can promise that you'll be in
the saddle again in a month or two."

"Oh no, Doctor! no!" exclaimed Mrs. Gaston,
"George must not be imprudent! and you must not
deprive us of him; you know he will be such a comfort
to us this winter!"

Dr. Harrington carefully avoided looking toward Annie, but he listened acutely. Annie said nothing. But
there were tears in her eyes, and she was looking, he soon
saw, with a face full of sad sweetness at the invalid.

A month after these events George Cleave had risen
from his sick bed, put on a handsome dressing-gown,
lined with red silk and decorated with a golden cord and
tassel—made for him by his two guardian angels—slowly
descended to the drawing-room; and one evening about
twilight was sitting beside Annie on the sofa, holding
Miss Annie Bell's hand.

The expression of the young lady's face was singular.
It was sorrowful, tender, a little angry, with a decided
expression of pique, and, with the rest, mingled an

hesitating, doubtful, altogether agitated look, which had evidently been occasioned by some statement from her companion.

"So Dr. Harrington advised you, did he, George?"

"Yes, Annie."

"You are then close friends?"

"He's the best friend I have in the world."

Annie turned her head aside a little, and said in a low voice:

"I am not very sure that he proved himself such on this occasion. There is nothing in me to make it worth any one's while to think of me, George!"

The young man responded by protestations which it is unnecessary to repeat. Then he calmed down, and said earnestly:

"If there is nothing in you, Annie, what is there in *me?* I am a poor, unhappy fellow, not worth attention, and I am sure I do not know why you and cousin should have thought me worth troubling yourselves about; better have let me die of my hurt. I am nobody—all my merit is that I love you dearly, and I think without you I would rather die now!"

"O George!"

"What have I to live for without you? I am poor, very poor—for I shall give up Cleaveland. I have written to Allan Gartrell, and I have before me no future but one of dull, hopeless, cheerless toil to make my bread. I am no fit match for my dear Annie—I know that—but I must tell you all the same that I love you with my whole heart. I am so lonely and unhappy—even Ralph

Harrington in his solitary office is twice as fortunate as I am——"

"And he urged you, George, to—address me?" faltered Annie.

"Yes, yes, warmly."

Annie flushed to the roots of her hair.

"He thought it would be the happiest event of my life, and urged me when I objected—I must 'try' at all events. Well, Annie, I have *tried.* I have told you how much, how dearly I love you! that I am very unhappy and need your dear smile to brighten my life! Tell me at least that you love your poor George a little!"

He stopped, blushing and faltering. The night descended. There was no light in the room but that from the wood fire, before which, in the homely country fashion, a tea-kettle was simmering. The whole apartment was a picture of *home,* and George Cleave and Annie Bell were sitting close beside each other—the excellent Mrs. Gaston having carefully remained up-stairs. Annie began to pout a little. Then she cried silently. George Cleave drew her pretty head with its glossy ringlets toward him, and leaned his pale cheek against her roses. Then he turned her face toward him, and Miss Annie permitted herself to be kissed.

When Mrs. Gaston came down at last, coughing elaborately and rattling the knob of the door before entering, Miss Annie Bell went up-stairs, and George Cleave, with a face lit up by his happiness, said:

"Cousin, Annie and I are engaged, and hope you will give your consent!"

# CHAPTER XII.

## MR. BROWN.

ONE summer evening in the year succeeding these events Dr. Ralph Harrington came out of his office, and placing upon the door a card containing the words "Will return in half an hour," locked the door, and went over to the village tavern to tea.

Harrington was considerably thinner, and not so ruddy, which may have been attributable to the sultry weather. His step was not so firm and jaunty, and his lips had lost their lazy smile of easy good-humor, betraying formerly his health of body and tranquillity of mind. A close inspection indicated other changes. His eyes had black semi-circles beneath them, and their expression was uneasy and even painful. The mild and friendly light had faded from them as the smile had faded from the lips. There was nevertheless no indication of weakness in the face or figure. The walk was deliberate, the muscles of the countenance were firm, and the air of the man cool and composed. Something had evidently preyed upon his mind; but the resolute Ralph Harrington was as resolute as ever.

He went to the tavern, and was just entering when the

stage from the railroad station nearly twenty miles distant—for Waterford was out of the great routes of travel—clattered up to the door. It was a heavy old-fashioned vehicle, with the baggage behind, beneath a leathern apron. The jaunty driver cracked his whip, touched his off leader, rosetted and gallantly prancing, and the stage drew up at the door of the tavern enveloped in a cloud of dust, from which emerged two or three passengers.

Among these one attracted the attention of Harrington. He was a portly personage of fifty-five or sixty, and wore a brown travelling suit and a tall black beaver hat. The face under the hat was rubicund and jocose in expression, but a certain keenness in the glance of the stranger seemed to contradict this easy and careless demeanor. He flourished a large polished cane with the air of one well to do and used to taking his ease; and bestowed upon the group of village wiseacres at the door of the tavern an amiable smile, which seemed to say, "Well, here I am, my friends; you see before you a gentleman of respectability and means—nothing underhanded, all above board !"

When the landlord bowed and presented the portly gentleman with a pen, pushing at the same time the register before him for his signature, the portly gentleman said, smiling:

"Ah yes !"

And he inscribed upon the page the name and address: "John Brown, New York."

As he laid down the pen, Mr. Brown's face expanded

into a more amiable smile than before, and gently caressing his chin with his fat hand, he said to the landlord :

"Can you inform me, my friend, how far Mr. Allan
Gartrell lives from this place ?"

"But a short distance, sir," was the reply.  "His place
is called Cleaveland, and a very fine place it is.  I will
have you driven there if——"

"Yes, yes, thank you.  To-morrow.  A little purchase
of land is in view.  The timber is said to be very fine on
the river, and a lumber company in New York, whose
agent I am, wish to make arrangements with Mr. Gartrell—but this will not interest you, my dear sir.  A very
fine place you have here !  I particularly admired your
new church—hem !—and now, my friend, a room, and
some supper if convenient."

The landlord bowed to his respectable guest, gave an
order to a servant, who ducked his head with the elaborate politeness of the American "help" when there is
a prospect of coin, and Mr. Brown disappeared, leaving
the wiseacres to discuss him.  He had kindly furnished
them with a few data, as the reader has seen—taking
compassion upon their painful ignorance.  He was Mr.
Brown, of New York, agent of a lumber company who
wished to purchase timber land from Mr. Gartrell, proprietor of Cleveland ; and the village worthies discussed
this interesting fact for half an hour, agreed that Mr.
Brown was a respectable old fellow, evidently well to do
in his circumstances ; then they proceeded to muddle
their brains with toddy at the bar, and retired.

Harrington had found his eyes persistently wandering

toward Mr. Brown.   He was puzzling himself with a detail which seemed to have escaped the village critics—
the queer glance from Mr. Brown's eyes now and then;
a glance which seemed to contradict flatly the apparent
*bonhomie* and carelessness of the rest of his personal demeanor.   What did that glance mean?   Never was anything more piercing.

"Well," he muttered listlessly, "here I am worrying
my mind with a matter of no earthly importance to me,
and probably indulging in nothing but a foolish fancy.
I'll go up and see George.   I've not met him to-day."

And Harrington sauntered out and then up-stairs—not
walking with his old elastic step, but heavily and firmly.

On the next morning Mr. Brown made his appearance
at breakfast, the picture of health, enjoyment, and good-
nature.   He smiled on everybody, called the servants by
their names, and having finished his meal, declared
audibly that it was excellent.   An hour afterwards he
was on his way, in the landlord's open carriage, toward
Cleaveland, which he reached in about two hours.

"A fine place; a very fine place, indeed!" said Mr.
Brown as they drove up the long avenue.   "Mr. Gartrell
is indeed a fortunate individual."

"Yes, sah," was the reply of the darky driver, from
whom Mr. Brown had extracted on the way every known
detail in reference to the owner of Cleaveland.

The carriage stopped before the great portico, and the
driver got down, walked up the broad steps, and knocked.
A servant in elegant livery appeared.   Was Mr. Gartrell
at home?   Mr. Gartrell was at breakfast—information

which the liveried servant furnished in a somewhat supercilious tone.

"Give him my respects, and say Mr. Brown, of New York, has called to see him."

The servant hesitated, but ended by carrying the message. In five minutes he came back with the message that Mr. Gartrell was at breakfast—Mr. Brown could call again.

Mr. Brown smiled, but did not make any reply.

He put his hand into his breast, drew out a visiting card, took a pencil from his waistcoat pocket, and wrote upon the card.

"Give this to Mr. Gartrell," he said to the servant, who took the card, went in, and closed the door.

"Will you go back to Waterford, sah?" said the driver.

"Not yet, my friend," was the smiling reply; "perhaps Mr. Gartrell may see me after all."

Mr. Brown had already descended from the vehicle, and was taking out his purse.

"I know Mr. Gartrell will not turn me away, after all," he said, with his eternal smile; "here is the amount of my indebtedness to your master, my friend, and something for yourself."

The money was received with bows and grins.

"I will remain with Mr. Gartrell, probably, to-night. You can go back."

And Mr. Brown composedly walked up the broad steps, flourishing his cane. A moment afterwards he had passed through the broad door, which the same servant opened, and it closed behind him.

## CHAPTER XIII.

### WHICH BRINGS UP THE NARRATIVE.

THE fine estate of Cleaveland had come into possession of Mr. Allan Gartrell early in the spring.

Dissatisfied with the course proposed by Mr. Jobson—
that is to delay action, contest, compromise, do anything
rather than quietly give up the property—George Cleave
had decided the whole matter by ascertaining from Mr.
Gartrell's letters to his uncle the address of his banker,
which proved to be Liverpool; written him fully,
announcing his intention of surrendering Cleaveland,
and then a second time to make quite sure; and the letters had been followed two or three months afterwards by
Mr. Gartrell's sudden appearance.

It may excite some surprise that, having become engaged to Annie, Cleave had not reconsidered his resolution and retained the property. He was unable to do so.
He attained his twenty-fifth year on the very day before
his engagement with Annie, and was debarred by the
terms of the codicil from retaining the estate. He therefore surrendered it to his cousin, who thanked him with
great cordiality, and very faintly suggested that he
should remain at Cleaveland—which George politely

declined—and on the next day he was installed in Mr.
Jobson's office, preparing himself for the practice of the
law.    He had collected some small resources, which
enabled him to live for the present at the village tavern ;
and, not greeting his change of fortune as seriously as
persons of more "strength of character" might have
done, the young man had resolutely gone to work, permitting himself no pleasures but a visit every few days to
Annie at The Hollies.

Harrington had ceased to visit there.   His practice, he
said, took up all his time.   He went, it is true, to The
Lodge, to see Jack Daintrees from time to time ; but
The Hollies he declared was a little out of his way, and
he was a creature of habit—he hoped no one would think
him unsociable.   In other words, Dr. Ralph Harrington
had conceived an ardent and now entirely hopeless love
for Annie Bell.   He had discovered the fact, as we have
seen, precisely at the moment when it was too late—the
accident which befell George Cleave had brought about
the rapid and unexpected denouement of the comedy—
and Harrington had retired in despair, shutting up his
misery in his own heart.   He had entirely ceased to
allude even to the inmates of The Hollies in his conversation with Cleave.   He turned the subject with a light
laugh—or an attempt at such—when George introduced
it ; declared that he was too old to occupy his mind with
such things ; congratulated his friend in a somewhat
stiff and unsympathizing manner, George thought, and
then introduced some other topic.

"Decidedly," Cleave would say after such interviews,

"Ralph has changed his whole character, and I don't know what to make of him."

The weeks passed on thus—Cleave assiduously studying—when one morning, not long before the visit of Mr. Brown to Waterford, one of the gossips casually alluded to the fact that Mr. Allan Gartrell was paying his addresses to Miss Ormby of Bayview.

This statement was made by one of the fair sex—an old maid residing at the tavern with her brother, a merchant of the place. It stung George Cleave to the quick, and he turned suddenly to the speaker—they were at table—and said :

"That must be a mere idle report, Miss Smith."

"Oh, no indeed !" giggled Miss Smith; "it is certainly so. He goes there every day ; and I heard all about it from Mrs. Jones, who heard it from Miss Primby—and she was at Bayview, and *knows* it, Mr. Cleave ! "

George Cleave went away from the table, and going up to his room, did not make his appearance again during the whole day. When he came forth on the next day he was quite pale, and did not utter a word to any one, even to Harrington.

The day afterwards, a lady visiting at The Hollies repeated the same intelligence in the hearing of Annie—adding that she had her own doubts, however, of the truth of the report, as young Dr. Ralph Harrington was also a frequent visitor at Bayview, and had the reputation of being a suitor of Miss Ormby's.

Thereat Miss Annie Bell flushed to her temples, after which her color faded suddenly, leaving her cheeks white.

"Is it possible?" said Mrs. Gaston, who had not observed the agitation of Annie; "Dr. Harrington is so
little of a lady's man that his visits are probably professional ones to some member of the family."

But this matter-of-fact explanation was promptly discarded by the lady-gossip. No, indeed!—Dr. Harrington's visits were to Miss Ormby, and wholly *un*-profes-
sional! There was no trusting these quiet people, like
Dr. Harrington! They were more given to such things
than any other class!

And the lady-gossip flowed on in ceaseless garrulity
for an hour, supplementing her facts with her imagina-
tions.

Annie had glided out of the room soon after the allusion to Dr. Harrington, and gone up to her chamber.
She walked with heavy steps, and her face—thinner and
paler than when we saw it last—was quite agitated. She
gained her chamber, sank down upon a low coach, leaned
her cheek upon the pillow, and, covering her face with
her hand, sobbed out:

"Oh me!—oh me!"

# CHAPTER XIV.

## MR. DAINTREES MAKES AN ELABORATE TOILET AND VISITS THE HOLLIES.

MR. JACK DAINTREES had carefully gone over his face with his razor three distinct times, but not yet satisfied with his personal appearance, applied a new covering of shaving cream, strapped his razor anew, and again mowed down the refractory remnants of his beard. He then passed his hand over his face, found the surface like satin, seemed satisfied, and proceeded to array himself in full visiting costume.

When he went to the door where his riding horse, a fine animal, with a coat as glossy as silk, stood awaiting him, Mr. Jack Daintrees was the picture of a gallant, and he proceeded to vault into the saddle with the activity of eighteen.

Now why had Mr. Jack Daintrees, that incorrigible fox-hunter and careless bachelor, indulged in all this personal adornment? Why had he shaved thrice and then a fourth time to eradicate every ungraceful hirsute remnant? Why had he selected his best coat, his most gorgeous waistcoat, his tightest boots, and drawn his pantaloons so closely at the waist that he was red in the face ?

Let us follow Mr. Daintrees, and perhaps we shall discover the meaning of this coquettish care for his personal appearance. He rode away, turned toward The Hollies, and after half an hour's ride found himself in sight of that female Paradise—one mass of flowers and foliage now, and quite a picture.

Mr. Daintrees rode on, congratulating himself as he looked at the sky that he was near shelter. It was late in the afternoon, and the heavens were overcast with black clouds. One of those violent thunder-storms which burst upon Virginia in the month of August was evidently approaching, and Mr. Jack Daintrees had reached that period of life when human beings carefully consider the disagreeable results of exposure to a torrent of rain, with the additional risk from lightning. The demon of rheumatism had indeed more than once seized on the limbs of the gay and jaunty Jack, he had a horror of lumbago. He therefore cantered on with visions of a charming evening in the society of a certain lady at The Hollies, with alabaster lamps diffusing a romantic light, the rain pouring without, his horse housed comfortably in the stable, whither country etiquette would have him quickly led, and he, Mr. Jack Daintrees, compelled by circumstances over which he had no control, to pass the night in that nest of doves, The Hollies !

Mr. Daintrees rode in, dismounted, and went to the door, at which he gave a modest knock.

It was opened in a moment by Annie, who had been

listlessly reading a magazine in the drawing-room. Annie was not so rosy as when we saw her last, and a settled sadness dwelt in the sweet eyes, once so bright and laughing.

"Walk in, Mr. Daintrees, I am very glad to see you," she said ; "I really believe I was moping."

"Moping !" exclaimed Mr. Jack Daintrees, "is it possible that a young bird of paradise like yourself, Miss Annie, ever *mopes !*"

"Yes, indeed."

"You should leave that to the old gentlemen—like myself," said Mr. Daintrees. "What were you reading ?"

They had taken their seats in the drawing-room, and Mr. Daintrees was waiting for—the rest of the household.

"Oh ! only this magazine," said Annie. "There is a love story appearing in it—it is very dull. I really hate love stories !"

"Is it possible ? At your age, and under the circumstances."

A covert smile accompanied these words.

"I should think," added Mr. Daintrees, "that they would appeal with peculiar force to—to—a young lady who is engaged to be married !"

Annie became very red, and then the color all faded.

"I am sorry aunt is not at home, Mr. Daintrees," she said with a sort of desperate feeling that something must be said, and anxious only to turn the conversation. She certainly succeeded. The words fell upon Mr. Jack

Daintrees like a death knell. All the charms of The Hollies faded and grew colorless.

"Not at home? ah? I am sorry. She is probably out visiting?"

Mr. Daintrees was actually confused, and began to stammer. Annie was too sad, it seemed, to notice the fact; and that spirit of fun which formerly made her laugh at everything, had plainly deserted her.

"Auntie went to Waterford to do some shopping," she said. "Uncle Jake drove her in the carriage. It is nearly time for her return, I think."

Mr. Daintrees looked through the window. The sky was as black as night—the night itself was coming—and long zigzags of lightning began to flicker from the horizon to the zenith, followed by low mutterings.

"A storm is coming; Mrs. Gaston will be exposed to it, I fear——"

He stopped suddenly.

"And the Swamp!" he added quickly; "does she know that the rains have swollen it nearly to the level of the trestle bridge?"

"They must have passed over it."

"Yes, yes—certainly! But this storm will raise the waters in a quarter of an hour. She may run serious risk!"

Mr. Daintrees rose quickly.

"I'll tell you what I will do, Miss Annie!" he said; "I'll ride as far as the Swamp—it is only a mile or two for that matter—and take a look at it. If it is dangerous I will warn your aunt not to attempt it!"

Annie was now seriously alarmed.

"Oh, yes! Mr. Daintrees, I wish you would!" she exclaimed. "I quite forgot! Do go—but you will be drenched!"

Mr. Jack Daintrees rushed forth, exclaiming gallantly—

"In the service of the ladies!"

Let us redeem the character of Mr. Daintrees, however, from the charge of utter thoughtlessness and indifference, to his elaborate toilet. He captured on his way to the door a long water-proof cloak, of light brown material, which he declared might be needed by Mrs. Gaston, mounted his horse, and setting the spurs into his sides, rode away at a gallop, waving his hat to Annie with all the grace of a lover.

There was but one circumstance that detracted from the gallant and romantic character of this proceeding—the fact that Mr. Jack Daintrees, bestriding with his portly limbs his flying steed, with his coat skirts floating backward in the cool gusts of the approaching storm, bore a close resemblance to a personage of history, or rather poetry—his namesake, Jack Gilpin, riding his famous race.

# CHAPTER XV

## IN THE SWAMP.

"THE SWAMP," to which Mr. Daintrees had alluded, was one of those sluggish streams frequently met with in Tidewater Virginia, the despair of agriculturists and roadmakers. In the dry season it was simply a lazy, lingering thread of muddy water which stole along through the grass-covered low grounds; but so low was the surface that the least rain swelled this slight current, made a dozen others, then covered the whole save where a sort of island here and there rose, and made the passage well nigh impossible.

On the road to Waterford a long wooden bridge, raised a few feet above the bush-grass on trestles, had accordingly been constructed; and on this somewhat rickety structure vehicles of all sorts could pass over the treacherous ooze.

Unfortunately, heavy rains had recently taken place, and the swamp was greatly swollen. Mrs. Gaston had passed over the bridge in the morning when the water, now completely covering the swamp, except in certain spots, was within a foot of the roadway. The driver had

declared it safe, as indeed it proved, but it was equally
certain that an additional rain-storm would seriously en-
danger the bridge.

Jack Daintrees thought of all this as he hastened on,
his horse frightened and flying along as the thunder
rumbled overhead.   Would Mrs. Gaston attempt to cross?
Would she arrive in time?   Might not the storm burst
before —— ?

The bridge was in sight—a long, low, insecure affair,
lashed by the now galloping waters of the whilom lazy,
lingering swamp.   The tall grass, nearly submerged,
dashed to and fro in the current, the hanging boughs of
some trees on a small island at the middle of the bridge
dipped to the water; the swamp was on a frolic, and—
worst of all—Mrs. Gaston's coach was seen approaching
the bridge.

At the same moment the rain dashed down, and the
waters seemed to rise before Mr. Daintrees's eyes.   He
spurred upon the bridge, which tottered and groaned beneath his horse's feet; made signals to the driver of Mrs.
Gaston's carriage not to venture upon it; reached the
middle—and saw the carriage coming on rapidly over the
bridge beyond.

The catastrophe followed.   Scarcely had the vehicle
reached the island when the bridge behind gave way.
Mrs. Gaston threw open the door and leaped out, exclaiming, "Oh! Mr. Daintrees!" in an accent which
sent a thrill of joy through the bosom of that gentleman—when the crowning event of this eventful day came
to put the finishing touch to everything.   Mrs. Gaston

had leaped from the carriage while it was in motion—the old driver, in his excitement, had not been aware of the fact, and had continued his way, entering on the last half of the bridge—all at once, as he was near the shore, that too sank under the vehicle ; and it was only by violent lashing that old Jake, plunging through grass, water, and mud, succeeded in forcing his way up the bank to firm ground.

Mrs. Gaston and Mr. Jack Daintrees were on an island in the middle of the swamp—the bridge was washed away on the right and the left—the storm was roaring down, the lightning setting the darkness on fire, the thunder discharging its big guns ; and the "weaker vessel," overcome and sobbing with terror, clung unconsciously to the "lord of creation," who supported her heroically with his encircling arm !

## CHAPTER XVI.

### BESIDE THE FIRE IN THE SWAMP.

"OH! Mr. Daintrees!"

"Don't be alarmed, my dear Mrs. Gaston!
don't be alarmed!"

"But—oh! we shall be drowned!"

"OH! MR. DAINTREES!"

"I think not," said Mr. Daintrees, "and I hope for
your sake more than for my own—yes! more than for

my own," repeated Mr. Jack Daintrees resolutely, as if
some one had contradicted him, "that no harm will
happen to one—hem!—one whom—I regard as my best
friend."

"Oh! indeed it is I who need a friend! Just look!
The water is rising!"

"But the storm is ceasing!" said Mr. Daintrees.

"There is no serious, real danger then!"

"I can't say that, madam; but one thing I can say,
that whatever that danger may be I am determined to
share it with you."

A grateful look repaid him. It was heroic in Mr. Daintrees. For might he not have mounted, plunged into
the current, and gained—as novelists say—the opposing
shore?

"I have long felt," said Mr. Daintrees, "that our fates
were or ought to be united, my dear Mrs. Gaston! See
how the very elements combine to throw us together!
We are here alone together on a lonely island in the midst
of a raging current, and—but be not uneasy. I will
rescue you or share your fate!"

Whether Mr. Daintrees had been reading romances or
not, we cannot say; but at least he was in earnest. His
earnestness, indeed, was so great that—unconsciously, no
doubt—he drew the graceful form of Mrs. Gaston toward
him, looked at her with deep devotion, and said:

"Let me wrap you in this cloak!"

It was an abrupt descent from the idea of perishing together; but an agreeable descent it seemed to Mrs. Gaston.
She permitted herself to be enveloped in the waterproof,

withdrew in a quiet manner from Mr. Daintrees's arm, and said :

" But oh ! Mr. Daintrees—what shall we do ? "

Having ceased to enjoy the pleasure of supporting his fair companion, and seeing no prospect of a renewal of that romantic proceeding, Mr. Daintrees looked at the " situation" in a strictly business-like light, and said :

" Let me reflect a moment, my dear madam, and think what is best. First, there is no prospect of the swamp falling even sufficiently to carry you over behind me—that is, not to-night ; and you see night has come. We must therefore be rescued—you at least."

" You can call to Uncle Jake !"

" My dear Mrs. Gaston, you fill me with admiration ! I knew the treasures of your heart—ahem—and now I find your good-sense equally admirable. Jake !"

The last word was uttered in a stentorian voice, and Jake responding, he was directed to hasten to the house of a neighbor and procure assistance. Jake promptly obeyed. He unhitched one of the horses, mounted, and was heard clattering off in the darkness.

" And now, for your comfort in the meantime ! The night is growing chill !" said Mr. Daintrees.

He took from his pocket a match-case, for so old a smoker never was without that convenience ; collected some dry sticks and dead limbs, lit them, and soon a cheerful blaze soared aloft, lighting up the wild and gloomy scene. The rain had ceased, and the storm had muttered away into the distance ; but the angry waters of the swamp were seen and heard roaring around them ;

drift-wood dashed by with dangerous velocity; there was even some reason to doubt whether the small patch of firm land occupied by Mrs. Gaston, Mr. Daintrees, and his horse, would not be overflowed.

"If it should be, madam," said Mr. Daintrees, "there is but one course to pursue. I will mount and swim to shore with you in my arms!"

Mrs. Gaston blushed. She presented a very handsome spectacle at the moment. She was half-reclining, wrapped in the water-proof, by the blaze, her fair hair all in disorder on her handsome neck, her small feet peeping from her wet skirt, and her whole attitude shrinking, timid, confiding. Mr. Jack Daintrees was nearly overcome!

"If we are saved," said Mrs. Gaston, with her little glance and blush, "I shall owe you my life!"

And Mrs. Gaston with her pretty hand put back a curl from her pretty face.

Mr. Daintrees was overcome!

"If I could only be permitted to take charge of that beloved life!" exclaimed Mr. Daintrees, seizing the hand. "If I was only worthy—if such presumption would not make you laugh at me—— !"

"Oh! Mr. Daintrees!" murmured pretty Mrs. Gaston.

"Am I wrong—indelicate—to speak of this on such an occasion—when we are thus alone together on this deserted isle?" said Mr. Daintrees. "Only tell me, dearest madam—only speak one word—and I will stop at once!"

But Mrs. Gaston seemed too much agitated to speak the word—whereat Mr. Daintrees thrilled with joy.

"I am not presumptuous then!—you do not forbid me!—I may hope then—— !"

Mr. Daintrees looked the picture of joy.

"Then I may take charge of the fate of one——"

A sudden halloo from the shore made them start, and looking up, they saw the blaze of torches.

"Only one word!" cried Mr. Daintrees, "only one word!"

Mrs. Gaston raised her eyes, looked at Mr. Daintrees for precisely the one hundredth part of one second, and then permitting the long lashes to fall upon her cheek, said in a whisper, with a blush and a smile:

"I would rather say that word—if I am to say it—at The Hollies!"

A resounding shout came, drowning Mr. Daintrees's rapturous response; hammers were heard constructing a raft of drift-wood, and precisely one hour afterwards Mrs. Gaston was placed upon this impromptu contrivance; it was pushed through the water, which proved not to be very deep, and Mr. Jack Daintrees having plunged through on horseback, they were all soon safely on shore.

Mrs. Gaston then got into her carriage—which had sustained no injury—thanked her kind neighbor, Mr. Page, who had come with all his men so promptly to her rescue; and then, with the last mutterings of the storm still resounding, rolled away toward The Hollies.

Mr. Daintrees had determined to return homeward, and had said with an air of common-place politeness:

"I shall do myself the pleasure of calling to-morrow, madam, to ascertain if you have caught cold."

The astute Mr. Jack Daintrees had supposed that he would thus compel Mrs. Gaston to say : "I shall be very glad to see you."

Mrs. Gaston simply replied—but with the ghost of a side-glance at Mr. Daintrees—

"Thank you, sir !"

# CHAPTER XVII.

## THE PHYSICIAN IN SPITE OF HIMSELF.

HALF a mile from The Hollies Mrs. Gaston was startled by an exclamation from the old driver, and the carriage suddenly stopped.

"What is the matter?" she exclaimed.

"It is nobody but me, Auntie," said a voice in the darkness, and Mrs. Gaston recognized Annie, who came and opened the door before the old coachman could descend for that purpose.

"Why, Annie! my dear child!" exclaimed Mrs. Gaston as the young lady entered the carriage, "what *could* have made you come out? you are soaking wet!"

"I was so uneasy about you, Auntie! I could not sit still! So I just walked out and went on until—— "

"With nothing on your head, and only this scarf around you! And your feet are wringing wet! Oh! my dear child."

"It is nothing, Auntie. But how did you get over, and where is Mr. Daintrees?"

The carriage had continued its way, and Mrs. Gaston having wrapped Annie in her own shawl, related her adventures, accidentally omitting any allusion to the somewhat peculiar character of her interview with the proprietor of The Lodge.

"That was just like Mr. Daintrees!" exclaimed Annie; "he is the best friend we have!"

"Do you like him, my dear?"

"Indeed I do—and so do you, my little auntie," returned Annie with a slight laugh.

Mrs. Gaston blushed in the darkness and said:

"Well, you know, my child—one can not help regarding as a friend a gentleman who comes so frequently! Ever since your accident last year, Mr. Daintrees has been very intimate with us, and has called every week."

"Every week!" exclaimed Annie with a momentary return of her constitutional gayety; "Every day you might say! But I won't tease you, Auntie, I am so glad you are safe, and I love you very much, and I believe I will kiss you!"

An embrace followed, then Annie suddenly coughed.

"You have taken cold, Annie!"

"A little, I'm afraid, Auntie. But it is nothing!"

It proved to be something, and by no means a slight something. The young lady had become drenched, her feet saturated in the mud and water of the high road, and on the next morning she complained of a pain in her side, and was ordered by Mrs. Gaston to remain in her chamber.

"Why what a nervous, fearful, and absurd little

auntie you are !" she exclaimed ; "why should I not go down ?"

"You may be sick."

"*I* sick !" what an idea ! And how do you think The Hollies will get along without me, madam ?"

"It will get along very well. I will take care of the flowers, and if George or anybody comes I will try to entertain them."

"George ?"

"Yes, you know he will certainly come, as he has not been here for two days."

A singular expression came to Annie's face, and she said quickly :

"Well, I suppose you are right, Auntie, and I will remain in my room."

Mrs. Gaston looked at the speaker who had thus promptly yielded, but Annie's face was impenetrable. The fair widow therefore left the young lady, and went to send up her breakfast.

Annie had no appetite, and coughed a good deal.

About noon Mrs. Gaston became a little uneasy, and thought of sending for a doctor, when Mr. Daintrees and George Cleave made their appearance—they had reached The Hollies by accident at the same moment.

Mr. Daintrees looked a little crestfallen—the presence of George was unlucky—and as the young man seemed to be in no haste to retire, Mr. Daintrees, utterly disappointed in the object of his visit, rose, took leave, and went away maligning his bad fortune. George remained for an hour or two, expressing much regret at Annie's indisposition, but not as much as Mrs. Gaston thought he ought to have expressed. At length he too went away, promising to return.

Toward evening Annie's cough seemed worse, and she had some fever. Mrs. Gaston then became alarmed, and, without telling Annie, wrote a note to Dr. Williams, her old family physician at Waterford, requesting him to come and see the invalid.

"If Dr. Williams is absent, request Dr. Harrington to come," she said to the servant.

And toward evening Dr. Harrington made his appearance, Dr. Williams having been called to some distance to see a patient.

Mrs. Gaston stood for a moment looking at Ralph Harrington, whom she had not seen for a long time. It was impossible not to be struck with the contrast between his present and his former self. All his jaunty air had disappeared; his cheeks were thin, and he looked wan and old.

"Why, what is the matter, Doctor!" exclaimed the lady.

"The matter, madam?"

"You are so much thinner and paler!"

Harrington smiled—it was rather a sad smile.

"Our profession is exacting, madam—night riding will tell upon the health. Miss Bell, I hope, is better?"

He very plainly desired to change the subject, and after informing him of Annie's symptoms, Mrs. Gaston went up to announce the doctor's presence. The young lady was lying in a morning wrapper upon a pile of pillows, with her hair in some disorder, and her flushed cheek resting upon one hand.

"Dr. Harrington has come, my dear," said Mrs. Gaston. "Shall I invite him up?"

"Dr. Harrington!" exclaimed Annie, turning redder than before.

"Yes, my child. Dr. Williams was absent."

"Dr. Harrington!"

"Do you object to seeing him? It is nothing. His visit is purely professional, and——"

"Dr. Harrington!"

Each of these exclamations had been uttered as it were unconsciously.

"I can understand your feelings, Annie," said Mrs. Gaston. "The doctor has been heretofore a young gentleman visitor in your eyes, and his new character startles you. But you need medical advice——"

"Oh! no, no, Auntie!"

"I really must insist, my dear."

She went firmly toward the door.

"At least wait a few minutes, Auntie—my toilet! Think of my toilet!"

Mrs. Gaston closed the door. No sooner had she done so than Annie rose quickly, ran to the mirror, bound up her hair, and had just completed these preparations and taken a seat upon a sofa when Mrs. Gaston and Dr. Harrington made their appearance.

Ralph Harrington was scarcely able to assume his professional coolness, but he did assume it, and said quietly:

"I am sorry to find you unwell, Miss Annie ; a trifle, I hope. Allow me to feel your pulse."

"Oh ! it is nothing, I assure you !" she exclaimed with a forced laugh. "Auntie is absurdly uneasy whenever I have a finger-ache !"

She held out her hand, and Dr. Harrington touched the blue vein on the wrist with his index and middle fingers.

"A little fever," he said, "resulting from simple cold. You will be well, I hope, to-morrow, Miss Annie."

Mrs. Gaston's countenance indicated the immense relief afforded her by these words.

"Then there is no danger of pneumonia, Doctor ?"

"None at all, madam, and you may dismiss all fears."

"How happy you make me !" exclaimed the lady ; "and George will be as glad as I am. Will you tell him on your return, Doctor ? He was here this morning."

A singular expression came to Harrington's face. He inclined his head rather stiffly, and said :

"I will, with great pleasure, madam."

He then rose, and said :

"I will leave a prescription. Can I write it downstairs, madam ?"

"Yes, Doctor."

Harrington turned toward Annie and their eyes met. For an instant they remained motionless, gazing at each other, and a slight tremor passed through the young lady's frame. Harrington's pale face flushed ; his lips opened, but no words issued from them. He simply bowed, and went out with Mrs. Gaston.

As the door closed, Annie's head fell upon the arm of the sofa, and she burst into tears.

On the next morning Dr. Williams made his appearance at The Hollies. He had been to see a patient ten or fifteen miles from Waterford, he said, when about midnight Dr. Harrington had reached the house and informed him of Miss Bell's indisposition, expressing a wish that, as he, Dr. Williams, was the family physician of Mrs. Gaston, he would treat the case.

" A mere cold, my dear madam," he said to Mrs. Gaston, after feeling Annie's pulse ; " and Miss Annie will be well in three days."

The interview had taken place in the parlor, whither Annie had insisted upon going. Had she expected Dr. Ralph Harrington ? An hour after the departure of the old physician, Annie was looking out of the window when she saw George Cleave ride into the grounds. Her proceeding thereupon was singular. In the morning she had declared herself perfectly well. She now rose quietly and said :

" Auntie, I believe I feel a little badly, and would rather not see any company. Will you tell George ?"

Having made this request, Miss Annie Bell strolled out of the room. Once in the passage she began to walk rapidly. Then as Cleave approached the house she flew up-stairs, and disappeared in her chamber, closing the door behind her.

## CHAPTER XVIII.

HARRINGTON ANNOUNCES HIS INTENTION TO LEAVE
WATERFORD.

THREE days after these scenes, Dr. Ralph Harrington was walking up and down in his office, about
twilight, smoking a cigar and evidently reflecting. His
habit of smoking had grown upon him of late, and he
was seldom without a pipe or a cigar between his lips.

The slow and measured promenade to and fro had continued for some time, when the door opened and George
Cleave came in.

"Take a seat, George," said Harrington; "you'll find
a cigar on the table."

He then continued his walk, Cleave seating himself
but declining the cigar.

"I am glad you came, old fellow," said Harrington,
"as I want to talk with somebody. I am going to leave
Waterford."

Cleave turned his head quickly.

"Leave Waterford?"

Harrington nodded.

"The fact is, I can't afford to stay. I am not doing

as well as I think I can do elsewhere. Sorry to go, but
I am compelled to."

Cleave's countenance, at this announcement, expressed
the greatest consternation and regret.

"You can't be in earnest, Ralph !" he exclaimed.
"Why, you are·succeeding better than any young doctor
in the country—everybody says that ! It is absurd to be
going away. Leave Waterford ? You astonish me !"

Harrington shook his head.

"Can't stay," he said coolly. "Every man must look
out for his career, my dear fellow. I am only dragging
along here, losing my best years. I don't like to leave
you, kind friends all, but I must pull up stakes, my son !"

Harrington spoke in his habitual tone of lazy indifference, and seemed to be smiling. Cleave looked at him
as well as the dim light would permit. He was quite
thin and pale, but all his old spirit of brave resolution
was plainly in him.

"What's the use of staying ?" he added. "I have
some talent they say, and some day I may wish—to
marry. What probability is there of making sufficient
income for that here ? True, marriage is not the chief
end of existence, but then the fancy takes a man with
almost absolute certainty before he's forty, to indulge in
that dangerous luxury, and it may seize upon *me !*"

The slight accent of irony, satire, whatever word expressed it, was plainer in the voice.

"True, I don't think of it now," Harrington added
again, "but—but here I am boring you, old fellow. I
must go."

Cleave had listened without a word. It was perfectly evident that he was watching the speaker.

"Well," he said quietly, "let us not speak any further of this at the moment. To come to another subject— my own affairs."

"*Your* affairs?"

"If anybody goes away, I think it ought to be *me.*"

"You? What an absurdity! You are the luckiest fellow I know, George. You are engaged to be married to—to the woman you love—and you know my opinion of her."

"You forget my poverty."

"That's nothing."

"Which proves, Ralph, that you are the most consistent of reasoners. Just now you argued triumphantly, in your own estimation, that money was necessary to marriage, and *you* must go elsewhere to make money."

"The case is different."

"It is the same. But to cease that discussion, I want to speak of my own affairs, as I said."

"Well, speak, George."

"I am going to request Miss Annie Bell to terminate our engagement."

"*What?*"

Cleave repeated his words.

"Well," said Harrington, a little agitated, "wonders never cease!"

He had stopped abruptly in his promenade at George's words. He now resumed his deliberate walk.

"Is it possible," he said, "that you are going to a

young lady to say, ' I love you no longer, and can't marry you ? ' "

" No, I am going to say, ' *You* love *me* no longer, and wish to be released from an engagement which you regret.' "

Harrington shook his head. When he spoke, his voice faltered a little.

" Take care, George. This is a ticklish business. What reason have you to think Miss Bell is anxious to be off ? "

" A hundred reasons, which it is unnecessary to state—among the rest, that she avoids me whenever she can do so ; is everything that an engaged young lady ought *not* to be ; and only does not *speak* because she shrinks from an apparent breach of faith ! "

Harrington continued to walk up and down in silence.

" Well," he said at length, in a low tone, " and *you*—what will you do, my dear fellow ? Blow out your brains ? "

Cleave did not reply for some moments.

" Do you remember what you told me the other day about Marian Ormby ? " he said at length in a very low voice.

" What was that ? "

" That she had acted under constraint in breaking off with me—had been forced by the tyranny of her father to deny herself when I came ? "

" Well, yes—and I said more ; that the poor thing was breaking her heart at the prospect of being forced to marry this Mr. Gartrell, whom she abhors."

George Cleave nodded.

"Now, then, you ought to know whether I am willing or unwilling to be off with Annie. The simple fact is, that engagement was an awful blunder. I was piqued, angry, wretched, and at The Hollies I found consolation; Annie *took pity* on me—that's all. The crowning misfortune is that—I love Marian Ormby more than ever."

Harrington knit his brows, but could not suppress the joy in his eyes.

"And you are going to say so?"

"Yes."

"To—Annie?"

"Yes."

Harrington controlled the throbbing of his heart by an effort, and said :

"Well, the interview, I think, will be curious; something like a story book ! You must act after your own views, George; I can't advise you. Suppose you come and tell me the result ?"

"I will, most certainly."

The darkness had come. Harrington's cigar glowed quickly and nervously, puff by puff.

"It will interest a cool, careless old fellow like me to hear how it turns out, George," he said.

## CHAPTER XIX.

### THE WOES OF DAINTREES.

THROUGHOUT the whole following day George Cleave was in the most absent frame of mind conceivable, and his eyes would remain fixed for hours together upon the same page of the law-book which he was reading—even upon the same sentence.

He sat in one corner of Mr. Jobson's office, where his studies were prosecuted. Before the great green-baize table sat Mr. Jobson.

Mr. Jobson raised his head.

"I don't like this Mr. Gartrell," he said aloud, addressing the walls of his office; "and who is this *Brown?*"

Cleave raised his eyes.

"What did you say, Mr. Jobson?"

The old lawyer rose.

"I say, I don't like your cousin, Mr. Allan Gartrell; and I don't like Brown! Brown is still there. What is he doing there?"

This was a poser. George smiled and said:

"He is agent of a lumber company, I believe, and came to buy timber."

"He is nothing of the sort, my dear sir," said Mr. Jobson, knitting his brows and wiping his pen. "There is some mystery about Brown, and I wish to heaven we had not given up that estate."

Mr. Jobson said "We." His feeling toward George was really paternal now, when the young man's fortunes were under a cloud; and he had attempted vainly to induce him to come and live with him—the amount for his board and lodging to be paid when convenient; say in twenty years—without interest.

"Very well," said Mr. Jobson, after gazing with extreme sternness upon an opposite book-shelf where the demon of dust seemed to have taken up its reign; "I'll say no more at the present time on the subject of Gartrell and—*Brown*. I am now going to see Mrs. Gaston. There is just time to return before dark."

"You have business with her, Mr. Jobson?"

"Yes; to read her the rough draft of a deed for some land she is about to purchase."

George closed his book.

"I will go with you."

The ghost of a smile flitted across the parchment face of Mr. Jobson.

"Your business, I suppose, will be with—the other members of the family."

"Yes," said George quietly.

Mr. Jobson groaned.

"To think that you might have kept Cleaveland if you had only arranged that affair in time!" he said.

Everything was an "affair" with Mr. Jobson.

"There was not time," returned Cleave in the same quiet tone; "and now as you are getting ready, I'll order my horse and go with you."

The sun was sinking toward the woods as Mr. Jobson and George rode up to The Hollies, where masses of foliage, flowers, and emerald sward were bathed in the rich, red light. They saw a horse at the rack—and George smiled. They dismounted and entered—there was Mr. Jack Daintrees, who had not arrived more than three minutes before them. Mrs. Gaston had not had time since his arrival to come down-stairs.

When Mr. Jack Daintrees beheld the forms of the two visitors, a muttered exclamation might have been distinguished by any one in his immediate vicinity; and an expression of the deepest gloom diffused itself over his countenance. The reason was that Mr. Jack Daintrees was the victim of misfortune, the sport of fate, a puppet in the unrelenting hand of destiny. Day after day he had vainly essayed to secure that much-desired private interview with Mrs. Gaston. What had that fair lady said, beside the fire in the swamp? Why, that if she *had* to utter a certain "word" ardently desired by Mr. Daintrees, she should prefer to utter it "*at The Hollies!*" What had the "glance of her eye" indicated as she rolled away homeward on that night? An unmistakable intention *not* to say "No!"

And ever since that stormy but brilliant moment, Mr. Jack Daintrees had been struggling to secure the desired interview—and incessantly something had occurred to prevent it; Annie's sickness, George's visits, a severe headache under which Mrs. Gaston labored — always something! On this evening, Mr. Daintrees had regarded his success as certain. No one had preceded him; Annie was well; the servant said Mrs. Gaston was quite well; and Mrs. Gaston had sent word that she would be down in a few minutes.

And now!— Here was George, and the hated Jobson! Jobson on "business," no doubt! *Business* at such a moment!

When Mrs. Gaston made her appearance in a few minutes, clad in an exquisite evening dress, with a bow of pink ribbon clearly relieved against her pretty neck, a white rose in her braided hair, and a faint smile just dimpling her blushing cheeks, Mr. Jack Daintrees experienced sensations which were too deep for words, and felt a violent desire to fall upon Mr. George Cleave and Mr. Jobson, and put them to death then and there!

Mr. Jobson having bowed stiffly and exchanged a few commonplaces on the subject of the weather, said :

"I have come as you requested, madam, but rather late, I am afraid. The deed you wish proved a more difficult matter than I supposed. It will require your attention for two or three hours, I fear."

Mr. Daintrees nearly groaned aloud.   He glanced round.   The sun was on the horizon, and its last rays darted through the window.   George and Annie had disappeared—with the view of looking at the flowers—and Mr. Daintrees was plainly *de trop*.   With a heavy heart and the most plaintive of expressions, he rose, declaring that as he had simply called to inquire after Mrs. Gaston's health on his way home—which was a fearful false-hood—he would continue his ride, doing himself the pleasure to call again.

What thereupon did Mrs. Gaston do ? Mrs. Gaston sent Mr. Jack Daintrees away with a bosom expanding with joy. The fair lady rose, gave him her small hand, pressed his own—actually pressed it—blushed, and murmured *sotto voce*, unheard by Mr. Jobson :

" I am sorry that—you can not—stay."

A glance accompanied the words which flooded the soul of Mr. Jack Daintrees with happiness unspeakable. He bowed low over the hand, threw an expression of sad and uncomplaining tenderness into his eyes, and went away in triumph.

George and Annie were nowhere to be seen.

## CHAPTER XX.

**P**RECISELY at midnight George Cleave opened the
door of Ralph Harrington's office, and entered,
closing the door after him.   Harrington was half reclin-
ing in an arm-chair, smoking as usual.   Through the
window streamed a flood of moonlight—the only light in
the apartment.

"Well, old fellow," said Harrington with an unwonted
tremor in his voice, "here you are, and you have had the
luck to catch me just as I was going to turn in.   Sit
down!"

Cleave did so, and replied :

"Let us leave all sorts of pretences, Ralph, and have
no concealments!   You know you were waiting for me,
and that you are dying to know the result of my interview at The Hollies!"

Harrington attempted a short laugh.

"What a suspicious fellow you are, my boy!   *I* dying
to know how affairs have turned out yonder between you
and your sweetheart?   What have I to do with it beyond

mere friendship for you ; the simple desire, certainly a natural one in a friend, to see you well out of this—love snarl ?"

Cleave looked at his friend, whose face utterly belied his words.

" My dear Ralph," he said, " do you think that I am like the persons spoken of in the Scriptures, who have eyes and see not, ears and hear not ? You have grown pale and thin ; your voice, once so strong and hearty, has lost its old tones. I can see and hear that. But let us leave this subject for the present."

" Most willingly. The fact is, George, you are dreaming !"

Unfortunately Harrington's face and voice completely justified Cleave's criticisms. The face was agitated and the voice shook a little.

" What you allude to, George," he added, " is easily explained. I am overworked, and nothing pulls a man down like loss of rest. The inhabitants of this agreeable neighborhood insist on being taken sick invariably in the night ; and I have no sooner turned in, congratulating myself upon at least one night's rest, than a ring comes at my night bell, and there I'm in the saddle for a ride of ten miles, perhaps !"

" I thought we had agreed to drop the discussion of that point, my dear Ralph."

" True ; excuse me."

" Let me tell you about my interview with Annie."

" Well," said Harrington in a low voice, " let us hear about that."

"Everything was explained, arranged, and ended in an hour. I walked out with Annie, and when we were out of sight of the house in the grove, made a clean breast of it, Ralph. I told her that it was perfectly plain that she regretted her engagement; that reflection and observation had convinced me that she had promised to marry me from compassion and pitying tenderness for me in my forlorn condition; and that such a union, on such a basis, would prove miserable to us both—a blunder which could never be righted. As her friend and adopted brother, therefore, I released her from her engagement."

"Yes," said Harrington.

"Then came the reply, Ralph. I won't repeat Annie's words, words full of affection and uttered in her frank, true, earnest voice. In the most delicate but the plainest manner, she informed me that I had truthfully read her heart; perhaps it *would* be better to terminate the engagement—was I sure that it would not distress me? She hoped not? She loved me dearly!—— then came some tears, and renewed assurances of affection which, as they were simply of *sisterly* regard, I can allude to, Ralph."

"You did not allude then to Marian?" came in the same low voice from Harrington.

Cleave colored and tried to laugh.

"I did not utter her name. Why say to Annie, 'I am too much attached to some one else to wish my engagement with you to continue?' Her own disinclination was reason enough."

"You are right."

"I am glad you think so."

"So—your engagement with Miss Annie is definitely at an end?"

Harrington could not suppress a tremor of the voice, through which broke forth a great and sudden joy.

"Completely at an end, and I assure you, Ralph, I feel all the satisfaction of a man who has extricated himself from a false position."

"And—Miss Bell?"

"I am compelled to say, unflattering as the avowal is to myself, that Annie could not conceal her happiness!"

Harrington was silent, but Cleave could hear him drawing long breaths.

"There was no sort of doubt about my little *sister's* satisfaction," added Cleave, "and I assure you she never looked so beautiful, and she *is* beautiful."

"*Very* beautiful!" muttered Harrington.

"And now I have the pleasure of knowing that my visits will not make her run up-stairs to avoid me, I shall always have a charming little friend to tell my troubles to—to go to for consolation. You should try, yourself, to secure such a friend, Ralph."

"I!"

"Why not? What for instance would be more rational than that you should give Annie the opportunity of brightening *two* people? You are pining away here for want of female society. Come! ride with me to-morrow to The Hollies."

"I!—to The Hollies!"

"Why not?"

Harrington's face filled with blood.

"The family are your excellent good friends. Their smiles will cheer you."

A strange agitation passed through the frame of the young physician. Joy was infusing itself like a subtle essence into his life.

"I will—I will think of it, George," he said.

Cleave, in spite of his own sadness, could not suppress a smile.

"You may as well pass your time as agreeably as possible before—you leave Waterford."

Harrington turned suddenly and exclaimed:

"Why should I be playing a part with you, George? Why am I making a fool of myself? Now that I know your engagement is broken, I can tell you what perhaps you know—that I love the very ground *she* walks upon! That I have been breaking my heart about her!"

"Well—that is now useless, Ralph; and listen!—try if you can't arrange with my little sister to be—my brother-in-law!"

Harrington thrilled suddenly.

"I don't dare to think of it! Let us speak of *your* affairs, George. I am going to Bayview to-morrow, and I will tell somebody there all about you. Don't despair! Patience, and shuffle the cards!"

Harrington uttered a laugh so young and joyful that it sounded like a boy's.

"I believe you have made me ten years younger, old fellow!" he exclaimed.

## CHAPTER XXI.

### ALLAN GARTRELL, ESQ.

ON the morning after this interview between Harrington and Cleave Mr. Allan Gartrell came out of his fine mansion of Cleaveland, drew on a handsome pair of riding gauntlets, mounted a superb horse held respectfully by his groom, and set off at a rapid gallop in the direction of Bayview.

Allan Gartrell, Esq., was what is called a "fine-looking man," about twenty-eight, with a ruddy countenance indicative of high living, a vigorous person, and English side whiskers, black and curling. Mr. Gartrell might have been called a "fine-looking man," though his appearance was rather rakish, and the only thing that detracted from his personal charms, was an ugly-looking scar upon his right temple. He was clad in the height of the fashion, and had a joyous air which seemed the result of a good conscience and a good digestion. He went on rapidly humming the air of a little French song, and in due time reached Bayview, from which, as Mr. Gartrell entered, issued Dr. Ralph Harrington.

Harrington's frequent visits to Bayview had aroused

that gossiping report that he was paying his addresses to Marian. His business was much more prosaic. A valued servant had been taken sick, some time before, and as Mr. Ormby had conceived a great dislike to old Dr. Williams, Dr. Harrington had been sent for, and had continued to attend the sick servant.

The two men coolly saluted each other with that indefinable reserve which clearly indicates all want of sympathy. Each felt that the other was not to his taste. Harrington did not fancy Mr. Allan Gartrell, and Mr. Allan Gartrell seemed to understand the fact perfectly. They therefore bowed coolly, the physician departed, and the last new-comer entered.

Opening the library door with the air of a man entirely at home, Mr. Gartrell found himself face to face with Mr. Jobson, who was sitting with one leg crossed over the other, his spectacles on his nose, a paper in his hand, and engaged in conversation with Mr. Ormby. A single glance at Mr. Ormby was sufficient to show that that gentleman was in an extremely gloomy state of mind. His brow was lowering, his general expression downcast. He rose hastily as Mr. Gartrell came in, and greeted him with some confusion, adding that he would probably find the drawing-room more pleasant—Miss Ormby would— there Mr. Ormby stopped, clearing his throat.

Mr. Gartrell bowed and smiled. He was evidently a gentleman of tact.

"Don't let me disturb you, my dear sir. I really beg pardon, business is business, and," he added with a light laugh, "I must say, at the expense of politeness, that I would rather see Miss Ormby than even two such worthy gentlemen as yourself and Mr. Jobson, Mr. Ormby!"

The old lawyer did not respond to this pleasantry. He looked at Mr. Gartrell out of the upper part of his eyes above his spectacles, and said nothing.

The airy Mr. Gartrell did not or would not see the lawyer's cool glance. He sauntered into the parlor, and having summoned a servant, who was directed to inform Miss Ormby of Mr. Gartrell's presence, Mr. Ormby returned to the library, closing the door carefully behind him.

"And the decree is now final, decisive, not to be assailed? Good heavens, sir!" said Mr. Ormby, losing all his habitual pomposity.

"Entirely," replied Mr. Jobson, "the motion for a new trial has been overruled, and I consider it my duty to say, Mr. Ormby, that an appeal will result in nothing; the slight remnant of your property which the plaintiff in this action is willing to release will go, if you appeal, and that I understand you to say is all you can look to for the support of your family."

"The sole means left! and that a mere pittance!"

Mr. Ormby sank back in his seat, the picture of despair.

"Is there no hope?" he exclaimed.

"None, I am truly sorry to say, Mr. Ormby. It is my duty to tell you that there is no means whatever of preventing the sale of Bayview, and your only course is to accept the proposition of Mr. Russell, surrender the property, and take what he offers you. There may be a moderate sum after the payment of the debt, and I would suggest to you the purchase of the small house and grounds near Waterford.   You will then have a home, if an humble one."

Mr. Ormby covered his face with his hands and groaned.   He was at last face to face with ruin.   He had heavily encumbered his estate nearly twenty years before, the interest had accumulated from year to year, and his creditor had at last demanded payment, and Bayview must go.

Mr. Ormby remained silent for half an hour, during which time Mr. Jobson closely scanned the paper which he held.

"There is no hope whatever," the lawyer said at length, "and I had better inform Mr. Russell's counsel that his proposition is accepted."

"Wait till to-morrow!" groaned Mr. Ormby; "I will then call and see you.   I must reflect.   Perhaps—yes, yes!" he added eagerly.   "Wait until to-morrow, Mr. Jobson!"

And again he murmured the word "perhaps—" looking as he did so toward the drawing-room.

Was he thinking of Mr. Gartrell?

Mr. Jobson bowed and took his leave.   As he disappeared, Mr. Ormby rang for a servant.

"Tell Mr. Gartrell that I should be glad to see him before he goes," he said.

# CHAPTER XXII.

## WHAT MONEY-TROUBLE BRINGS SOME MEN TO.

THE interview between Mr. Gartrell and Marian Ormby on this morning was of a painful character—so painful that we shall spare the reader a detailed account of it.

For some time now Mr. Gartrell had been the avowed suitor of the young lady. When he made his appearance and took possession of Cleaveland, Mr. Ormby had visited him, invited him to Bayview—and this invitation Mr. Gartrell had promptly accepted. A week afterwards he repeated his visit, expressed himself delighted with the place, the house, the elegance of everything at Bayview—and thereafter his visits became still more frequent, and it was perfectly obvious that these visits were paid to Marian Ormby.

The poor girl was pale and thin, but very beautiful; and Mr. Gartrell no doubt concluded that a young lady of such attractions, high position, and worldly advantages as the only child of the wealthy Mr. Ormby would make a most appropriate mistress of the Cleaveland establishment. He, therefore, coolly proposed himself to Mr.

Ormby as his future son-in-law, received a response approving of his proposition; then he redoubled his attentions, and on this morning offered himself in an impassioned speech to the young lady.

Marian flushed to her temples and promptly refused him. Up to this moment she had struggled against her father's despotic authority in silence; had listened in a sort of dumb despair to his arguments in favor of Mr. Gartrell, and had not flatly refused obedience. Awed and crushed well nigh by this tyrannical will, she had not dared to rebel; but now when the question of actual union with one whom she absolutely disliked was presented to her she discarded every other thought, and gave Mr. Allan Gartrell a "No!" so distinct and unmistakable that he colored with anger.

"Well, madam!" he exclaimed, "I see I need say no more! I will, therefore, bid you good morning!"

"Good morning, sir," said Marian, rising and slightly inclining her pale face.

Mr. Gartrell went out of the drawing-room, and was about to leave the house in a rage, when a servant in the hall gave him the message from Mr. Ormby. He hesitated, a singular expression of cunning came to his face, and he went into the library.

An hour afterwards Mr. Allan Gartrell came out of the library, and going to the place where his horse stood mounted and rode away.

Then Mr. Ormby, who had been standing at the window of the library looking after him, rang the bell; a servant came and Mr. Ormby said:

" Say to Miss Ormby that I wish to see her."

Marian promptly came ; the door closed, and with the exception of some stifled sobs from the library, no sound for the next hour disturbed the stillness at Bayview.

Then the door again opened, the girl came out looking as pale as death and went up-stairs, and Mr. Ormby made

"GOOD MORNING, SIR," SAID MARIAN, RISING.

his appearance behind her, red, flurried, gloomy, and indeed the picture of despair.

"There was no other course !" he muttered. "No other course !"

And taking his stick from its place in the corner, from

the force of long habit, he went through the front door, and out upon the lawn, trembling, breathing heavily, and indeed appearing to be about to suffocate.

What had taken place in these two interviews? In this world—outside the pages of romances—men are not entirely bad as they are not entirely good. Mr. Ormby was a mixture, and—driven to the wall by his pecuniary troubles—allowed the bad to get the mastery of him for the time. He had learned from Mr. Gartrell the result of the interview with Marian; pooh-poohed the idea of abandoning the affair in consequence of the mere caprice of a girl; assured the suitor that a few words from himself would set matters to rights, and dismissed Mr. Gartrell with the assurance that he might call again in two days, when all the trouble would have disappeared.

Mr. Ormby loved his daughter, and believed perhaps that he was acting for her real welfare. Her union with Cleave he regarded as out of the question, her marriage with Gartrell even at the expense of some disinclination as the better course; she would be the mistress of a fine establishment, and not be dragged down with his own falling fortunes. So he sent Mr. Allan Gartrell away with that understanding—not alluding even to his money difficulties, and sending for Marian proceeded to "use his parental authority."

Let us pass over this interview as over the first. When Mr. Ormby had demonstrated his good-sense and real affection by urging the marriage with Gartrell, and Marian declared that nothing would ever induce her to take such a step, Mr. Ormby grew angry and insisted.

When Marian exclaimed that she could not and would not, Mr. Ormby, more angry than before, threatened her with his parental displeasure. When she still refused, he bade her go and reflect upon his words, and prepare to obey him.

Marian had then gone to her room, flushed and trembling, and Mr. Ormby no less flushed and trembling even more had walked out to indulge his wretchedness where no eye could see him.

Once in her chamber, the unfortunate young lady sat down, leaned her elbow on the arm of her chair, her forehead in her hand, and remained for more than an hour, gazing with fixed and vacant eyes upon the carpet. What was passing in her mind ?   No sound escaped from her lips to indicate the current of her secret thoughts, but the laboring bosom as she drew long breaths, the flushed cheeks, and the tearless eyes fixed in that vacant stare seemed to indicate that she was slowly approaching some resolution from which she shrank, but which every instant gathered strength.

When at length she rose and looked around her with a vague, yearning, piteous glance, these words issued from her lips :

" Nothing else is left me ! "

# CHAPTER XXIII.

WHEN Mr. Allan Gartrell reached Cleaveland after his return from Bayview, he beheld the portly Mr. Brown slowly promenading upon the great portico in front of the mansion, flourishing his cane, swinging his shoulders, and gazing around him with a smile full of friendly good-humor.

Mr. Brown seemed to have found his quarters at Cleaveland agreeable, and not to contemplate an early departure. He had, indeed, the air of a gentleman perfectly satisfied with his surroundings, in no haste to change them and entirely "at home." As he gazed upon the fertile fields extending in front of the great mansion perched upon its lofty hill, and allowed his idle glance to wander to the distant river seen through a vista of the woods, his appearance was that of a wealthy landed proprietor, not ill-pleased at surveying his ample possessions.

As soon as Mr. Gartrell's horse's hoofs resounded upon the avenue a groom appeared, and was ready to receive his horse, which the rider abandoned to him, walking rapidly thereafter up the broad, marble steps.

Mr. Brown had walked half the length of the portico, and was now between the two middle pillars which rose on each side of the steps. His cane was held perpendicular, the ferule resting upon the porch ; his ample waistcoat protruded in front ; his head, surmounted by its tall, black, beaver hat, was slightly bent toward one shoulder, and Mr. Brown smiled.

"Ah ! ah !" said Mr. Brown in a jocose voice. "So here we are, my young friend ! We have been riding abroad to see our sweetheart ?"

"Yes," said Mr. Gartrell, cutting some atoms of dust from his elegant boots with his ivory-handled riding-whip, "and a cursed slow business it has been, my dear Brown !"

"Slow, eh ?" said Mr. Brown inquiringly.

"With the young lady at least," said Mr. Gartrell walking toward the front door. "The fact is, my dear friend, I have been flatly refused—think of *my* being refused !"

"It is incredible !"

"But luckily, the paterfamilias intervened—declared that the damsel's views were not his views, that young ladies never knew their own minds—and the affair is where it was before or in a better condition. Mere maiden modesty, you see, on her part."

"So you are going to be a married man after all, eh ? my dear Gartrell ?"

"I think so."

"You are going to be the happy mate of this handsome damsel—you say she is handsome."

" Yes, very."

" And the owner of her papa's acres, since he has no other children."

Mr. Gartrell knit his brows and was silent for a moment.

"I really don't know about that, or at least what the extent of the said acres will be.  I had an interview with papa—a lawyer was there when I arrived.  Do you know, Brown, the fancy strikes me that the old man is embarrassed."

" Embarrassed ? "

" Yes, and that will never do."

Mr. Brown smiled sweetly.

" You are right, but perhaps you are mistaken."

" It is possible, but come in.  This is dry talk, and I'm as thirsty as a fish.  Any one called ? "

" Nobody, my dear Allan ; let me call you by your first name !  I yearn to do so.  My affection for you, my dear Allan !  but you will laugh at me.  Come, I think you said champagne !  'Tis my favorite beverage."

Mr. Gartrell laughed a rather reckless laugh, and led the way into the superb dining-room, where a silent and respectful servant quickly opened a bottle of champagne, and then another, and then another.

It was an interesting spectacle to behold Mr. Brown partaking of this liquid.  He held out his glass, watched the sparkling beverage flowing into it, raised the glass as the liquid foamed to the brim, said : " Thank you, my friend ! " to the servant ; and then, having first inspected the color of the wine by holding it up between his eye and the light, permitted it slowly to disappear down his ample throat.

"How obliging in your late worthy uncle to provide this charming vintage for his dear nephew, yourself," said Mr. Brown smiling; "excellent man! his taste in wines was irreproachable."

"He never thought of me, my dear Brown," said Mr.

"HIS HEALTH!"

Gartrell, laughing; "my cousin George was his favorite, as you no doubt know. A good boy, my cousin George! His health!"

And Mr. Gartrell emptied his second bottle and grew red in the face. Mr. Brown's countenance was not flushed. That gentleman never changed. Sometimes—

after his fourth or fifth bottle—he grew solemn and gave serious advice; he never grew tipsy, which Mr. Gartrell was now becoming.

"By the by, Brown," said Mr. Gartrell, "I met Mr. Daintrees, a gentleman of the neighborhood, to-day, and he invited me to dine with him, with some friends, to-morrow."

"Ah?" said Mr. Brown.

"I accepted, and told him that I had a very dear friend on a visit to my house—I said a very dear friend, Brown!"

"Why not? And I am invited?"

"You are invited!" said Mr. Gartrell, with imposing solemnity, steadying himself by grasping a corner of the table.

"How gratified I feel!" said Mr. Brown, laying his hand upon his waistcoat and smiling.

"You ought to be, you know, Brown," said Mr. Gartrell in a voice which had grown a little thick—"for the first time, you are moving in good society, Brown—your origin, Brown, is—excuse me, Brown—your origin, you know, is—low! Anybody can see that."

Mr. Brown laughed heartily.

"You are right, my dear friend," he said, "and I am only too proud to associate on equal terms with so elegant a young gentleman as yourself."

Mr. Gartrell staggered slightly, and suddenly scowling, observed:

"Curse you—Brown—you are always laughing at a man!"

"Laughing, my dear fellow? Not in the least. Why should I laugh?"

"You had better not—I'd punch your old nob, Brown! What do you mean by laughing at me, I say?"

And Mr. Allan Gartrell poured out another glass of champagne, which he drained; after which he burst into loud laughter.

"*Vive la joie!* old fellow!" he exclaimed. "What a jolly good thing it is to have you here, Brown! You are my best friend—I love you, Brown; I love you like a brother!"

Mr. Brown wiped his eyes with a yellow bandanna handkerchief.

"Don't talk so, my dear friend!—you move me to tears!"

"Fact! And you—take an interest—I—that is you— jolly good fellows—every one—ha! ha!"

After which Mr. Gartrell permitted his head to decline upon the arm of his red velvet chair, and muttering inarticulately slept.

Mr. Brown placed his glass upon the table and gazed at Mr. Gartrell for some moments in silence. His expression was singular, and very difficult to describe. He ended by nodding his head slowly about six times, smiling sweetly, and leaving the apartment.

As he did so, a servant came into the hall bringing the letter bag. There were but two letters, one for Mr. Gartrell on some neighborhood business—a fact which Mr. Brown ascertained after the departure of the servant, by adroitly opening it without in the least tearing the envelope, and then re-sealing it skilfully—and one to himself. This he read with close attention, as also a paper enclosed in it; after which he drew from his pocket a match-case, lit a match, and carefully burned the letter.

"Well, the game is in my own hands now," he said. "Shall I play my trump?"

## CHAPTER XXIV.

JACK DAINTREES ENTERTAINS SOME FRIENDS.

WHEN Mr. Jack Daintrees invited his friends to a bachelor dinner at The Lodge he prepared for that festivity with the utmost care. On the present occasion his saddle of mutton was superb, his old ham beyond all praise, his fowls puffed out with fat, and his wines and stronger drinks adapted to the most fastidious palates.

It was Mr. Daintrees's habit to give about four dinners a year, and to invite every gentleman of the neighborhood. On this occasion, as we have seen, he had included Mr. Gartrell, whom he scarcely knew, and Mr. Gartrell's friend, Mr. Brown. These gentlemen arriving late completed the party, and the *convives* having duly observed the bad ceremony of drinking toddy on their arrival, sat down to dinner ; after which they adjourned to the drawing-room, and lighting cigars, began to play whist.

A bowl of punch had been brewed in a huge variegated China affair, an heirloom in the Daintrees family, as was the antique silver ladle used to fill the glasses ; and this inspiring liquid soon began to tell upon the tongues and in the faces of the guests. They laughed, uttered an hundred jests, and a gay hubbub ensued, which all at once, however, became stilled—the company gathering around a table in one corner, where Mr. Allan Gartrell and a wealthy young planter of the neighborhood were playing a game of cards to themselves.

On the table before them lay a large pile of bank-notes, and the figures "100" on a number of these notes indicated that the players were playing for high stakes. The group around them was striking. The gentlemen of the party, unused to such betting, lost sight of their jests and fixed their eyes intently upon the players. Every face was earnest, and more than one person protested in a low voice at this introduction of so exciting a mode of playing into the quiet assemblage of friends and neighbors. One personage only seemed to be highly amused at the proceeding, and this personage was Mr. Brown. He stood with the thumb of his right hand inserted in the armhole of his ample waistcoat ; a quiet smile upon his face ; his eyes fixed steadily, without winking, upon Mr. Gartrell ; with a slight drawing down of the corners of his lips, which was very striking.

Suddenly the young planter threw down his cards, exclaiming :

"I'll play no more ! You have the devil's own luck. sir !"

He rose from the table, turning red and then pale. The amount which he had lost exceeded two thousand dollars, received on that day from the sale of his wheat.

Mr. Gartrell quietly thrust the bank-notes into his pocket, rose in his turn, and approaching the speaker, said :

"What do you mean by that expression, sir ?—that I have played unfairly !"

The young planter was about to reply when a solid

'NO OFFENCE IS MEANT BY EITHER GENTLEMAN, I AM SURE."

figure interposed between him and his adversary—the figure of Mr. Brown ; and that gentleman said quietly :

"No offence is meant by either gentleman, I am sure."

Half turning to Mr. Gartrell Mr. Brown added with a peculiar shutting down of his eyelids, and a glance, keen, penetrating, and rapid as a flash of lightning,

"Am I wrong?"

Gartrell could not sustain the glance. His eyes fell and he muttered,

"No offence meant!"

"Honor is satisfied," Mr. Brown said coolly; "and now, Mr. Gartrell, as it is late, shall we return, sir?"

Gartrell looked moody and reluctant; but a second glance from Mr. Brown decided him. He bowed stiffly to the company and went out with his companion, accompanied to the door by the hospitable Mr. Daintrees.

No sooner had the two horsemen gotten out of sight of the house than Mr. Brown said:

"How much did you win, my dear young friend?"

"Two thousand dollars."

"The old trick?"

Mr. Gartrell was silent a minute.

"Well, yes—you are the very devil for keen eyes, Brown?"

"That is my reputation, my dear sir; and now I'll trouble you to hand me the roll of notes—a mere loan which, of course, I will repay."

"Hand you the notes!"

"If agreeable."

Mr. Gartrell burst forth into imprecations, in the midst of which Mr. Brown uttered a few quiet words in a very low tone. These words seemed to produce a remarkable effect upon Mr. Gartrell. He ceased to rage, uttered an expiring growl, and drew forth the bank-notes, which he handed to his companion.

Mr. Brown's proceeding thereupon was not compli-mentary.   He carefully counted the notes and said :

" Eighteen hundred—now for the other two !"

Mr. Gartrell drew them from his sleeve with a low curse, and they were politely taken by Mr. Brown, who placed the entire amount in his breast-pocket—revealing as he did so the handle of a small revolver.

" Well, that is done with, my dear friend," said Mr. Brown ; " and now let us talk.   I must lecture you a little on your imprudence."

# CHAPTER XXV.

## THE LAWYER AND THE LUMBER-AGENT.

WHEN Mr. Brown rose on the following morning, and after an elaborate toilet descended to the breakfast-room, he was the picture of smiling enjoyment, and beamed on all around him with serene good-humor.

Not seeing his host, he inquired in a friendly manner of the silent and respectful dining-room servant whether his master had risen, and receiving the information that Mr. Gartrell had breakfasted an hour before, and ridden out to see the manager of his estate, Mr. Brown smiled once more, said, " Well, James, I find I must breakfast by myself," and proceeded to partake of that meal with an excellent appetite.

Mr. Brown then rose, and uttering a little sigh of content, strolled forth upon the portico, looking around him with a pleased expression upon the landscape.

" My young friend Gartrell has a really admirable property here," soliloquized the worthy Mr. Brown, indulging as he did so in his blandest smile; " how fortunate he is! what a fine thing it is to be born with a silver spoon in one's mouth! I think my young friend must have made his appearance in this world with a roll of bank-notes in his infantile grasp! And that reminds me—I think I have about me something of that description !"

Mr. Brown inserted his hand between his ample waist-coat and his shirt, deftly unbuttoned a secret belt which never left him, and drew forth the bank-notes won on the day before by Mr. Gartrell. These he now proceeded to count ; after which he quickly restored them to their hiding-place.

"All right, as I supposed," he said ; "my door was locked as usual during the night, but accidents some-times happen !"

Mr. Brown then went into the hall, put on his tall, black hat, took his large cane, and coming out again proceeded to walk to and fro upon the long portico, with the air of a gentleman enjoying and endeavoring to pro-mote still further a mild digestion. He had gone twice the length of the portico and had turned to continue his promenade, when the sound of hoofs upon the avenue attracted his attention. He looked up, saw a person on horseback, and this person dismounted and came up the steps, saying as he did so, in a stiff and formal voice :

" Mr. Brown, I believe ? "

"At your service, sir," said Mr. Brown with a polite air ; "may I ask —— ? "

" My name is Jobson—attorney-at-law from Water-ford."

"Ah ! my dear sir, I am really delighted—have often heard of you—and as a gentleman of the highest char-acter. Walk in, Mr. Jobson."

Mr. Brown waved his hand in a cordial way ; ushered

Mr. Jobson into the drawing-room; and they seated themselves in two easy chairs by the centre-table. Mr. Jobson looked more wiry than usual, and his glance was piercing and suspicious. Mr. Brown on the contrary was all smiles and sweetness—a bland good-humor expanded itself over his full and smiling countenance, and his portly figure, even.

"I called to see Mr. Gartrell on business, sir," said Mr. Jobson.

"I regret to say that he is temporarily absent," said Mr. Brown.

"Humph!" said Mr. Jobson.

"But perhaps I might take his place, my dear sir," said Mr. Brown. "The proposal may surprise you, but I am an old and intimate friend of young Mr. Gartrell. I may say I am quite well acquainted with his private affairs, and I think I may add, Mr. Jobson, that he seldom takes any business step, if I am near, without consulting me."

Mr. Jobson's glance had not lost its suspicion, but there was a smiling frankness in Mr. Brown's manner which affected him in spite of himself.

"Well, sir," he said, "I don't know that what I have to say to Mr. Gartrell is very confidential; and as he is governed so much by your advice, I will proceed to speak of the business that has brought me."

"Do so, my dear sir," said Mr. Brown. "I appreciate your confidence."

"You are probably aware, sir," continued Mr. Jobson, "of the somewhat extraordinary character of the late Mr. Cleave's will or rather of a codicil subsequently discovered. In his will this estate was left to Mr. Cleave, Junior, his nephew; in the codicil it was made, however, a condition that Mr. Cleave, Junior, should marry a Miss Bell before his twenty-fifth year or surrender the property to another nephew, Mr. Allan Gartrell."

"I had heard of the codicil, my dear sir."

"Well, sir, there was one defect in it. It was not worth the paper it was written upon, for there were no witnesses to the instrument—it was waste paper; and yet young Mr. Cleave, acting from a mistaken sense of delicacy, surrendered the estate, and is now nearly penniless !"

At this statement Mr. Brown lost all his smiles, and looked at the speaker with unaffected astonishment.

"Is it possible !" he said.

"Yes," said Mr. Jobson, "and Mr. Gartrell takes the estate; supplants Mr. Cleave with a young lady, Miss Ormby, to whom he was engaged to be married ; sees his cousin sunk in poverty without a care ; and does not give a thought to the fact that Mr. Cleave might have had this codicil set aside by simply moving his finger, in any court in this commonwealth."

"Humph ! humph ! humph !" said Mr. Brown; "I am sorry to say, Mr. Jobson, that this makes out our friend Mr. Gartrell something like—I must say it—a—rascal !"

Mr. Jobson rose in his chair, exclaiming :

"I honor you, sir ! Yes, it was a most discreditable proceeding in Mr. Gartrell—most discreditable—and I have come here to-day, without Mr. Cleave's knowledge or consent, to say to Mr. Gartrell that he is bound in common honesty to release to his cousin a portion of this property—to make some fair compromise; it is not yet too late, I meant to tell him, to file a bill in chancery and open upon this whole question!"

Mr. Brown listened in silence. His face was thoughtful, and he slowly scraped his cheek with his fat fingers. Then he shook his head.

"Mr. Jobson," he said, "you are an honest man."

Mr. Jobson grunted a slight acknowledgment.

"Shall I give you some advice?"

"What is that, sir?"

"Leave this affair—to me."

"To *you*, sir?"

"To me. I will have something to say to you on the subject within—let me see—within, say the next ten days."

Mr. Jobson looked suspiciously at the speaker, but Mr. Brown's countenance was impenetrable.

"Upon one or two points," continued that gentleman, "I should be glad to have some information. Miss Ormby, you say, was engaged to be married to Mr. Cleave—why does she marry Mr. Gartrell?"

"Her father is forcing her to do so."

"Why?"

"Mr. Cleave is poor and Mr. Gartrell is rich."

"Ah, yes! what a rascally affair!" said Mr. Brown with great candor; "and I will find Miss Ormby at—that is to say, she resides at her father's?"

"Certainly."

"There is also another young lady concerned in this whole affair, sir; a Miss Bell, I think it is?"

"Yes, the adopted daughter of Mr. Cleave, Senior, whom he wished his nephew to marry."

"She is also a resident of this neighborhood?"

"She lives at The Hollies, the residence of her cousin, Mrs. Gaston, some miles from this place."

"The Hollies, eh? I can find it, I suppose."

"You wish to see Miss Bell?"

Mr. Brown smiled sweetly and appeared to remember himself.

"Not necessarily, my dear sir; not necessarily. I am an old gentleman, you see—quite alone in the world—and I like young faces. Well, I believe this is all. And now, while I think of it, you have probably heard of my errand to this neighborhood; can you inform me, my dear sir, of the price of *lumber* in this country?"

When Mr. Brown uttered the word *lumber* his face assumed an expression of the highest enjoyment, and his sweet smile gradually expanded into an unmistakable grin. When Mr. Jobson gave him a matter-of-fact reply to his question, he propounded others on the same subject, listened with the same air of enjoyment, and finally uttered a brief, husky but highly expressive laugh.

When Mr. Jobson took his leave at length, weary of waiting for Mr. Gartrell, that strange laugh was still in his ears.

# CHAPTER XXVI.

## WHAT OCCURRED AT THE HOLLIES ON A SUMMER NIGHT.

IT was an exquisite night, and The Hollies was bathed in a flood of moonlight which slept upon the trees weighed down with deep green foliage, on the sward as smooth as an emerald sea, and on the flowers which, grouped in clusters everywhere, seemed to open their fresh leaves and variegated blooms to the sweet and caressing airs of the summer night.

The Hollies was, indeed, a picture. The white trellises gleamed in the mellow splendor, the white gravel way around the circle resembled a band of silver, and some rustic seats scattered here and there beneath the great cedars and hollies cast picturesque shadows, reproducing on the grass the outlines of their gnarled and fantastic forms.

It was one of those nights, and one of those scenes, too, which seem made for lovers; and some personages who had either reached or were approaching the fairy land of love were enjoying its tranquil splendors.

On the portico sat Mrs. Gaston not far from Mr. Jack Daintrees. But—oh! horror!—an excellent lady of the neighborhood with her two charming daughters, respectively thirty-four and thirty-eight, had called to spend the evening, and was crazing the unfortunate and tantalized Mr. Daintrees with all the gossip of the day. Mr. Daintrees said nothing. He was engaged in calculating how long this thing could continue—whether there was any possibility of its ceasing before midnight. Long experience told him that there was little or no probability thereof; and with gloomy eyes he gazed most enviously upon a couple seated upon one of the rustic seats, half in moonlight, half in shadow.

These two persons were Ralph Harrington and Annie. The young lady was looking at the moon with a coquettish smile upon her lips, and Harrington was leaning his elbow upon the back of the rustic seat. He had his face turned toward her, and the expression of his countenance was as timid as that of a boy approaching his first avowal.

In three days this wonder had been accomplished by that ruler of the world—love. Harrington was no longer recognizable. He had been easy, negligent, prone to satirical comment, and rather too self-possessed and "jaunty" to impress you with a very exalted idea of his modesty. He was now as shrinking as a girl—was actually coloring; and Annie was smiling mischievously.

"I am glad to see your health and joy have come back! You look so beautiful as you sit now in the moonlight!"

It was even more the tone than the words that brought the quick blush to Annie's cheeks.

"And you too, sir," she said looking at him for a single instant and then back to the moon, "you too look a great deal stronger than you did."

"I am happier!"

Annie said nothing.

"I was not happy, and it made me thin and pale. You do not know it—I hope you never will—but unhappiness causes that."

"I know it," Annie said, "but we must not think of past troubles."

Harrington looked at her quickly. What lover ever lived who did not fancy that the nothings uttered by the beloved one had a secret meaning?

"I have forgotten all about my distress," said Harrington blushing and faltering. "You alone could——"

"And I," said Annie laughing, "have no recollection of my wetting or my cough, or anything! I am happy to say that I never felt better than I do now—my appetite is enormous—and Auntie says I am nō longer in the least interesting."

The reason why Miss Annie gave this prosaic turn to the conversation was that she had not the least intention that Dr. Ralph Harrington should ask her a certain question—which it was perfectly plain to her feminine instinct he intended to ask—in so public a place, and so very soon after his resumption of friendly visits at The Hollies. This young lady had indeed determined to lead the young gentleman a long and weary chase—to tantalize him with doubt—nay, if the fancy seized her, to refuse him—at first.

And the gay, the self-possessed, the satirical Dr. Ralph

Harrington was like wax in the hands of this little "country girl!" She laughed, looked over her shoulder at him, out of the corner of her eyes, enjoyed exquisitely his blushes and timidity, and when he was rendered desperate and seized her hand, then it was that the young witch proved finally too adroit for her lover.

"There is Auntie calling us!" she exclaimed. "The ice-cream! the ice-cream! You don't know how delicious it is! I mixed it myself—it is strawberry! The very last!"

Then was beheld the spectacle of a fairy clad in the last fashion, flitting through the moonlight toward the house, followed ruefully by a male figure whose face was very much downcast. The fairy laughed a low laugh of triumph as she disappeared up the steps; her companion blushed, and forgetting that he was the cool, the self-possessed, the superior Dr. Ralph Harrington, looked as awkward as a school-boy!

"As I told you, my dear Mrs. Gaston, there is no doubt about the fact that Miss Quigby *did* encourage old Mr. Welby. Just to think! he is at least sixty years of age, and what Miss Quigby could mean by setting her cap at such an old gentleman, who has grandchildren as old as she is nearly and puts his feet in flannel to drive off the rheumatism whenever it is the least cold, I leave it to you, my dear Mrs. Gaston, to say, and I know you will think with me that——"

This was the species of conversation which our friend Mr. Daintrees had been listening to for precisely two hours and three quarters. His mind was slowly giving way. He struggled against the spell in vain. He endeavored to reflect upon other things, and not to listen— useless. He swore internally, and might have done something desperate, when Mrs. Gaston rose, and interrupting the ceaseless flow of words said sweetly to her lady visitor:

"May I give you some ice-cream?"

The ice-cream had the desired effect. It checked the torrent. There is indeed some occult property in country ice-cream, rich and pervaded by strawberries, which on summer evenings temporarily paralyzes the oral powers of the most talkative. Mrs. Gaston's was served in a great cut glass bowl, towering above a slender stem, and the saucers were covered with flowers in their natural colors, upon which the exquisite substance reposed in conscious loveliness. The lady visitor and her daughters partook of three saucers each, and as they rose thereafter and declared that they must really return home, a sudden gleam of joy darted across the soul of Mr. Jack Daintrees.

His opportunity had come, or would come on the departure of these excellent people. Fate at last was propitious. Even Dr. Ralph Harrington would not be in his way. That gentleman had finished his ice-cream; invited Miss Annie to walk with him in the moonlight, received for reply a polite regret that she could not venture out so late just after being sick; and thereupon Dr. Ralph Harrington, sad, but resigned and willing to await a more favorable opportunity, took leave of the company, and rode away toward Waterford.

The crowning joy for Mr. Jack Daintrees succeeded.

Mrs. Gaston's lady visitors put on their bonnets; assumed, after the fashion of ladies, the air of persons just on the point of departure; remained in that attitude conversing for half an hour precisely; and at last, as the carriage had been waiting for some time, entered upon the final ceremonies of feminine leave-taking. These consisted in kissing Mrs. Gaston and Annie, and in saying they would be " *so* glad " to see them—they " really *must* come soon," and then a brief conversation of not more than a quarter of an hour followed as the visitors descended the steps.

Never was Mr. Jack Daintrees more delighted than in offering his assistance to the ladies on this occasion. He bowed with the sweetest smiles, gently pushed the somewhat angular elbows of the three ladies as they got into the carriage, closed the door with a sigh of delight, and saw the vehicle roll away with the devoutest thanks.

At last! His hour had come! The carriage had rolled around the circle, passed through the tall gateway which closed with a clang, and was heard rattling away. Even Annie seemed to feel that it would be heartless in her to remain down-stairs, and ran by Mrs. Gaston with a wicked smile upon her lips, which brought a rosy blush to the face of the pretty Mrs. Gaston, exclaiming as she did so:

"I must go and fix my hair, Auntie! It's tumbled down, and will take me—at least an hour!"

Mr. Jack Daintrees could have embraced the speaker out of pure gratitude. But he had no thoughts now for any one but the pretty widow. There she stood in the moonlight with her rosy cheeks, her pouting lips, her little white hand raising to those lips the small lace handkerchief, while with the other hand, on which a diamond sparkled, she rearranged the white rose in her hair.

To state that Mr. Daintrees was flooded, well nigh drowned in happiness, as he gazed upon this figure, would be scarcely to express the whole truth. He was the most fortunate of men! Who but must envy his lot? Had not a hundred glances from those eyes informed him that he was not indifferent to their owner? Had not he poured forth his love in the swamp? Had not his angel then glanced sweetly at him, cast down her eyes, and when he besought her to utter but "one word," replied with blushes that she would prefer uttering it "at The Hollies?" What other meaning could she have than this, that the answer would be "yes?" It was with such thoughts passing through his mind that Mr. Jack Daintrees now approached the pretty Mrs. Gaston as she stood in the moonlight watching the gate through which her visitors had just disappeared; and eager, ardent, thrilling with the near approach of the supremely happy moment, stretched out his hand to take the pretty hand of the widow.

It would please the writer of this page to leave the figures thus—to discontinue the narrative—and to let fall the veil of *convenance* before Mr. Daintrees and Mrs. Gaston, leaving the rest to the imagination.

But such a proceeding is impossible. Events occurred suddenly which must be recorded. Fate rushed upon Daintrees.

Just as he stretched out his hand to take Mrs. Gaston's, cries were heard one or two hundred yards in front of The Hollies, and the alarmed character of the outcries in question was unmistakable.

" Oh me ! " exclaimed Mrs. Gaston, " something has

CRIES WERE HEARD ONE OR TWO HUNDRED YARDS IN FRONT OF THE HOLLIES.

happened ! An accident ! Perhaps fatal ! *Do* make haste Mr. Daintrees —— ! "

Mr. Daintrees groaned. He was not an unamiable person, but he went somewhat deliberately. In fact he met the three lady visitors walking back toward The Hollies.

"Oh! my *dear* Daintrees! such a terrible accident! My poor nerves!—just to think, and there is Mrs. Gaston running to meet us, and Miss Annie! Oh! my *dear* Mrs. Gaston! it is a Providence that we were not all killed! The wheel, my dear Mrs. Gaston! the wheel! It suddenly fell to pieces with a crash! Thomas the driver says it was *dished!* What is 'dished?' I only know that we have mercifully escaped death!"

Having presented a very slight portion of the excellent lady's observations we proceed to state in one sentence that the front wheel of the carriage had run over a rock and broken to pieces, thereby disabling the vehicle.

The result was that the lady visitors were compelled to spend the night at The Hollies—Mrs. Gaston promising to send them home on the next morning in her carriage, if their own was irreparable. To this they consented, and having seated herself comfortably in the drawing-room, the worthy old lady proceeded to narrate once more, with every particular and at extreme length, her fearful accident and providential escape.

Mr. Daintrees did not hear this narrative. Uttering a groan which might have melted the heart of his bitterest enemy, he had taken his leave, and was—we are sorry to say—*swearing* on his way back to The Lodge.

# CHAPTER XXVII.

### WHAT OCCURRED AT BAYVIEW.

ON the day after this scene, at about noon, Mr. Ormby was seated in his library, reading a law-paper. The unfortunate man was the ghost of himself. In a few days he seemed to have grown ten years older, and his appearance no longer indicated, in the remotest degree, that patronizing feeling of superiority which he had formerly indulged upon all occasions.

Pecuniary trouble and domestic discord had changed Mr. Ormby. He was sullen, gloomy, gruff, and scowled when people spoke to him. The sale of Bayview seemed unavoidable unless some means could be devised to satisfy, or at least temporarily soften his inexorable creditor. But what means were possible to him ? His credit was utterly gone—he could not borrow upon real estate already covered by a lien to the extent of its value—but one resource was left him ; the marriage of Marian and Allan Gartrell. If that could be effected, he would be able to gain time. His creditor would indulge him a little longer, if hopes were held out of payment, through the instrumentality of so wealthy a son-in-law. That was the sole and only means—the single barrier between him and utter bankruptcy ; he owed it to his family, to his daughter herself—the unhappy man reflected—to effect the match : and Mr. Ormby, who had let the law-paper fall from his grasp, to indulge in this train of gloomy thought, saw all at once through the window the approaching figure of Mr. Allan Gartrell.

Mr. Gartrell was met at the door by Mr. Ormby, and conducted into the library, where a prolonged interview took place between them. With a sort of sinking at his heart Mr. Ormby perceived, or thought that he perceived, a decided diminution in Mr. Allan Gartrell's anxiety to consummate the marriage with his daughter. The truth was that Allan Gartrell, Esq., had spent some hours in profound reflection, after hearing certain rumors of Mr. Ormby's pecuniary troubles, and had come to the conclusion that perhaps it would not be so very desirable after all to wed the daughter of a possible bankrupt. This he dissembled, however, simply protesting against the employment of any means of coercing the young lady's action—he could not consent, he said, to force himself upon *any* family. To which Mr. Ormby responded that his daughter was actuated simply by caprice—there could and would be no real difficulty—and, leaving the matter in that ambiguous condition, Mr. Allan Gartrell bowed and departed.

This interview drove the depressed, angry, and nervous Mr. Ormby well-nigh to frenzy. Here was the rich suitor already suspicious and growing cool ! He had no doubt heard the rumor of the approaching sale of Bayview. Or if he had not heard it, he *would* hear it ! There was no time to be lost.

Thereupon Mr. Ormby rose nervously, jerked down the bell-cord, a servant ran, and a message was sent to Marian that her father wished to see her in the library.

Ten minutes afterwards the poor girl, as white as a ghost, and fearfully thin, made her appearance, slowly dragging her steps toward her father. At sight of her pale face his heart bled within him ; but nerving himself with the coolness of a ruined and despairing man, he announced his will—that she should prepare to marry Mr. Gartrell in three days from that time.

Marian did not reply. She stood looking at the floor, and twisting backward and forward in her thin fingers a paper which she was unconscious of holding—it was a note written her by George Cleave during their engagement. When Mr. Ormby, who had spoken in a low and hoarse, but determined voice, ended what he had to say, reiterating his fixed will and order, Marian raised her eyes, fixed them for a moment upon her father, seemed to understand in a dull sort of way that the interview was over, and without speaking turned and went with the same slow, dragging steps out of the room.

As she reached the hall, the sound of steps attracted her attention. She slowly raised her eyes. At the front door stood a portly individual in an ample waistcoat, grasping a stick, and wearing an enormous black hat. This gentleman had been smiling benevolently. At sight of the young lady, with her frightful pallor and her attenuated figure, all these smiles disappeared, and the face of Mr. Brown, for it was that gentleman, grew cold and stern.

"Your father, Miss ——?"

He uttered the words almost unconsciously, and Marian simply moved her thin hand in a mechanical man-

"YOUR FATHER, MISS——?"

ner toward the library. Then she dragged her slow steps up-stairs, and disappeared.

Mr. Brown stood perfectly motionless for some moments gazing after her. His expression was singular.

It was a mixture of deep pity, indignation, and sternness. All at once he heard a step ; Mr. Ormby came out
of the library, and with a stiff bow Mr. Brown asked if
he had the pleasure of addressing Mr. Ormby.

" You have, sir," said Mr. Ormby with a temporary
return of his habitual hauteur. " May I ask the occasion
of your visit, sir ? "

" I wish to know if you have any timber upon this
estate which you wish to sell standing, and if so, on what
terms you will dispose of it," said Mr. Brown, eyeing his
companion with a keen and fixed glance.

Mr. Ormby cleared his throat and was about to grasp
at this offer, to secure ready money. But a moment's
reflection told him that the sale of the timber was not
practicable. It would alarm his creditor, and hasten
harsh measures ; in addition to which, the proceeding
would not be precisely honest.

" I have none for sale, sir," he said stiffly.

Mr. Brown bowed as stiffly, and said :

" I will then bid you good morning, sir."

With which words he went out and mounted his horse.

" That man's very look disgusts me ! " he said.  " To
come into these sweet rural scenes, as the poet says, and
find such people ! Well, I am a little tired of my visit
to Virginia. I will bring my business here to an end
without loss of time. That poor girl ! and they are
going to force her into a marriage that she hates ! Well !
I won't swear ; but they count without—John Brown ! "

Having uttered these words John Brown rode on and
disappeared.

Marian did not come down to dinner, and only toward night glided into her mother's room. The poor lady, who was completely overawed by her harsh husband, had been unable to afford the girl any consolation or hope ; and Marian did not seem to expect any now. She sat down beside her mother on a cricket, leaned her head upon the feeble knees, and drawing her mother's hand to her,‘placed it on her head, holding it there for some time. During this time her lips moved, and she seemed to be praying. At last she rose, stood for an instant gazing at her mother with inflamed eyes, and then putting her arms around her, kissed her on her lips, her cheeks, and her gray hair, and went slowly back to her chamber, the door of which she closed behind her.

On the next morning, the young lady did not come down to breakfast, and Mr. Ormby sent a maid to summon her.

The maid came back with a frightened face, and said that Miss Marian was not in her chamber, and her bed had not been slept in.

"Not slept in!" cried the unhappy man.

"No, sir."

"Oh!"

And with a deep groan the miserable father let his head fall upon the table.

Marian Ormby had indeed fled from her home—whither no one could divine.

# CHAPTER XXVIII.

## MR. BROWN PRONOUNCES SENTENCE.

A LLAN GARTRELL, Esq., after his interview with Mr. Ormby, had ridden toward The Lodge to pay a visit to Mr. Jack Daintrees—one of the few gentlemen of the neighborhood who had invited him to their houses. Not finding Mr. Daintrees at home, Mr. Gartrell experienced a sensation of *ennui*, and returning to Cleaveland, proceeded to indulge in the amusement of becoming tipsy, through the instrumentality of champagne—a large supply of which he had discovered in the cellars of Mr. Hamilton Cleave.

The effort made by Mr. Gartrell to dispel his weariness had eminently succeeded. At the end of his second bottle he became comfortably careless of all human ills— had routed the fiend *ennui*—laughed, sang, and was ready to quarrel.

He had reached this point, and was contemplating in a muddled and hazy manner the propriety of ordering up another bottle, when Mr. Brown, who had ridden back through Waterford to see Mr. Jobson for a few moments, made his appearance. The incident was greeted by Mr. Gartrell with great satisfaction.

"Take some champagne, Brown," said Mr. Gartrell in a thick voice; "I want a little talk with you, my good Mr. Brown."

The gentleman thus addressed bestowed a penetrating glance upon Mr. Gartrell, smiled according to his wont, and said:

"Champagne? With pleasure, my dear Gartrell. And conversation? Nothing could please me better."

"Brown," said Mr. Gartrell scowling, "you are a fool."

This observation appearing even to the muddled intellect of Mr. Gartrell liable to the criticism of being somewhat irrelevant, he proceeded to explain it by the further statement that Mr. Brown was a "stuck-up puppy."

Mr. Brown bestowed upon the speaker a glance which he did not seem to observe—a curious, very curious glance.

"A puppy, my dear Mr. Allan Gartrell?—and a fool too? Well, I was never before regarded as a fool precisely; but come! we are talking in a friendly way—why am I a fool?"

"You think you are master here!"

"Master?"

"You put on your cursed familiar airs! I say *familiar!* And I say I have had enough of it, Brown!"

"You are then desirous that my visit should terminate, eh, my dear Mr. Gartrell?"

"I am!" said Mr. Gartrell scowling.

"Very well," said Mr. Brown benevolently; "but it is not friendly in me to leave you, without asking how you are getting on, my dear Gartrell. Your matrimonial projects, I hope, are in good train. At Bayview, you know—all right there, eh ?"

"No, sir !" responded Mr. Gartrell with extreme hauteur, "they are *not* all right. They are all wrong. The old man is trying to hook me."

"To hook you ?"

"I say to hook me ! A miserable bankrupt ! A penniless adventurer !" said Mr. Gartrell.

Mr. Brown serenely sipped his champagne, smiling.

"You are unfortunate, my dear Gartrell," he said sweetly; "do you know that I was prepared to lay any amount that you would make a good thing of that ? But I fear you are unlucky. Now I will tell you what perhaps you are ignorant of—that I never back unlucky men. In fact, I am like the rest of the world ; I am ready to do my part to ruin them."

Muddled as was the brain of Mr. Allan Gartrell, he vaguely realized a hidden menace in these words. He had finished his third bottle, however, and had grown pugnacious.

"What do you mean by that, Brown ?" he said.

"A mere jest, my dear friend," said Mr. Brown smiling, but watching his companion keenly.

"Because if you mean to insult me, Brown——"

Here Mr. Gartrell grasped an empty bottle of champagne, and expressed his feelings further by a volley of the most shocking expressions.

"Come, come, my dear sir," said Mr. Brown, laughing, but continuing to watch his companion ; "what is

the use of all this? Are we not the closest, dearest
friends. Take care, my dear Mr. Gartrell—let me assist
you—you are, I fear, a little overcome by this excellent
beverage. Ah! here is James. James, Mr. Gartrell is
a little unwell. Perhaps it would be as well to assist him
to a sofa in the drawing-room. These little attacks are
soon slept off."

And rising, with his sweetest smile upon his lips,
while the grinning James supported his staggering
master to a sofa, Mr. Brown went out, put on his hat,
and walking up and down the portico, reflected deeply.
At the end of an hour he stopped, smiled slightly, and
said:

"I am tired at last of trifling with this gentleman.
His hour has come!"

# CHAPTER XXIX.

### SKIRMISHING AT THE HOLLIES.

THAT nest of doves, The Hollies, on the night of this same day was a scene of fairy enchantment —of moonlight, variegated lanterns, white muslin, jewels, rosy cheeks, and sparkling eyes.

Pretty Mrs. Gaston was giving her annual party. The fair widow was an enormous favourite with the young ladies of the neighborhood. It seemed the most natural thing in the world to them to encircle her waist with their arms whenever they were in her presence, and for some weeks before this graceful proceeding on the part of the blooming young maidens had been followed regularly by the exclamation, "*Oh !* Mrs. Gaston !—*do* give a party !— You know you said you would !"

Kisses, bright glances, caressing words, and laughter succeeded ; all attempts to extricate herself from the fondly encircling arms were resisted, for the very school girls tyrannized over pretty Mrs. Gaston ; the victim could only laugh, blush, declare that they were plagues ; after which the evening for the party was duly fixed, as the teazing maidens knew it would be.

When Annie was informed of her intention by Mrs.

Gaston, the young lady glowed with joy, and, forgetting all the dignity of eighteen, proceeded to clap her hands. Then she rushed upon Mrs. Gaston, seized that lady in her arms, and having kissed her rapturously declared that of all the little aunties that anybody had ever possessed this small auntie was the paragon—the flower of flowers.

" Because you are to have a dance, you little witch !" said Mrs. Gaston ; " did anybody ever see such sly, interested creatures as you girls are !"

" Oh !" exclaimed Miss Annie, " Grandma is talking so demurely ! *Girls !*—I'd like to know if there is anybody younger than my small auntie, in her feelings—and her face too !"

" Go away, you flatterer, I am an old woman and will never be able to keep you young things in order. But what in the world are we to do for music ? The piano will not do."

This obstacle was promptly met. There was an excellent fiddle in the neighborhood, and if he disappointed them, Mr. Daintrees, who was famous for his skill as a performer on the violin, would play for them.

" Mr.—Daintrees ? " said Mrs. Gaston, coloring a little, " but perhaps it would not be agreeable to Mr. Daintrees."

Annie looked at pretty Mrs. Gaston, who at the moment was carefully polishing a silver sugar-dish with a tea-cloth, after breakfast ; and a mischievous smile was seen upon the maiden's lips—heralding the approaching shaft.

" Not agreeable to Mr. Daintrees ? " said Miss Annie,

"I will make sure of that gentleman, and warrant that it will be agreeable."

"You?"

"With one word."

"What do you mean, my dear?"

"I will tell Mr.—that is to say my future Uncle Jack——"

"Annie!"

"That—*my little auntie requests him to play for us!* Oh! how you are blushing!"

And in the midst of declarations from Mrs. Gaston that she was "a goose," and the "absurdest creature," Miss Annie made the breakfast-room ring with laughter.

"You shall tell Mr. Daintrees nothing of the sort," said the lady with her little timid smile; "and now as we have done washing up let us go and make a list of persons to be invited."

It was quite a pretty group—the fair lady of thirty-five and the maiden of eighteen bending down, with their handsome heads close together, over the sheet upon which name after name was written. They had nearly exhausted the neighborhood, when Mrs. Gaston said:

"Just to think! We have forgotten Dr. Harrington!"

Pretty Mrs. Gaston had her revenge, at last. Miss Annie Bell suddenly colored.

"Pshaw!" she said, "of course he will come."

"Without an invitation? Fie! my dear, you must have a very bad opinion of Dr. Harrington's manners. And now, as I have alluded to the subject"—Mrs. Gaston paused an instant, assumed an innocent expres-

sion, and glanced with a slight smile at Annie—" I think
I have observed my dear, that—you have a positive anti-
pathy to Dr. Ralph Harrington !"

The fair lady had taken her revenge. The shaft went
home, and the laughing Miss Annie Bell betrayed unmistakable confusion. This was quickly succeeded,
however, by a burst of laughter, and the young lady
exclaimed :

" You are right, Auntie ! I can't bear your conceited
friend ! He is really overpowering with his lofty airs—
and you may invite him or not just as you please. I
assure you *I* don't care."

With a toss of her head the young lady added :

" If he comes to-day I will tell him so."

Mrs. Gaston raised her hand and pointed through the
window.

" There he is, my dear, and you will have an excellent
opportunity."

In fact, Dr. Harrington was riding in on his return
from a professional visit. Annie tried to break away
from Mrs. Gaston, who mischievously held her fast.

" Where are you going ?—then you will not see him ?"
she said.

Miss Annie struggled.

" Let me go, Auntie !"

" Where are you going ?"

" Can you ask !—going ? I am going up-stairs to fix
my hair, and to change this horrid old thing I have on !"

The horrid old thing was a morning wrapper, and
having changed it, the maiden descended the stairs with

a prim and demure air, humming a little song, unconsciously as it were, to express polite surprise at the
presence of the visitor. Her polite air continued as she
conversed—with every door wide open—on the subject
of the weather, appealing repeatedly to Mrs. Gaston,
and thus keeping that lady in the room. When Dr.
Ralph Harrington suggested a walk in the grounds,
Miss Bell declined; when he made speeches indicative of
a desire to direct the conversation in another channel,
Miss Bell "snubbed" him; and when at last he departed,
his face indicated anything but pleasure.

Miss Annie Bell's proceeding thereupon was singular.
She concealed herself behind the lace curtain of the
drawing-room, peeped at the gentleman as he walked
around the circle and mounted his horse; continued to
watch him with the closest attention until he passed
through the gate; and when he disappeared this incomprehensible young lady burst into laughter—after which
she sighed. She then ran to the piano, and began to
play a waltz, in the midst of which Mrs. Gaston came in,
and said:

"Well, my dear, did you have a pleasant visit·from
Dr. Harrington? I hope he made himself agreeable?"

"Agreeable!" exclaimed Annie turning round on the
piano stool; "he made himself just as stupid!—Oh,
Auntie, *how* stupid!"

"I hope you invited him to the party?"

"Y—e—s," said Miss Annie in a hesitating voice;
"You know, Auntie, common politeness required me to
do *that!*"

# CHAPTER XXX.

## A GENERAL ENGAGEMENT.

THE Hollies on the evening of the party was, as we have said, a scene of positive enchantment. As the moon did not rise until nearly midnight, Mrs. Gaston had procured a number of variegated paper lanterns, which were suspended from the drooping boughs of the cedars, among the burnished leaves of The Hollies, and even high up amid the delicate leaflets of a willow beneath which a rustic seat, conveniently in shadow, afforded a refuge for lovers seeking privacy for their romantic interviews.

Seen by the mild and subdued light of the variegated lanterns, The Hollies was a picture. The outlines of foliage were clear cut against the stars; the white trellises gleamed; the nooks beneath the trees, where couples occupied seats, were full of quiet laughter; the green circle glimmered; along the veranda flowed to and fro a stream of promenaders, to hasten in when the notes of the violin announced the "next set;" and all about The Hollies laughed and sparkled, catching as they fled the joyous splendor of the hours.

The headlong violin rushed onward in a maze of cotillons, waltzes, polkas, and galops, until supper was served,

when the gay young people proceeded to the apartment
where Mrs. Gaston had exhausted her skill—quite famous
in the neighborhood—on her entertainment; and then,
this agreeable ceremony being over, the dancing recom-
menced; the honest old country house was full of a
mirth and laughter greater than before.    And suddenly
the full-orbed moon was rolled into the sky, like a golden
shield above the dreamy fringes of the trees.

From the house, the grounds, and the landscape let
us pass now to a figure or two and a scene which took
place on this evening.    The grace and beauty of a neighborhood quite famous for such, had assembled at The
Hollies on this evening; but it may be fairly questioned
whether any of the little beauties were more beautiful
than Annie—it might well nigh be added—than pretty
Mrs. Gaston.

How shall we describe the fair widow as she appeared
on this evening?    She was a rose in full bloom, with all
the freshness of the morning dew upon it!    She wore a
dress of lilac silk and a little modest lace collar which
was not whiter than her neck.    In her hair was a white
rose, and red roses were in her cheeks—for that habit of
blushing which she indulged in the privacy of her family
was all the more observable now, when she was called
upon to occupy the prominent position of hostess.    It
was astonishing how popular that little blush made Mrs.
Gaston, and pleasant to see how the very little girls just
"coming out" flocked to her, and figuratively took her
under their protection!    They gathered about her whenever she appeared—kissed her upon the least or upon no

provocation; even the young gentlemen with budding mustaches teased her to dance with them, and she was compelled to hasten away, as the only means of resisting their solicitations.

It was doubtless with the view of extricating pretty Mrs. Gaston from these annoyances that, during a cotillon which drew into its merry mazes nearly all the company, Mr. Jack Daintrees gallantly arranged a light scarf around the lady's shoulders, issued forth with her upon the veranda, and after a few moments spent in persuasive reasoning, induced his fair companion to descend to the sward, in order to enjoy the beauty of the full-orbed moon.

And Annie—what shall be said of Annie? Having nearly grown enthusiastic in that previous portraiture, we fear we shall become absurd if we dwell long upon the appearance of the little beauty of The Hollies. She was like a vision of youth and joy. Her pure oval face was brushed by a few curls; her eyes sparkled with supreme enjoyment; she wore a white muslin dress, over which fell a cloud of what we believe is styled "illusion," looped up with pink rosebuds;—a little *bouquet du corsage*—and from the falling sleeves of her dress emerged two round white arms on which shone a pair of gold bracelets.

The cotillon ended, and the couples scattered themselves over the lawn—leaving only a few inveterate dancers to the headlong enjoyment of the galop. For some time the young ladies who had gone out to the lawn with their partners were seen strolling to and fro in the moonlight; then the couples disappeared one by one; then the murmur of voices, mingled with "fairy laughter," was heard from the rustic seats beneath the shadows of the trees—and the genius of flirtation spread his wings above The Hollies.

At the risk of incurring the proverbial fate of eaves-droppers, let us listen to what one of these couples are saying, on a gnarled and fantastic seat beneath the drooping foliage of a great ash, which rises from some mossy rocks nearly at the extremity of the grounds.

The speaker at the moment is a man, and his voice is firm and earnest. Not a tremor interrupts the grave, strong accents, which are deep and low—his voice is of that sort which comes from and speaks to the heart.

"I have told you everything, now, Annie, and you know me as well as I know myself. I have intended to tell you this for a long time, but thought—why should I? It is only to the woman a man loves that he can say such things—and—and—why use any ceremony now? You know how dearly—how deeply—I love you."

An inarticulate murmur, so faint that it might have been taken for the whisper of the summer wind in the ash overhead, came from the listener—a young girl with her head drooping, and her white hands opening and closing a little variegated fan upon which her eyes were fixed.

"Every man's life comes to this at last," the speaker went on in a voice growing deeper and more earnest as he spoke. "He may laugh, jest, make his satirical comments on women, and amuse himself at their expense.

Then, some day, he finds that he loves some one with his whole heart and soul; and forgets his laughter, and —if he loves her as he should—speaks to her as I have spoken to you!"

The earnest voice seemed to draw, against her own will as it were, the eyes of the young lady to her companion's face. She raised her eyes, and for a single instant they were fixed upon his own—her cheeks full of blushes, her bosom heaving—then they fell again.

"I have concealed nothing," he went on. "I have told you my life—that I am only a poor gentleman, but. at least a gentleman, and I hope a Christian. I claim no merit for that—to be indifferent, even, in such things has been from my very childhood monstrous in my eyes. To live in this beautiful world, surrounded by so many marvels—to have the love of a mother—of friends—to see the moon rise, and the grass and flowers grow, and live through all like a dumb animal—that at least I could not do! and in my hard life—it has been a hard one sometimes—I can say, and I would say it to *you* only, that I have never forgotten the prayers I learned with my head on my mother's knees."

He stopped for a single instant and then went on:

"I have said enough of this—far more than I intended to say. But I am loyal—I say that proudly. I dare not conceal anything, and have opened my whole heart to you. The rest you know. You know how we met first —how I tried and succeeded in making George offer you his hand—how I found then that I loved you, and you need not be told that the result was utter misery to me.

I resolved not to come near you, and the most wretched hour of my life was that visit to you when you were unwell, and I was called upon to take in my own the hand—that belonged to George Cleave. The rest followed—your engagement ended—I had the right to love you then—I had not the right before, and I loved you, I love you, Annie, with all the strength of my being! I am not a boy—I am a man, and a hard one, in some things. I will conceal nothing from you—refuse me and I will not go and drown my misery in drink, or coarse company, or give up my career. I will work, and work harder than I ever did. I defy misery to crush me—it can not crush Ralph Harrington!"

The head of the speaker rose with something proud and resolute in the very poise of it. A moment afterwards it dropped.

"I am talking absurdly," he murmured; "it is because my thoughts rise to my lips, and I mean to show you my very heart! I am blundering on all about what I will do if you refuse me—but do not refuse me, Annie! I was only boasting, perhaps—I think I should die without you!"

Two hands which were near each other seemed to approach, unconsciously, and were clasped together. A little head with brown ringlets rose slowly, and a pair of moist eyes were fixed with a long, earnest, trusting gaze upon his own.

The lips of the beautiful girl uttered not the slightest sound; but in that long, earnest look was written without room for doubt—"surrender."

Suddenly the headlong violin within The Hollies struck up a reel—the merriest of all the reels since time began—and the whole moonlit lawn was quickly alive with figures hastening in to take their places. The prying moon had witnessed a number of romantic scenes— what it lingered upon now, the last of all, was the spec-

THE PRYING MOON—WHAT IT LINGERED UPON NOW.

tacle of a girl clasped in her lover's arms, her lips pressed to his own in a long, lingering kiss.

"Only another moment, Annie!"

"I must go now—Ralph!"

And Miss Annie Bell, with cheeks the color of the red rose at her corsage, flitted away, her little satin slippers gleaming in the moonlight.

"Mrs. Gaston! where is Mrs. Gaston!" cried a youthful gentleman, rushing forth from the veranda.     "She's engaged to dance the reel with me!   Oh—h—h—h! Mrs. Gaston!"

What spectacle was it that then greeted the bright eyes of youths and maidens whose attention had been attracted by the youthful gentleman's outcries?   We said that the moon had seen the last of the romantic couples, but were quite mistaken.    From a clump of shrubs, beyond which stood a rustic chair under a holly, suddenly appeared—the pretty Mrs. Gaston and Mr. Jack Daintrees!   The former was blushing as she had perhaps never blushed before; the latter walked with his head erect and triumphant.   In fact we can only describe the demeanor of Mr. Daintrees by saying that he resembled a warrior returning from a successful campaign, in front of whom the bands are playing, "See the conquering hero comes!"

How pretty Mrs. Gaston got through the reel that night was a mystery to herself, and she never remembered anything about it afterwards.     Fortunately her habit of blushing served to explain the permanent roses in her cheeks, or the rapid motion was credited with the phenomenon.   Certain it is that everybody admired Mrs. Gaston and Annie, as they went together from end to end of the reel; and the hearts of Jack Daintrees and Ralph Harrington beat time to the music.

For the "skirmishing at The Hollies" had been succeeded by "a general engagement"—and an unconditional surrender.

# CHAPTER XXXI.

### THE CYPRESS LEAF—AND THE SUNSHINE.

IT was three o'clock in the morning and the revellers had begun to disperse.

On the high road near The Hollies the moon was pouring its solemn splendor.

No sound was heard but the low sigh of the night wind in some shrubbery skirting the road; but all at once a human sigh was mingled with the inarticulate murmur of the foliage; and this low, piteous sigh issued from the lips of a crouching figure, lost like a shadow in the shadow of the shrubs, and shrinking lower as the guests went by in carriages or on horseback toward their homes.

The shadow in the shadow scarcely moved. It was crouching, shrinking, shuddering, and seemed about to faint and fall.

It had glided out of Bayview, and an hour past midnight, scarcely knowing in what direction it went; tottered with weak steps across fields and through forest paths, with the vague thought of going somewhere—anywhere; and going on and on, with the same faint, feeble, tottering steps, had sunk down weak and powerless at the very gateway almost of The Hollies.

An hour afterwards Marian Ormby was in bed at The Hollies, with Mrs. Gaston and Annie seated by her, holding her poor hands and weeping.

Ralph Harrington was standing at the foot of the bed, looking gravely at her. It was he who had discovered the poor girl as he passed, the last guest of all, on his way back to Waterford. Hearing a low sob in the shrubbery beside the road, he had dismounted, gone to the spot, found Marian stretched nearly lifeless on the ground, and had hurriedly questioned her, demanding an explanation of her presence there. In a faint and broken voice she had tried to give him this explanation. She was going—she meant to go—her aunt lived only a few miles—then the poor girl burst into tears and hid her face in her hands.

Ralph Harrington had no difficulty in understanding the whole mystery. Marian had left her father's home to take refuge at her aunt's—had sunk down on the way; a hot fever had seized upon her, he saw, and with gentle force he bore her into The Hollies, just as Annie and Mrs. Gaston were extinguishing the lights.

It was the cypress leaf that mingles fatally with the orange flowers of life.

At daylight a note was dispatched to Mr. Ormby; and this note reached him an hour after his discovery of his daughter's flight. Mounting his horse he rode at full speed to The Hollies; and, without waiting to be announced, abandoning all ceremony, driven by the one passionate thought that his child was there, the unhappy father, with his pride all broken in his breast, hastened up the staircase, opened the door, beyond which he heard voices, and an instant afterwards was holding Marian in his arms, kissing and fondling her with sobs and tears, and promises to love and cherish her always if she would only live and love him. So mighty is the father's heart under all the sordid trappings of a worldly philosophy !

Mrs. Gaston had truly informed Mr. Ormby in her note that Marian had a very dangerous attack of fever; and as the day wore on the fever gathered strength. When night came the poor girl was delirious, and talked incessantly of George Cleave, of her father, and of some one whose name she did not pronounce—from actual disgust it seemed—who could have been none other than Mr. Gartrell. Then her mind wandered to her night walk—to the scene on the highway—and so the sick girl muttered on and on, watched by her friends, but more than all by Mr. and Mrs. Ormby, whose very hearts seemed breaking.

Harrington had ridden to Waterford in the forenoon and returned to The Hollies with Dr. Williams and— George.

The young man was quite pale and still. He sat on the veranda, his eyes fixed upon the lawn, the scene so short a time before of mirth and laughter ; and this gaze was so immovable and apathetic that it was plain the youth was nearly stunned. From time to time, as

Harrington descended to mix some medicine, he turned his head and fixed his eyes upon his friend's face.

"A fever, George—from exposure and agitation. Bad, to be frank with you—but not serious—yet."

Harrington would then go up-stairs again; and so the day, then the night, then the next day, and the next night passed, George Cleave remaining almost all his waking hours upon the veranda listening. He had taken up his abode at The Hollies, by Mrs. Gaston's request. He waited for the decision which he felt would be life or death to his heart.

This decision came on the night of the third day. Marian fell asleep at dusk; and Harrington sat watching her with a fixed, immovable gaze which indicated plainly his profound anxiety. An hour passed, then another; there was still no change, and the young physician grew more and more anxious, his gaze more fixed and intense. At last he drew a long breath of relief. An almost imperceptible alteration had taken place in the appearance of the sleeper. The hot blood in her cheeks seemed slowly to retire ; her pulse, when he lightly laid his finger upon it, throbbed less violently, and toward midnight a slight, pearly moisture diffused itself over the white forehead.

The crisis of the fever was passed. Harrington announced the fact to her father, who had scarcely left her day or night.

"All depends now upon moral influences," added Harrington. "I have informed you, Mr. Ormby, that the real origin of this attack was obviously mental distress.

If you are aware of the cause of that distress, I advise you to remove it."

Mr. Ormby moved his head slowly up and down. As he did so, Marian opened her eyes, and when her father came to her, she placed her arms around his neck, smiled faintly, and kissed him.

He laid the thin cheek against his own, his eyes filled with tears, and he whispered:

"Shall I go and tell—George—that your father and mother consent to—your marriage with him?"

The sunshine in the poor girl's eyes rendered any reply unnecessary.

"I will go tell him now—this very moment. I am not so bad a father as you think, my dear, my own Marian!"

And ten minutes afterwards George Cleave knew two things—that Marian would recover, and that she would be his wife.

## CHAPTER XXXII.

### MR. BROWN DEPARTS.

WHEN Mr. Allan Gartrell woke after the slight attack of drowsiness consequent upon drinking that moderate supply of champagne—only three bottles— which we have alluded to, he stretched himself, yawned, experienced a slight headache, and what was equally disagreeable, a vague, uneasy consciousness that he had done something excessively imprudent.

What was this imprudence? Oh yes!—and Mr. Gartrell turned a little pale. He had insulted his friend Mr. Brown; insulted him; had characterized him as a "puppy," and, unless his memory was treacherous, had hurled, or been about to hurl a bottle at his head!

The remembrance of this scene caused a slight perspiration to gather upon Mr. Gartrell's forehead. It was plain that he had offered a gross indignity to his dear friend, and having swallowed nearly half a tumbler of brandy to fortify his shattered nerves, Mr. Gartrell rang the bell, to send for Mr. Brown and apologize.

"Tell Mr. Brown I will be glad to see him for a few moments," he said to the servant, "and mind, you rascal! be polite! Mr. Brown is one of my best friends!"

The servant did not go, whereupon Mr. Gartrell burst into vituperative epithets demanding why he stood there like a calf.

"Mr. Brown is gone away, sir. He left a letter on the mantel-piece."

"Gone away!"

"He had the light carriage hitched up, and Joe drove him to Waterford, sir. Afterwards, in the evening, Joe drove him, he says, to the railroad, and he went away on the cars."

Mr. Gartrell seized the letter, forgetting in his agitation to utter a single oath. It ran as follows:

"AMIABLE MR. ALLAN GARTRELL: Your unappreciated friend, Mr. John Brown, presents his compliments, and begs to state that not finding a longer stay at your hospitable mansion agreeable to his feelings, he has reluctantly concluded to tear himself away.

"You will readily conceive that *under the peculiar circumstances*, he, your friend Brown, would not have come to this determination without good reasons. But insults have been uttered, taunts employed, intimations made, that a further sojourn on the part of Mr. Brown at the residence of Mr. Gartrell would be unwelcome to the proprietor of the establishment.

"So for the present Mr. Brown defers the further prosecution of the business which brought him to this country—the purchase, that is to say, of lumber for sale in the New York market. Whether Mr. Brown will be able so far to command his feelings as to forget the unpleasant scene above obscurely alluded to, and return to the mansion of Mr. Gartrell, the future will determine.

"At present, with a heart deeply wounded, feelings lacerated, and a melancholy which causes his tears to flow, he presents his respects to Mr. Gartrell, and subscribes himself Mr. Gartrell's

"Most obedient humble servant,

"JOHN BROWN."

Mr. Allan Gartrell perused this note with an expression of unmistakable terror. Having read it slowly through once, he went back and read it through again; studying it, as it were, sentence by sentence and word by word.

If an opinion could be formed from the appearance of Mr. Gartrell's countenance, his effort to discover what he sought was unsuccessful. He sat there for a long time, gazing stupidly at the paper, knitting his brows, and looking extremely gloomy.

At last he started up, and uttered a violent oath.

"Curse him! let him go!" he growled. "Let him try——! I defy him to——"

He stopped, muttering. Then he went and poured out some more brandy.

"What a devil of a man that Brown is!" he said with a reckless laugh; "and decidedly I think I will miss the old muff!"

.    .    .    .    .    .    .    .    .    .    .

On the morning after this scene, as Mr. Gartrell was drinking brandy as usual, a step was heard upon the portico, a knock resounded, and a moment afterwards the attentive James announced Mr. Jobson, who came into the apartment.

At sight of the lawyer Mr. Gartrell assumed a stiff and formal air.

"You wish to see me—Mr. Jobson, from Waterford, I think?"

"Yes, sir."

"Your business, sir?"

Mr. Jobson had not been invited to sit down, but he now proceeded to do so, looking at Mr. Gartrell over his spectacles.

"I called to see you once before, sir," he said quietly, "but did not find you at home. My business is to have a few words on the subject of the codicil to the late Mr. Cleave's will, which I beg to inform you, before going further, was not worth the paper it was written on, as it was not witnessed."

Thereupon Mr. Jobson proceeded, with great coolness, to business; spoke of the extreme hardship of not releasing to George Cleave, after his magnanimous surrender of the estate, any portion of it; and ended by urging upon Mr. Gartrell, as a course dictated by common propriety, some provision for his cousin.

Mr. Jobson had visited Mr. Allan Gartrell at an unfortunate moment—which does not, however, involve the statement that under any circumstances his course would have been other than that which he now pursued.

"Curse my cousin!" said Mr. Gartrell, scowling; "what the devil have I to do with him? My uncle left me this property if that marriage did not take place—with Miss Bell; well, has he married her?"

"You know the circumstances, Mr. Gartrell——"

"Curse the circumstances!" interrupted Mr. Allan Gartrell, becoming angry; "are you sent here by Cleave to do his begging?"

"I am not, sir," said Mr. Jobson with unalterable sang froid, bestowing a curious glance upon the speaker over his spectacles. There was something so singular in this look that even Mr. Gartrell noticed it. It might almost have been said that Mr. Jobson was doing what he never did—smiling.

"What brought you, then, old parchment-face?" said Mr. Gartrell with a sudden access of humor, due to the brandy; "any money in the affair, do you think—eh?"

"I expect none, sir."

"Come! speak out, old black-gown! Say *half;* will that do?"

Mr. Gartrell burst into sudden laughter, adding:

"Well, I see we can't come to an understanding. Have some brandy, Jobson?"

Mr. Jobson politely declined and rose.

"Mr. Gartrell," he said quietly, with the former ghost of a smile upon his thin lips, "I do not often throw away my time, but I have deliberately done so to-day, I see. I will not further trouble you on this business this morning. Is Mr. Brown here? A most worthy gentleman—your friend Mr. Brown!"

And with the air of a personage who has perpetrated an excellent jest, Mr. Jobson put on his hat and took his departure. For some moments Mr. Gartrell looked after him in silence. Then he muttered with an uneasy air :

"Brown ? Does he know Brown ? Is there something under all this ? That old wooden-head was laughing at something ! What was it ?"

# CHAPTER XXXIII.

### WHICH TREATS OF THE MYSTERIOUS MOVEMENTS OF MR. JOBSON.

ALL the way back to Waterford Mr. Jobson continued to indulge in that covert smile, and once or twice a low sound escaped from his lips which actually resembled a chuckle.

Having reached the town he rode up the main street with the air of a gentleman at peace with himself and all the world ; stopped in front of his office ; dismounted, hitched his horse to an old rack, much gnawed by the horses of clients ; and going into the office found himself face to face with George Cleave, who held a law-book before him and was—thinking of Marian.

"Well, my young friend," said Mr. Jobson, "a fine day, and you seem to be deep in the law. That's well— a hard mistress, and requires, says a great man, the *lucubrationes viginti annorum.*"

" Which will bring me to forty-five—nearly as old as you are, Mr. Jobson !"

The young man's face was radiant ; his voice like music. A few moments on the veranda at The Hollies had caused that.

"As old as I am! I am sixty—every day of it! I am an old law parchment—did not my dear friend, Mr. Gartrell, say as much?—and you, you are a nosegay with the dew on it!"

Having indulged in this unwonted outburst of poetry, Mr. Jobson came up to George Cleave, sat down beside him, drew his chair close, leaned over, and looking at the young man over his spectacles, said in a low tone:

"Are you discreet? Can you keep a little secret?—for twenty-four hours?"

"A secret, Mr. Jobson! I think I can."

"Listen then!"

And in a whisper Mr. Jobson made a hurried communication at which Cleave visibly started. His eyes were fixed upon Mr. Jobson with the profoundest surprise; the law-book escaped from his grasp, and he did not pick it up; and, with this air of stupefaction almost, he remained silent, listening to the end.

"Good heavens—!" he exclaimed, at last.

"That's enough!" said Mr. Jobson, suddenly rising. "Keep quiet, and remember—to-morrow at noon!"

"Yes, yes!"

Thereupon Mr. Jobson went out of his office, walked down the street, and, reaching the office of Dr. Ralph Harrington, opened the door without ceremony and went in.

Harrington had just come back from The Hollies, and never was the fulness of joy more plainly written on the human face. This human being seemed to have had some elixir of life suddenly infused into his frame. His

pale cheeks had grown ruddy ; his dull eyes as brilliant
as light itself ; and the lips which so recently had expressed only disgust and weariness with all around him,
seemed never done with smiling.    Ralph Harrington
was, indeed, the picture of abounding joy—a joy which
had come to him like a burst of sunshine, on that moonlight night at The Hollies.

" Well, Doctor !"

" Come in, come in, my dear friend ! Delighted to see
you.    What news ?"

" The news that miracles have not ceased—that a man
as thin as a shadow and as white as a ghost can be made
a stout fellow with the reddest cheeks I ever saw, in a
week !"

Harrington laughed like a boy.

" Well, such miracles take place sometimes !"

"I see one !"

"I *feel* one !"

" So you and George Cleave are going to marry your
sweethearts—the right ones—after all, eh ?"

"I hope so ! what would you have, my dear Mr. Jobson ?  It is a man's fate to be entrapped—to be induced
reluctantly to perpetrate matrimony at some period,
sooner or later, in his mortal existence !  A hard fate,
my dear friend—but how are we to avoid it ?  Struggle
as you will—make all the good resolutions imaginable—
resolve that you will not desert the noble army of
bachelors—and some day you find that your fate is sealed
—that you are tied tightly to the apron string of some
little Blue Eyes !"

" Annie's eyes are not blue," said Mr. Jobson, putting in his protest.

Thereat Ralph Harrington burst into laughter once more, and actually colored a little.

" You are a terrible personage," he said, " and I see that nobody can mislead you. Well, yes, yes ! my dear Mr. Jobson, let me cease my jests and say that I am as happy as a child this morning. I have had trouble enough in the last few months to break down the strongest, but Heaven be thanked it is over—yes, my dear sir, I shall be married, I hope, to a person you know in a month ! "

" Good—very good ! " said Mr. Jobson. " A fortunate thing for both ; and if I am not very much mistaken, the noble army of bachelors will miss *three* of its recruits instead of two—the third being Mr. J. Daintrees."

" Yes—it is as good as announced. An excellent fellow—Daintrees."

" As honest a man as I know, and has a good estate, as you have a good professional income, which is equivalent. Now for George Cleave. He is the only poor bridegroom. Let us come to George Cleave, and let me tell you what I have just told him."

Mr. Jobson then proceeded to make a communication to Dr. Ralph Harrington, which caused that gentleman to stop suddenly as he was lighting a cigar, and gaze at the speaker with astounded eyes.

" You are surely not in earnest ! "

" I was never more in earnest in my life."

" And—to-morrow ? "

" At noon.   Don't fail."

And Mr. Jobson went out of the office without further words.   He stopped then for a moment and looked around in a hesitating manner.

" Yes—it is best I suppose," he muttered.

He then walked down the street, stopped in front of the county jail, the iron-studded door revolved at his knock, and he disappeared within.   A quarter of an hour afterwards he came out, went to his own residence— a comfortable house in the outskirts of the town—and entering, ascended the stairs.   As he reached the second floor, Mrs. Jobson, a buxom dame in a cap, came out of her chamber, and exclaimed :

" Oh ! Mr. Jobson !"

" Well, madam," said Mr. Jobson, looking at the lady over his large spectacles.

" Oh ! Mr. Jobson !" repeated the lady, breathing quickly in an extremely agitated manner.

" That is not an observation from which it is possible to derive any precise information," said Mr. Jobson with unwonted humor.

" Oh ! there's somebody in the green-room !   There is no doubt of it, Mr. Jobson !   We heard him walking about !"

" Him ? why not *her ?*" said Mr. Jobson.

" The steps were too heavy ! and the door is locked, for Molly tried it ! and—and—you seem to think nothing of my agitation, Mr. Jobson ! you don't believe me ! and yet I *heard !*—Mr. Jobson, there's somebody in that room !"

"Nonsense, Mrs. Jobson," was the cool reply. "I have always told you that your nerves would be the death of you. You fill me with anxiety, Mrs. Jobson! Your pale and wasted appearance leaves no doubt of the state of your nervous system. You require a doctor, Mrs. Jobson!"

Which was the crowning joke of Mr. Jobson on this day of unwonted jocosity—for the good lady was as plump and ruddy as he was wiry and parchment-like in countenance.

"There," he suddenly said, "I see your friend Mrs. Jones is coming up the steps, madam, to make you a visit."

"Mrs. Jones! I must change my dress! she is so particular, and notices everything!"

The lady hastened into her chamber, and closed the door. Then it suddenly opened again, and she exclaimed :

"There's somebody in that room, Mr. Jobson! I heard them with my own ears!"

Then the chamber door closed—this time finally.

As soon as Mr. Jobson was satisfied that the enemy had retreated he went to the door of the mysterious apartment, gave a peculiar knock, said, "It is I!" and the door opened, closed upon him, and was locked again.

The consequence was that when Mrs. Jobson came forth in full toilet, prepared for further allusions to the noise in the green-room, Mr. Jobson was nowhere to be seen.

## CHAPTER XXXIV.

### WAITING.

A T about half-past eleven in the forenoon, on the
day after these scenes, Mrs. Gaston and Annie
Bell were seated in the drawing-room at The Hollies,
looking intently through the windows opening on the
veranda, and evidently awaiting the arrival of some
person or persons.

The two gracious and beautiful creatures seemed to
suit the place and time. They might have been taken
for sisters, so youthful did the rich complexion of her
rosy cheeks and the shrinking little smile of Mrs. Gaston
make their owner appear—and this resemblance was increased by the dresses which they wore ; dresses made of
precisely the same material and cut—by orders from
Miss Annie—in the very same fashion. This identity in
costume was Miss Annie Bell's fantasy, and she despoti-
cally carried out her caprice down to the least details.
Each wore a little bow of pink ribbon above the corsage ;
each skirt was flounced and ornamented with rosettes ;
and crowning triumph of despotism !—supreme indication of the fact that the pretty Mrs. Gaston was wax in
her companion's hands !—the hair of the fair widow had

been arranged by Annie in the last fashion, and a rose-bud nestled there, as one nestled in her own glossy ringlets.

The faces smiled and were as fresh as the rosebuds. And The Hollies smiled too. A bright August sun poured its glory on the trees ; a slight wind pushed the white clouds across the sea of blue ; and the birds were singing and the flowers blooming as they seemed to sing and bloom nowhere else in all the world, except here at this nest of doves—The Hollies !

So The Hollies that day and its inmates were a charming spectacle. But listen !—this poetic repose is about to be disturbed. Hoofs are heard on the road beyond the grounds ; the rider approaches the gate ; it opens and shuts with a clang, and Mr. Jack Daintrees dismounts and approaches the house.

Annie looks at Mrs. Gaston with her wicked and mis-chievous smile—at pretty Mrs. Gaston, whose cheeks re-semble peonies in full bloom.

"I think I have left my handkerchief up-stairs, Auntie !"

"You little goose !" is the murmured reply, "there it is in your belt !"

"Oh yes !—I didn't mean my handkerchief ! My work-basket ! my work-basket !"

"No, Annie !—no ! I do not wish——"

"But—my Uncle Jack ! Think, Auntie ! what will my Uncle Jack say if he—sees me idle !"

"No—— !"

And Mrs. Gaston holds the young witch by her dress.

" Let me go, Auntie !"

" No—no ! "

Suddenly Mrs. Gaston smiles and quietly releases her.

" Well, go, as you are so anxious to do so !"

Annie laughs in immense enjoyment and is about to dart away.

"I suppose I can entertain *both*, my dear !"

And Mrs. Gaston smiles.

" *Both*, Auntie ? "

"I mean Dr. Harrington, too. I see him just coming through the gate !"

Annie suddenly stops and turns her head toward the window. Dr. Ralph Harrington is dismounting and approaches the house.

" You will scarcely have time to get your work-basket, dear !" says Mrs. Gaston, with a little laugh, which makes her charming ; whereat Miss Annie darts at her and exclaims : " You are the sliest, most improper, most ——Oh ! what an absurd small auntie I have !"

She then vanishes from the apartment, as though to disappear up-stairs ; but in some mysterious manner she happens to be at the door when Ralph Harrington reaches it. A little murmur is heard—a slight noise of a singular sort ; a brief, quick, incomprehensible sound, as if—but the sound is indescribable ; and then Dr. Harrington enters and salutes Mrs. Gaston and Mr. Daintrees—Miss Annie making her appearance about five minutes afterwards, singing innocently as she trips *downstairs*, and into the room, where she politely salutes the gentlemen.

# CHAPTER XXXV.

## IN CONCLAVE.

THE HOLLIES on this morning seemed destined to be overwhelmed with visitors.

No sooner had Dr. Harrington and Mr. Daintrees taken their seats than the front gate again revolved on its hinges, and Mr. Ormby came in, Mrs. Ormby being up-stairs already with Marian.

And then Mr. Ormby had scarcely finished his polite and elaborate greeting of the company, when that perpetual motion of a gate once more opened, and George Cleave made his appearance with Mr. Jobson.

The personages thus assembled at The Hollies—with the single exception of Mr. Jobson—looked at each other with an astonishment which every moment increased. There was evidently some mystery under this singular meeting of so many persons at the same place and at the same hour. Each looked at the other, as though to demand an explanation; but no one seemed able to give this explanation; and a sudden silence ensued — one of those "awful pauses" which prove mortal to social enjoyment in a drawing-room.

At this critical moment, Mr. Jack Daintrees rushed gallantly to the rescue. Clearing his throat in order to hear his own voice and give himself courage, Mr. Daintrees assumed a winning smile, crossed one leg with an easy and jaunty air over the other, and said :

"It really would appear that we had all met here by appointment."

"Yes, really," said some one.

"That this was a general rendezvous arranged beforehand," continued Mr. Jack Daintrees, habituated now to the sound of his voice and gathering courage.

"It certainly does seem so," from another of the company.

"But what is the explanation ?" said Mr. Daintrees extending one finger argumentatively. "It is impossible that everybody could have visited The Hollies to-day for the reason which has brought me."

At these words a smothered laugh was heard ; and looking in the direction of the laugh, the company perceived Miss Annie Bell concealing her laughing countenance with her little lace-fringed handkerchief. All eyes again turned to Mr. Daintrees. Mr. Daintrees was so very red in the face that he seemed in danger of apoplexy. In fact, Mr. Daintrees's reasons for visiting The Hollies might be conjectured !

"That is—hem —!"

Mr. Daintrees laughed rather faintly.

"Suppose we each inform our friends here assembled, if there *is* any appointment."

This proposal of Mr. Daintrees was not destined to

result in an explanation at that moment of the mysterious gathering. As he spoke, the gate again opened, a horseman came in and dismounted; and this horseman, as he drew near, was seen to be no less an individual than—Mr. Allan Gartrell.

As Mr. Gartrell approached the veranda, Mr. Jobson rose gravely, and said:

"I have listened in silence to your conjectures, my friends, not regarding it as necessary to explain an assemblage which I may as well now say I am responsible for. Each guest of Mrs. Gaston's here assembled has come in consequence of a note or request from myself, to be present at an interview of the gravest and most important character. One person only has come at the invitation of another—Mr. Ormby wrote asking the presence of Mr. Gartrell. He has arrived, and now the number will soon be complete."

Mr. Gartrell entered, and bowed stiffly. The number of persons present evidently astonished him. Observing Mr. Ormby, who was seated in a large arm-chair near the rear window, he approached him, took his seat with an easy air, or what was meant to be such, and said:

"I received your note, sir, asking me to call and see you here, and here I am."

The last words were uttered with a slight accent of defiance. Mr. Allan Gartrell evidently began to feel uneasy, and had recourse in consequence of that fact to his air of indifference—as of one who cared nothing for the friendship or hostility of any one present.

While he was speaking the eternal gate once more

opened to admit a last visitor. This time, however, the latch made no noise, or the voice of Mr. Gartrell prevented it from attracting the attention of the company. Mr. Ormby did not offer at the instant any definite explanation, such as Mr. Gartrell's observation seemed to demand ; but he cleared his throat in a loud, resounding, and elaborate manner, which was perhaps the reason why a step upon the veranda was not heard.

Thereat Mr. Gartrell seemed to become irritated, and exhibited unmistakable evidences of patrician hauteur. He grew red in the face, rose from his chair, pushing it back angrily as he did so, and said :

"I did not come here, sir, to sit and be stared at by you and your friends ! You wrote saying that you wished to see me. Here I am—what is your business with me ?"

"I will answer that question," said a voice at the door. "All these little mysteries will be soon explained, my dear Mr. *Wilkes !* "

And the smiling, the benevolent, the beaming Mr. John Brown came into the apartment.

# CHAPTER XXXVI.

## MR. BROWN BEGINS.

IT is wholly impossible to convey an adequate idea of the extreme benevolence with which Mr. Brown beamed upon the assembled company. This benevolence overflowed in his eyes and shone in his smile. The thumb of his left hand was inserted in the armhole of his ample waistcoat; his right hand was extended with a gentle, persuasive, and touching grace—he had the air of the stage-father who says, "Bless you, my children!"

The good Mr. Brown even beamed upon Mr. Allan Gartrell, or—as he had called him, no doubt, through inadvertence or forgetfulness—Mr. Wilkes. But Mr. Gartrell, or Mr. Wilkes, was so unfriendly as not to reciprocate this sentiment; he suddenly started up, grew very pale, and was evidently revolving the question in his mind whether he should not rush upon Mr. Brown, overturn him, and make his exit safely from the room.

"No," said Mr. Brown, extending his hand toward Mr. Gartrell, and shaking his head slowly from side to side, with a sweet smile upon his lips, "No—don't try *that*, my dear young friend. It will not do. The thing will hang fire. I am able myself to deal with you—perfectly able—but in order to save myself that trouble I have a friend in the passage. I have just heard him enter. He came in by my request at the back door, and I now hear him coughing modestly behind his hand, and think I see him there with a stick beneath his arm."

In fact, a slight cough was heard from the passage without, which cough issued from the lips of a gentleman resembling a bull dog—a friend of Mr. Jobson's from the county jail.

"Life," said Mr. Brown, with a smiling and didactic air, "is full of mysteries; but, sooner or later, these mysteries are cleared up, and I have come this morning to this most agreeable residence to clear up one of the most interesting that I have ever met with during twenty years spent in arduous labor as—a member of the detective police in Scotland Yard, London."

In the midst of a stir of astonishment Mr. Brown continued :

"Up to the present moment, my friends, it is probable that no one of this company has indulged a surmise even upon the subject of the identity or non-identity of the gentleman sitting yonder, and passing under the name of Allan Gartrell, Esq. It is my agreeable duty now to throw light upon his real name and character. My friend's baptismal and family designations are not Allan Gartrell, but Charles, or familiarly, Charley Wilkes. He is not the nephew of the late Mr. Hamilton Cleave, of Cleaveland, but one of the most brilliant, the most skilful, and I will add most elegant and popular of the fast men, and —burglars—of London."

As Mr. Gartrell, or rather Mr. Wilkes, who had sunk again into his seat, suddenly rose again at these words, Mr. Brown drew forth a large bandanna handkerchief from the inner left breast-pocket of his coat, displaying, casually, as he did so, the handle of his revolver.

"Sit down, my friend," he said benevolently; "it will be useless to attempt anything in the way of resistance. I have a little persuader about me, which I am used to handling; and even if you fired upon me—I see you are armed—my friend in the passage would secure you."

"You have no warrant!" came in a furious growl from the pale Mr. Gartrell-Wilkes.

"Oh! what a mistake!" returned Mr. Brown, drawing a paper from his pocket. "I have one in due form— from ministerial headquarters—all regular. But we are losing time. Let me proceed, my friend. The company I see is impatient, and I have a most interesting series of events to relate."

Overcome by Mr. Brown's sang froid, or convinced that all resistance was impossible, Mr. Gartrell-Wilkes sat down, leaned back in his chair, assumed a careless and defiant expression, and did not offer any further interruption.

"Ah!" said Mr. Brown, "I see that you are a man of reason after all, my dear sir. You know when to assume the offensive and when to observe a masterly inactivity. Remain silent therefore, and let me tell my interesting story. There are portions of it which will be new to you, my friend, as well as to this honorable company, I think!"

# CHAPTER XXXVII.

## MR. BROWN CONTINUES.

CLEARING his throat, gazing around him more benevolently than before, and assuming his sweetest tones, Mr. Brown continued :

"Let me adopt the style of my English literary friends —as follows : On a handsome street of Liverpool stands the banking house of Thompson Brothers, and on a pleasant afternoon, a stranger of distinguished appearance might have been seen entering the banking house and presenting a check, calling for the payment to the bearer of the sum of one thousand pounds sterling. Let me describe more particularly the appearance of the distinguished stranger—but no, I shall grow tedious if I adopt the literary style. Let me be terse, my friends— terse as my favorite novel writer. The check for one thousand pounds was promptly paid, as it was drawn by one of the most prominent merchants of Liverpool, and it was only two days afterwards that it was discovered to be a forgery. Thereupon Thompson Brothers telegraphed to London for a detective—as the Liverpool police could do nothing for them—and I was sent down. The case was an embarrassing one. There seemed no possibility of identifying the distinguished stranger; all that the clerk could say was that he had observed a singular scar upon one of the gentleman's temples. This fact was only mentioned on the day after my arrival, in the most casual manner; but it gave me at once the clue. I well knew a gentleman with a scar on his temple—a fast gentleman about London, who had been mixed up in some ugly affairs, but had slipped out of them. It occurred to me in a word that the forger was Mr. Charley Wilkes, whom I had not seen for sometime, in his old haunts, and I began my hunt for that gentleman.

"It would weary you, my friends, to expatiate upon the methods employed by the respectable corps to which I belong—I refer to the detective police—to follow up an affair of this description. Suffice it to say that I tracked my friend to London, found that he had left that city two days before my arrival; then I went over to France, discovered that he had not landed at Calais; came on his track again at Brussels, which he had reached by way of Antwerp, and thence followed him by means of the passport office through Germany to the Prussian frontier, where his passport had been *visèd*, to Berlin.

"At Berlin I found everything in commotion at the banking house of Stralsund & Company. A check, drawn by the wealthiest dealer in hides in all Berlin, had been presented at the bank in which their funds were deposited, paid without suspicion, and the bank suddenly discovered itself *minus* the sum of two thousand thalers,

paid to a forged check. When they sought for the distinguished stranger who had presented the check, he was
nowhere to be found, and I only came upon his traces
again, always by means of that lucky system of passports,
at Vienna. When I intimate that I pursued the same
routes of travel adopted by my distinguished friend, and
was enabled to do so through the instrumentality of the
excellent, but sometimes embarrassing, passport system,
I do not mean that I ascertained at the passport bureaus
that Mr. Charles Wilkes, citizen of England, with residence at London, had left such a place at such a time
for such a city. I was too averse to losing my time to
indulge in any inquiries for "Mr. Charles Wilkes." I
requested everywhere a sight of the official records at the
passport offices, announcing my object; they were politely opened to my inspection, and I looked for a *signal-
ment* relating to a gentleman of from twenty-eight to
thirty, of ruddy complexion, vigorous stature, dark hair,
pleasing address, and—*with a scar upon his left temple.*
I was not left unrewarded. I found at Antwerp that the
Baron von Rahmburg, who had obtained a passport to
visit Berlin, was disfigured by the scar in question ; and
at Berlin by a remarkable coincidence the scar reappeared
in the passport description of Mr. John Wilson, a respectable English gentleman, who had set out two days before,
for Vienna.

"Well, at Vienna the police were in a state of real
fury, of mental prostration, approaching despair. The
princely *magasin* of Arnhoff & Co., Jewellers, had been
broken into on the night before. The persons sleeping

in the *magasin* had been deluged with chloroform, and plate and jewels to a fabulous value had been carried off by the burglars. The Austrian police, I regret to say, are rather too deliberate in their movements; they did not investigate this unfortunate affair until ten o'clock on the next day; and even then they were unable to discover the least traces of the perpetrators of this extensive burglary. All that one of the salesmen asleep in the store could say was that he had a dim recollection, just before losing consciousness under the effect of the chloroform, of seeing among the burglars a man with *a scar on his left temple*, who appeared to be the leader of the gang. I was present at the investigation; and when I heard this testimony I went directly to the office of passports. M. le Chevalier Gautry, who had obtained a passport to visit Geneva, on the day before, had, by the strangest of coincidences, *a scar on his left temple!*

"I need not say, my friends, that the affair of the burglary at Vienna had now ceased to interest me. I walked back toward my hotel, musing quietly upon the subject of M. le Chevalier Gautry, and was so lost in admiration of that gentleman and his proceedings that an unfortunate accident happened to me. The day was rainy, and the streets very slippery. I was passing from one side of the street to the other when the fine equipage of a young Viennese nobleman—or rather the horses—ran against me; I lost my footing, fell, the equipage went over me, and my leg was broken: to the great regret, I ought to say, of the young nobleman, who immediately checked his horses, leaped out, raised me up, and offered me a thousand apologies.

"Unfortunately these polite assurances of his very great regret did not heal the fracture in my leg. I was conveyed to my hotel, and remained on my back for a month—torturing myself, I must say, with the fear that my friend, the Chevalier Gautry, would not be at Geneva when I went to call upon him there. At last my broken bones were knit together again, I could walk by limping a little; whereupon I paid my bill, sent a line to headquarters in London, and took the railway for Geneva, where I arrived safely, and stopped at the handsome and well kept *Hotel Beau Rivage*, from which I moved however on the next day to the *Hotel Russie*."

## CHAPTER XXXVIII.

### MR. BROWN CONCLUDES HIS EXPLANATION.

WHEN Mr. Brown uttered the words "Hotel Russie," Mr. Allan Gartrell, if we may continue to address the gentleman by that name, exhibited very considerable interest, and looked at Mr. Brown with a dare-devil smile.

"Your narrative grows highly interesting, my good sir," he said; "continue—you have never told me about *Geneva*."

"I wished to reserve it as an agreeable surprise to you, my worthy friend," replied the smiling Mr. Brown. "There was little merit in my proceedings up to that moment—anybody might have followed the Baron von Rahmburg, Mr. John Wilson, and the Chevalier Gautry from Antwerp to Berlin, from Berlin to Vienna, and from Vienna to Geneva. That was all in the regular line of business—there were the passport offices, and a novice could not have blundered. But from and after Geneva the thing was different."

"Let us hear," said Mr. Gartrell with an easy air, "the story becomes exciting."

"Delighted to interest you, my dear friend," said Mr. Brown; "I will then continue. I mentioned, I believe, that I left the *Hotel Beau Rivage* on the day after my arrival at Geneva, to take up my quarters at the *Hotel Russie*. It is a charming hotel. The view like that from the *Beau Rivage*—but I must not linger on the charms of the landscape, of the handsome streets, of the—see *Murray*—I will continue.

"My motive for transferring myself and my luggage to the *Hotel Russie* was the discovery at the office of passports that the Chevalier Gautry, from Vienna, had a month before taken up his residence there; and as the records did not exhibit the fact that the Chevalier had left Geneva, I committed what, I must say, was a great blunder in concluding that, for that reason, the Chevalier was still at the *Hotel Russie*.

"I am very sorry to say that I discovered that the Chevalier had disappeared about two weeks before; and as my smiling friend, the landlord, seemed to have a a plenty of leisure on his hands, and to be fond of talking, I encouraged him to communicate any items of interest relating to the Chevalier, which might be in his possession. I was amply rewarded for this chance suggestion. My friend, the landlord, suddenly glowed with interest. Anything relating to the Chevalier Gautry!—he exclaimed. He could tell me a thousand things—a hundred anecdotes of this charming, this ravishing young nobleman! He threw his money about like water! he never looked at the items in a bill!—he ordered the oldest wines, and paid for them without a word !—he was a prince ! a prince ! I give you my word of honor, monsieur !—and it was no wonder that the English Milor Allan Gartrell, who alas ! had expired of fever at the *Hotel Russie,* had become the Chevalier's bosom friend !

"At these words from my fat little host, I began to listen with the deepest attention. I encouraged my landlord to continue his remarks. I ascertained what follows : When the Chevalier Gautry reached the *Hotel Russie* a young Englishman, who had been on a visit to Rome, was lying very ill in the hotel. This young gentleman was a certain Mr. Allan Gartrell—evidently a person of ample means ; a very handsome and cordial person, and bore the strongest possible resemblance—a most extraordinary resemblance—to the Chevalier Gautry. Two days after the arrival of the Chevalier he had managed to become acquainted with ' Milor Gartrell,' and thenceforth scarcely an hour passed without a visit from the Chevalier to the sick man's apartment. The Chevalier watched over him, amused him, cheered him—was a veritable brother to the poor young Milor, my host assured me on his word of honor. Whenever any letters came the Chevalier would receive them and read them to his sick friend. Whenever the young Milor required an amanuensis the Chevalier was there to offer his services. He was a brother—a veritable brother !—Had my friend, the landlord, I inquired, ever chanced to observe the post-mark on any letters received ?—Yes, *one* he had observed, as it was the last the young Milor ever received. It had the post-mark of the United States of America upon it, and the Chevalier Gautry took it, as usual, and went with it up to his friend's room. They remained long together—conversing in reference to this letter it seemed, as in passing he, the landlord, had heard the rattle of paper mingling with the voices. This was nearly the last interview between Milor Gartrell and his friend. On that very night the young Englishman began to sink. The doctor was summoned, but before his arrival the young Milor was dead of his fever, brought from the Pontine marshes to Geneva.

"At this event, my landlord continued, the grief of the Chevalier Gautry was most touching. He wept, he cried aloud, he paid the funeral expenses of his friend without a word—and it was a magnificent funeral. Then, overwhelmed with grief, he paid his own large bill at the hotel, without looking at a single item, and left Geneva to return to England and inform Milor Gartrell's family of their irreparable loss."

Mr. Brown paused, and gazed around him with his blandest smile.

"Such, my friends," he said, "was the highly interesting narrative which I heard from my excellent host at the *Hotel Russie*, in Geneva. It caused me to reflect deeply. There was under all this very evidently, some deeply interesting plot of my friend, the Chevalier Rahmburg-Wilson-Gautry-Wilkes! And let me say at once with what I think you will regard, my friends, as modest and pardonable pride—let me say that in ten minutes, nay in one minute, I had discovered the Chevalier's daring *ruse*. The clue to this discovery was that extraordinary resemblance that he bore to Mr. Allan Gartrell, and I had not the least doubt that he had taken advantage of it for some purpose. You are obliged, my friends, in this singular trade of detecting criminals, to enter, as I may say, into the feelings and views of the person you are pursuing—and put yourself in his place. Now I knew that the Chevalier Gautry-Wilkes was a gentleman of great daring, and, above all, of vivid and kindling imagination—that to assume the name and character of a dead man would present itself with brilliant attractions to a person like himself—and I did not lose sight of the further fact that nothing could have been more desirable to him at the time than to assume a new *alias;* to disappear as Mr. Gautry-Wilkes, and reappear as Mr. Allan Gartrell.

"The only thing which puzzled me," continued Mr. Brown, "was to determine whither Mr. Wilkes, under his new name of Gartrell, had gone. Not to England— he was much too intelligent for that. Not even to Paris —there were many young Englishmen there who probably knew the late Mr. Gartrell. I therefore concluded that the letter from America had suggested an idea to my friend, the Chevalier; that he had been seized with an ardent desire to explore the magnificent natural scenery, and form his own opinion upon the complicated social relations of that great republic, the United States."

Mr. Brown smiled modestly, and added:

"You will perceive that I was *burning,* as the children say, my friends. I was right so far; but a long and

weary chase was still necessary ; greater trouble than
before to follow my friend. Good fortune came to my
aid, however—all the mystery was cleared up in a moment. I had proposed to visit New York first, from
which city *Mr. Allan Gartrell* would no doubt write to
his banker in England for remittances, in his ordinary
handwriting, so well known to his Geneva friend, the
Chevalier ! but after New York, the real trouble of following him would begin, as you have no passport system.
Well, I was revolving all this in my mind at the *Hotel
Russie*, Geneva, when—presto ! comes a letter for Allan
Gartrell, Esq., forwarded from his Liverpool bankers.
It was the *second* letter written by Mr. George Cleave
announcing his intention to surrender Cleaveland to his
cousin. I ascertained that fact by opening the letter—
my host had intrusted it to me for delivery to Mr. Gartrell's family in England, whither I told him I was going.

"Thenceforward, my friends, all was plain sailing. I
knew now, perfectly well, where I should find my friend
the Chevalier Wilkes-Gartrell. I came to New York, and
thence to Waterford and Cleaveland, where I announced
my real character—or rather recalled myself—to my
friend Mr. Wilkes. My stay was longer than I intended,
but I became interested in this friendly little neighborhood and its affairs—I enjoyed the hospitalities of my
friend Mr. Daintrees ; and I may add that I restored the
sum of two thousand dollars, through my friend Mr.
Jobson, to a young gentleman who lost it, owing to the
great *skill* at cards of Mr. Wilkes !

"A few words will finish this narrative, my friends,"

said Mr. Brown. "I have said that I remained in the hospitable abode of Mr. Wilkes-Gartrell much longer than I intended ; but I hope Mr. Cleave will not charge me for his champagne consumed there, in consideration of my present services ! Well, to end—I was much amused by my worthy friend's aim to ally himself with the honorable family of Mr. Ormby. I delayed further proceedings. I lingered, greatly interested, when one day Mr. Wilkes insisted on hurling a bottle at me, and I grew a little tired of him. I accordingly went away from his princely mansion—ostensibly departed on the railway for parts unknown ; but on the same night I made my way back to Waterford, and remained *perdu* in a private chamber of my excellent friend Mr. Jobson's, much to the agitation, I fear, of Mrs. Jobson. Need I say that everything had been arranged between myself and Mr. Jobson for this interesting explanation in the presence of everybody ? I called on him for that purpose on my way back one day from the residence of Mr. Ormby, and there, I must say, my heart bled at sight of a young lady who was pale, ill, fainting, dying nearly, from the brutal persistence of this man Wilkes to force her to marry him !"

No one would have supposed the benevolent countenance of Mr. Brown capable of assuming a look so stern and forbidding as it assumed when he uttered these words. All his smiles had disappeared—all the tone of banter had gone out of his voice. It was a stern and indignant judge that stood there, with his eyes fixed on the face of Mr. Gartrell-Wilkes.

And that gentleman betrayed an emotion, as the vibrating voice resounded, which he had not before displayed. His careless and ironical air deserted him, his face filled with blood, and his hand went with a sudden movement to his breast.

"A fine—a very fine sentiment!" he growled, "from —a common policeman."

Mr. Brown's eyes flashed.

"It is better to be a common policeman than to be a thief—and a heartless scoundrel, sir," he said.

"A scoundrel!—beware!"

"Beware of what? Of your displeasure? That might frighten children, my good sir; it is a small thing to me!"

"Take care—!"

Mr. Brown fixed his eyes upon the speaker with an expression of contempt, which evidently galled that gentleman extremely.

"Instead of measuring my words, my good Mr. Gautry-Wilkes," he said with immense disdain, "I will express my meaning a little more clearly than before! I came to this country with the simple view of performing my professional duty. I had no special dislike to you. I remained in your house, or rather in the house which you occupied, more amused than anything else with your skilful operations, and content to defer arresting you, until the humor to do so seized me. Your insolence to me was nothing—that is your nature. Your threats of personal violence were amusing, and I did not fear them. For your character I had, as I said, no very great dislike

—the result it may be of the fact that I am a 'common policeman.' As such I am used to forgers and burglars like yourself—have perhaps lost my disgust for them ; but for some offences in men I have no pity!"

Mr. Gartrell-Wilkes looked as black as night.

"Beware!" he said again.

"You are one of the swell-mob," continued Mr. Brown, "and to lie and steal is perfectly natural to you. But even the swell-mob gentlemen disdain to do some things. They are thieves, pickpockets, burglars, and laugh at the law. But I tell you, sir—and it will explain the great disgust I now feel toward you—that not the worst thief in London, the meanest pickpocket, would have been guilty of this heartless scheme to break the heart of a mere child like Miss Ormby—or acted, as you have acted, with this coarse cruelty and cowardice!"

The words and tones of the speaker were full of such extreme contempt that Mr. Gartrell-Wilkes was stung to the quick, and lost his head. Rage carried him away ; his hand darted to his breast, and drawing a long and murderous-looking knife, he threw himself upon the cool Mr. Brown. That gentleman was, however, ready for him. His own hand had gone no less rapidly to his breast pocket — the barrel of his revolver suddenly gleamed, and the muzzle was upon his enemy's breast.

But the knife raised aloft did not fall, nor was the pistol discharged. The individual resembling a bull-dog had listened with great attention from the passage to the conversation which has been recorded, had approached the door, had seen the knife gleam—and, all at once, a

heavy stick descended upon the head of Mr. Gartrell-
Wilkes, who staggered, reeled back, and ended by measuring his length upon the floor, where he was speedily
handcuffed and secured by the constable.

. The company had started up in confusion.  Mr. Brown

THE INDIVIDUAL RESEMBLING A BULL-DOG HAD LISTENED.

alone preserved his air of perfect composure.  He un-
cocked his revolver, restored it to his breast pocket, and
stood looking with philosophic interest upon the pros-
trate and handcuffed figure.

"A cool hand, a very cool hand—my friend, Mr.
Charley Wilkes!" he said in a moralizing tone; "one of

the coolest hands, in fact, I have ever known! His forgeries and burglaries did not distinguish him among the crowd of competitors—but this personation of a dead man indicated genius! What a pity that a 'common policeman' should interfere! Well, my hand is on him at last, and his game is played. He deserves his fate. A thief?—that is bad, but not the worst thing about my friend. The meanest thief I know would have been ashamed of what this rascal has attempted—to break the heart of a poor girl, whose face reminded me of a little girl of my own in England!"

## CHAPTER XXXIX.

### AND THE CURTAIN FALLS UPON THE COMEDY.

OUR comedy—as we venture to style this little history of "Pretty Mrs. Gaston"—naturally ends with the happy termination of the love affairs embraced in it, and with the discovery that George Cleave was still the proprietor of Cleaveland.

A few words on the subsequent fates of the personages may, however, interest the reader. Let us take them in turn.

George Cleave and Marian were married in the autumn, and went to live at Cleaveland as if nothing had happened. The young man's title to the property was unassailable upon either of two grounds. He had informally surrendered it under a paper which had no legal force, from the absence of witnesses to attest it ; and if his title had been lost, it was restored by the death of the real Allan Gartrell, from whom, as his nearest relative, he inherited. Thus Cleaveland was his own again, and as Mr. Ormby's property at Bayview was soon sold, that gentleman and Mrs. Ormby, at George's earnest request, came to live at Cleaveland, where Mr. Ormby for the next ten years promenaded on the long portico morning and evening, taking the landscape, as of old, under his protection.

Ralph Harrington and Annie, and Mr. Jack Daintrees and pretty Mrs. Gaston were married at the same time—The Hollies blazing with lights in honor of the occasion. Ralph lives at "Tree Hill," near Waterford, and is perfectly happy. And Mr. Jack Daintrees—but how shall we depict the bliss of Mr. Daintrees? He wonders how he ever remained a bachelor so long. He is henpecked in a fearful manner, but not aware of the fact. He does not live at The Lodge—he lives at The Hollies, where he went to reside after a long but ineffectual struggle. Mr. Daintrees does not hunt the fox any more. He gives the gayest dinners, but is even losing his taste for that. He lolls in a dressing-gown and gorgeous slippers, smokes a great deal, and has a taste for landscape gardening. When not thus employed, he may be seen holding his wife's worsted, while she rolls it into a ball, gazing meanwhile with admiring eyes into one of the prettiest faces in the world.

Of Mr. Jobson we need say nothing—these old law-machines run on in the same groove. And Mr. Brown and Mr. Wilkes may be dismissed in a few words. Mr. Brown went away with his friend in charge; but Mr. Wilkes was a "cool hand" indeed, as he soon proved. He eluded his friend at one of the stations on the railway—was no more seen—but is supposed to have been recognized as a prominent citizen of Poker Flat, on the coasts of the Pacific, where he secures an ample maintenance by his *skill* at games of cards.

The little neighborhood which we have visited, kind reader, soon settled down again and grew quiet. Everybody smiled at everybody, and plainly thought the world around Waterford the best of all possible worlds.

I had heard of these events and went thither to spend the autumn. I was a guest at Tree Hill, and basked in the sunshine of a pair of eyes, the brightest and sweetest I ever saw—the eyes of "Annie Bell," at present Mrs. Ralph Harrington. One day we went over to dine at The Hollies, and that smiling nest of doves, upon which a bachelor hawk had intruded, was in all its glory.

As the sun was setting behind a mass of piled-up orange clouds, I went with Mrs. Annie to a certain rustic seat of which I had heard—the seat where, on the night of the party, Ralph Harrington grew romantic. I smiled as I alluded to the scene, and Mrs. Annie blushed.

"Very well," she said, laughing through her roses, "but Auntie had a rustic seat, too ; yonder she comes— ask her if she did not !"

I looked up. Mr. and Mrs. Jack Daintrees were approaching across the lawn ; the lady with her little timid smile and shy manner—the gentleman fat, good-humored, and unromantic.

"What a very strange world we live in !" said Annie laughing.

"That is a sage observation—quite true in every particular—but your meaning, madam ?"

"I mean that—I am married to Ralph, and—"

She raised her hand, pointing to the approaching pair.

"And here is the end of 'Pretty Mrs. Gaston' !"

# ANNIE AT THE CORNER.

## CHAPTER I.

### FROM A WINDOW.

I AM not a married man, and I do not think that all my lady acquaintances are angels; consequently, I am a miserable old bachelor.

There is absolutely no doubt upon the subject, I am informed by my friends; and so, because I think that something more than the want of wings distinguishes the fair from the other class, and because I spend my life in a suit of apartments, undisturbed by the musical laughter of children—for these reasons, as I have said, I am a crusty, musty, miserable old unmarried misanthrope.

I have been substantially notified of the fact more than once, by Miss Tabitha Ringgold, who lives in the handsome house opposite; and though I am charitable, my friend, I should not be surprised if that fair lady were, at the present moment, directing her private spy-glass into my chamber from behind her white curtain, a corner of which is, I perceive, slightly raised : I would not be at all surprised if Miss Tabitha were there, looking through the open window here, and lamenting the failure of science to discover ear-trumpets, such as might be used to catch a distant conversation.

Miss Tabitha often arrays herself in her best finery, and leans from the window, with nods and smiles, and silent invitations to come in, when I chance to pass. I do not accept these invitations often, as you will understand, if you listen further; but sometimes I do go over and take a hand at whist in the small parlor; in consequence of which, I am considered, I believe, an admirer of Miss Tabitha, and more than once my cynical and discourteous bachelor companions have gone so far as to declare that Miss Tabitha has long been engaged in the pleasing occupation of setting her maiden cap at me and my six per cents. Of course I do not give any credit to these scandalous jests and rumors, and I invariably reprove Bob when he gives utterance to them. There is, of course, no truth in the charge, and I'm glad of it. I regret to say that, even if there were not other objections, I could not solicit the honor of a matrimonial alliance with Miss Tabitha—my affections being engaged.

Ah ! do you start a little ? Do you look at me with astonishment, and ask, with your eloquent eyes, if I am not uttering a pleasant jest ? *I* engaged—you seem to say with a change of the pronoun—I, the incorrigible old bachelor, the woman-hater, the misanthrope, the miserable, disagreeable, outrageous, old curmudgeon ! *My* affections engaged, when the utmost inquisition of feminine curiosity eternally on the watch, has never discovered the least loop to hang a report upon ? Well, my dear friend, perhaps there is some ground for surprise, and your astonishment is not singular. My engagement is certainly not exactly what the world would call binding—and yet it binds *me*. Such things must frequently result in a matrimonial alliance between the man and the woman—at least sometimes : now, *my* engagement will not probably have any such termination. Gossips talk about Corydon, when he goes constantly to visit Chloe, in glossy patent leathers, a flowery waistcoat, hair elegantly curled, and a perfumed handkerchief gently waved in a diamond-decorated hand. They talk a great deal about that young man, and the talk rises into a hubbub, when the watchful eyes perceive the youth finally emerging from the mansion of his love, with beaming eyes, and nose raised high aloft with triumph, while Chloe sends a golden smile toward him as he goes, from behind the curtain of the drawing-room. The gossips, I say, talk about Corydon's engagement for a month thereafter ; but the most inveterate and ferocious tattle never occupies itself with my little affair.

I never speak of it ; the object of my affections preserves silence, too ; and not even Miss Tabitha suspects our little arrangement. If I tell you all about it now, good friend of many years, I do so because 'tis scarcely loyal to our friendship to have aught of reserve ; but, above all, because my burden of thought and feeling cries aloud for utterance.

I linger on the threshold—let me linger a moment longer yet, and ask you if I have never seemed eccentric to you? Often in passing to your counting-house, you send me a friendly nod as I lean from my window in the sunshine; and, doubtless, you go on to your arduous toils, thinking what a happy fellow I am to afford to be idle, when you and your whole establishment will all day be struggling to balance the books of the firm. You honestly consider me idle at such moments: my friend, I am never busier. You think me solitary: I am surrounded by companions. The street may be wholly deserted; the city square yonder may not tempt a single child to enjoy its green sward and shadow—Miss Tabitha even may be busy at her invisible toilet, and her window deserted—yet I am not alone.

When the real figures of actual, living personages appear, however, they do not, by any means, disturb my revery. I am not at war with my kind, but often find in the forms of men, women, and children what pleases me, and heightens the zest of my recollections.

I lean upon the sill of my window, and, thrumming idly with my fingers, scan the different wayfarers with smiling attention. I see my friend Dives with his jingling watch-seals, his creaking boots, his spotless shirt bosom, and his dignified look, go by to his warehouse, saluted respectfully by the heads of our two "first families"—the Scribes and Pharisees—who sometimes invite me to their palaces up town. And, as Dives disappears like a moving bank round the corner, I perceive Lazarus, with his maimed limbs, swinging himself by, on his hands, inserted in wooden gloves—the shadow of his low figure mingling with that of Dives. Of course I do not know Lazarus, as I move in good society: yet I am glad to see him with the cheerful smile on his pale, thin face; and when he passes on this side of the street, I sometimes drop slyly a piece of money into his bosom, and laugh to myself, as I draw back, fancying his puzzled expression. I related this incident at dinner, the other day, to my friend Dives and his guests; but he raised the question whether such things were advisable, the public charities being amply sufficient for meritorious sufferers, while individual relief encouraged pauperism and idleness.

"But, my dear Dives," I said with a smile, "suppose the coin which I dropped bought some small articles for the children of Lazarus, and so gave them pleasure far greater than any I could have enjoyed by spending the money?"

"The principle in the thing," replied my friend, sipping his claret and shaking his head, "the principle is bad. As members of society, we are bound to observe the laws of society; and as, in a state of society, we must be governed by the rules and regulations of that society, so I think, as a member of that society, you were rather bound to have this individual sent to prison as a vagrant on society, than to encourage him in what must eventually render it necessary to make an example of him for the good of society."

Those were the words of Dives; and as my friend the Reverend A. Caiphas asked me at the moment to take wine, the discussion was not resumed. I am obstinate, nevertheless, and shall probably continue to outrage the rules and regulations of "society," if the whim seizes me, when Lazarus passes beneath my window.

I am running on pretty much at random, and shall not, at this rate, get to my story. But I take so much interest in my window observations, that I am led to weary you with them. A word more, and I shall get regularly to my narrative.

Besides Dives and Lazarus, I see many other figures pass on the street. I·see Strephon go by in the tightest boots, the finest kid gloves, and the glossiest hat, escorting Miss Almira, the daughter of old Two-per-cent; and I stand, or rather lean, in silent admiration of her gorgeous appearance, as she sails by, rustling in silks and satins, with a bird of paradise upon her bonnet. She has chosen to walk on account of the sunshine, and the great carriage, with its liveried driver and footman, rolls by, unoccupied. It is a pity that the poor girl yonder slinking round the corner, and looking so faint and weak, can not ride a little in it; and I fancy Strephon might procure this favor for her, as the weak girl exchanges a look with him, which seems to indicate acquaintance. The three figures pass on, and disappear; but somehow, the look of the pale, weak girl dwells in my memory, and haunts me. Well, I weary you, good friend, and another word ends my window pictures. In addition to the figures I have mentioned, my observant eyes descry the merry forms of children dancing over the velvet sward of the public square—rolling their hoops, playing by the fountain, and shouting at their play. Their sweet faces please me; and the bright eyes seem to make the day more brilliant, the deep blue sky of a softer azure. It is only in the afternoon that I see them, for in the morning they are at school.

One of them wears a blue dress, and a white chip hat, secured beneath her chin by a pink ribbon—and, thus accoutred, she passes every morning to school, directly opposite my window.

As I gaze, with my shoulders drooping, my fingers inveterately thrumming, my eyes half-closed, and my lips wreathed with smiles, a little sad, perhaps, in their expression, I see my little friend come tripping along by the row of elms, cased in their square boxes, and I am pleased to see her bright figure, lit up by the sunlight which dances on her curls, her straw hat, her checkered flag satchel, gaily swung upon the bare arm, and the little boots of crimson morocco, tightly fitting to her delicate ankles. I wait for her, and look for her appearance, and when she comes, I follow her with my eyes, as she arrives opposite, and then disappears round the corner. She is different from some other young ladies of my acquaintance, who pass on a similar errand. These latter look up as they pass, at my grizzled hair, my gray mustache, my carelessly thrumming fingers, and I know very well, that at such times, they are thinking who on earth the old fellow at the window can be; the curious old fellow, always leaning from the very same opening, in the very same way, and smiling as he beats his tattoo, with the very same idle and dreamy expression.

My little friend of the blue dress and white chip hat

does not treat me quite so cavalierly. As she passes, every morning, she raises her blue eyes, and smiles in the most winning way, nodding her head in token of recognition, and thus causing a profusion of brown curls to ripple around the brightest cheeks in the world. Having thus indicated the pleasure she experiences in seeing me smiling and well, my little friend kisses her hand, laughing, and tripping on more rapidly, to make up for lost time, vanishes round the corner, singing "Lucy Neal," or "Lily Dale," or some other melody dear to the hearts of organ-grinders.

This brief and fitting exchange of friendly attentions between myself and the child takes place every morning, and, when she disappears, I close my window, and leaning back in my favorite chair, the red velvet yonder, light my old meerschaum and ponder. I generally remain thus, silent and motionless, for an hour before I commence reading the newspapers, over whose contents it is my habit to growl and vituperate.

I am going now to tell you what I think about in these morning reveries, and to explain the circumstances which attended my engagement, which engagement unfortunately interferes with any matrimonial views in connection with my friend, Miss Tabitha. I see that the corner of her curtain has fallen, and so we are entirely to ourselves.

## CHAPTER II.

### A SCHOOL GIRL.

I REACHED the age of twenty-five without ever having been in love.

I do not deny, that two or three times I had fancied myself smitten by the charms of young ladies with pretty lips and rosy faces. I am sure, however, that I by no means loved them, and *that*, simply because their smiles or frowns neither pleased nor grieved me in any considerable measure—an excellent test, in my opinion, and one which quite satisfies me.

I tranquilly pursued my daily occupation, which was that of a clerk with a moderate salary, in the house of Wopper & Son, now dissolved; and after my routine in the counting-house, generally spent my evenings in strolling about and reflecting upon my prospects. I was an orphan, and there were very few congenial companions at the house where I boarded, so I was left pretty much to myself, and was not embarrassed in the selection of amusements, by any one's suggestions.

Thrown thus upon my own resources, I looked around for something to interest and occupy my mind, and I found this object of interest in a girl whom I met regularly every morning at the corner yonder, where my present little friend disappears on her way to school.

The figure of the maiden of old times was not unlike my little friend's to-day ; but the former one was much less gaily clad ; her face was covered with a green veil, and she was older—about seventeen.

Regularly every morning, after breakfast, as I went to Wopper & Son's with the punctuality of a clock, I met my friend coming round this corner, and the encounter became an expected pleasure, which I could not forego. I knew nothing of the girl, except that she, doubtless, liked blue tints, which everywhere appeared in her cheap and simple clothing. She generally walked with her head down, conning a school-book which she held beneath her green veil, and for some time she never encountered my eyes with her own.

At last, as we went by each other at the same hour every morning, and as my dress was seldom altered in those days, she noticed me, and we would exchange looks. Then I saw her, with her veil raised, come around the corner looking for my familiar figure, then we exchanged glances of half recognition.

Things had reached this stage, when, one day, as I was coming up to dinner, and just as I was crossing the street, half-way down the square yonder, by the little wooden house, my attention was attracted by a scream ; I raised my head quickly, and at the same moment saw the breast of a horse strike the form of a girl within two paces of me. I was an active young fellow then, and with a single motion of my hand caught the animal by the bit, forced his foaming mouth backward, and with the other arm supported the girl, who was near fainting. The horse was ridden by an urchin who could not manage him, and galloping down the street he had nearly crushed the girl.

She now half leaned upon my arm in an attitude of terror and weakness, and a glance at her countenance told me that she was my friend of the corner. I need not say that the circumstance did not displease me; and when she came to understand that her deliverer, as the romance writers say, was the owner of the face so familiar to her, too, I don't think she was less pleased than myself.

I asked where she lived; and she replied, in a hurried and timid tone, that the little wooden house you see yonder was her mother's, and that she was returning thither from school. I offered her my arm with that simplicity and sincere respect which sprung then, as it springs now, from my admiration for a pure woman, young or old; and, leaning upon the arm, the girl reached her mother's, and, in the same timid tone, asked me to enter.

I was very glad to obey, and found myself in a small apartment, very poorly and cheaply furnished, but with an air of respectability and neatness about it, which indicated taste and refinement in the occupants. In one corner sat an old lady in a black bombazine dress, busily knitting, which operation she followed with eyes covered with large spectacles.

The old lady looked very much frightened when the girl related her adventure ; and the expression of gratitude upon her thin countenance, when my part was described, remains with me even now as one of my most delightful recollections.

I will not lengthen out the description of this scene, when, for the first time, I made the " speaking acquaintance " of Annie Claston. Her mother was the widow of a poor clergyman, and managed, as I afterwards learned, by close and rigid labor and economy, to supply the wants of the little household and send Annie to school. The girl had protested, almost with tears, against this, declaring that she was old enough to help her mother and not be a burden ; but the old lady still preserved her ideas about training and education, and Annie was forced to submit.

The acquaintance thus auspiciously commenced was not suffered to languish. More than ever, I had an object of interest to occupy my thoughts, and soon it began to occupy my heart. I now looked more eagerly than ever to see Annie at the corner ; and I think I may add that judging from the bright expression of her countenance, she was also pleased at our meetings. We generally paused a moment to exchange a clasp of the hand and a few words and smiles, and then we passed on. I do not know that she thought of me again until we met next morning ; but I am very certain that her image never left my thoughts for fifteen consecutive minutes throughout the day. Old Wopper, more than once, had occasion to ask me if I was asleep, and whether the pile of goods would be shipped if I only stared them out of countenance; and I think, if my imagination had been a photographic medium, the ledgers of the firm would have been covered with ten thousand pictures of a young girl in a blue dress, with curls on her neck. These pictures would have pleased most persons more than the entries; and this introduces a brief outline of Annie.

She had deep blue eyes, brown hair, a complexion as white as snow, and lips as crimson as carnations—I have never seen any so red. A delicate pale rose tint touched the centre of each cheek, and the expression of her countenance was the perfection of modesty. Look! here is her miniature, taken long afterwards from a pencil sketch I made, and the likeness is excellent. Now that you see I have not painted a figure of my imagination, I will proceed.

A few days after the accident I called one evening, with a beating heart, at Annie's mother's—with a beating heart, I say, for those "long, long thoughts," as the poet says, and our regular meetings had suddenly, in a single night, as it were, blossomed into love.

I was warmly received by mother and daughter, who with the simplicity and confiding sincerity of elevated nature, did not doubt for an instant that I was what I seemed. I spent an evening, every moment of which appeared to me a separate and perfect world of happiness, and when I returned to my poor chamber I leaned my head upon my hand, and remained lost in thought for an hour, and when I lay down I dreamed of her, and woke thinking of the girl, and trying to ask God to bless and protect her. I am not ashamed of that prayer, friend of years, and do not doubt that it rose to the throne of the Almighty. Let what will happen—let things look as they may—I bow my head and submit myself, as a child, to Him who rules us, and sends the sunshine or the storm, as He wills.

I will not lengthen out this portion of my brief story either, but get on to the end of it. For some months I continued to visit Annie, almost every evening now; and as I met her as of old, at the corner yonder, her beauty and goodness filled my life, as it were, and riveted those chains which her loveliness and purity had bound me with. I loved her with all the deep and earnest passion of my nature, and she saw that I did, and was too innocent and destitute of art to feign indifference. I had, at the end of the time I have mentioned, the unspeakable happiness of knowing that I was as dear to her as she was to me; and now, looking back through a life of many decades, I recall no sensation approaching in blissful intensity of happiness that first throb of rapture, upon finding that the lovely and pure-hearted girl had dowered me with the whole affection of her nature. I think God gives us on this earth few purer or happier emotions, and I humbly thank Him for this gift to me, His unworthy creature.

I was Annie's accepted lover.

# CHAPTER III.

## TWO RIVALS.

WITH the exception of three or four elderly ladies of the neighborhood, reduced in circumstances, like Mrs. Claston, no one visited at the house to which I so regularly bent my way, but a young man named Lackland.

He was the son of a wealthy merchant, who had formerly been a parishioner of Annie's father, in the country, and his acquaintance with the young girl had commenced accidentally at a small evening party in the neighborhood. Lackland was about my own age, and might have been called handsome, but for the weak and irresolute expression of his lips, and the lurking and uneasy glance of his eye—characteristics which he vainly tried to conceal beneath a laughing and careless manner.

From the first moment of his meeting with Annie, he fell in love with her, as completely as was possible with him; and as his father's wealth was placed, in a great measure, at his disposal, he understood the advantage which the circumstance gave him, and used it.

I will tell you in a moment how he managed to impress upon the young girl the possession by himself of exactly what I lacked—an abundance of money. I will say first, that the young man dressed in the most splendid fashion; that his equipage was in the finest taste, and that every trait of his manner, down to the most unconscious movement, showed that he was accustomed to the highest and most fashionable society.

Nevertheless, he did not advance in the opinion of Annie, or her mother, and I had, what to a lover is the profoundest pleasure—the conviction that a moment of my society was more valued by Annie than an hour of his.

The wealthy young lover affected not to understand this, although it was plain to the commonest apprehension, I thought. In spite of everything he did not seem to understand that his visits were unwelcome, and persisted in frequently coming in the evenings, in spite of his cool reception. On these occasions he bowed with an easy air ; saluted me, when I was present, with friendly familiarity, and sat down, playing with his hat and smiling. It was impossible for Annie to treat any one discourteously, and though she had taken a dislike almost to Mr. Lackland, she did not betray this impression, but met all his advances with the most perfect and maidenly courtesy, but nothing more. I have never seen a more perfect exhibition of what is called the "high-bred air," than that of the girl on these occasions, and Lackland seemed to think as I did, that any man might be proud of such a wife.

The visits of the young man were continued as regularly after our engagement as before, and he had for some time been sending Annie very handsome presents, anonymously, and in such a way that they could not be returned but just with that transparent veil thrown over them which the eye easily pierced.

One evening a servant handed to the maid at the door a small box, and then disappeared without waiting for an answer, or leaving any gentleman's name. The box was succinctly addressed to "Miss Annie Claston," and contained a pair of magnificent bracelets.

When I came Annie showed me the jewels, and I at once recognized them, having seen Lackland purchase them that morning at White's. The young lady asked me to advise her what to do, as she was convinced that Mr. Lackland had sent them. I did not mention my meeting with him, and felt unpleasantly about it. I begged her not to give herself any annoyance, that I would return them, frankly informing Mr. Lackland of her disinclination; and on the next morning I did so.

I met my gentleman coming out of the Club, whither I had gone to seek him, and handing him the box, said that Miss Claston had commissioned me to thank him, but to beg him to receive back the jewels.

"Jewels!" said the young man, swinging his ivory-headed cane, and holding his other hand behind his back, "what can you mean, my dear fellow?"

"In the present instance, jewels means *bracelets*, Mr. Lackland," I replied calmly.

"Bracelets!" he returned, with an air of surprise.

"Yes, sir, bracelets which you sent to Miss Claston last evening."

"I!" he repeated in the same tone, "really, you are going too fast, sir."

I think, Mr. Lackland, I move at a pace exactly in accordance with my calling, which is that of a mercantile clerk. I am now on my way to the counting-house, and my time is valuable. I beg to repeat, that Miss Claston has commissioned me to thank you for these jewels, but begs that you will pardon her for returning them."

The irresolute and uneasy expression came to his face, and mingled itself with the irritation.

"Really, sir!" he said; "I am subjected to actual persecution. You wish to force me to receive back what I never sent."

"Mr. Lackland!" I said, profoundly astonished at this falsehood.

"Sir!" he said, stiffly.

"You will pardon me," I said satirically, "but I saw you purchase these very jewels yesterday morning at White's. Doubtless the circumstance has escaped your recollection."

His face turned crimson as I spoke, and an angry flash shot from his eyes.

"Well, sir!" he said angrily, "you seem to make it your business to keep watch over my movements! Suppose I *did* send that box, and suppose I *did* wish to conceal my agency in sending it—what concern is it of yours, sir?"

"I choose to make it my concern, sir," I replied

coldly, "and if you address another observation to me in that tone, you shall answer it elsewhere."

I never knew before that he was a coward. His cheek blanched, his eyes lowered themselves before my angry glance, and he did not reply.

"Mr. Lackland," I said, "I regret that this conversation should have taken a turn so unpleasant. I have not the least desire to quarrel with you, sir, and wish simply to discharge the commission which I have undertaken, as a friend of Miss Claston. She begs to thank you for this gift, but can not receive it, and I now return it."

With these words I placed the box in Lackland's hand, and bowed and left him. From that moment, as I knew afterwards, he hated me with all the bitterness and malice of a small and cunning nature. You will see how his hatred developed itself.

# CHAPTER IV.

### PARTING.

ANNIE and myself had entered into our engagement with that thoughtless precipitancy of youth
which older and wiser heads visit with so much reproba-
tion.  My salary was entirely insufficient for the comfortable support of two persons united in the holy bonds
of matrimony, and, after long and sad discussions upon
the subject, it was the conclusion of the little household
that we must wait for happier times.

Long engagements are a great evil; and they should, I
think, be avoided, if possible, in all cases.  To see the
phantom of married happiness constantly fly before you,
eluding your grasp, and laughing pitilessly at your
despair—this is sufficiently saddening.  But there is the
further consideration of the young lady's position.  The
knowledge of her engagement on the part of her asso-
ciates is more or less embarrassing, and I have known
many gentlemen who declared it impossible to enjoy the
society of such a lady—"talking to you at random, and
looking over your shoulder at her intended."  It is true
Annie did not give a thought to this, and she declared

her willingness to wait just as long as she lived; but altogether it was disheartening.

Just when we had arrived finally at the conclusion that we must wait, and that I must look around for some improvement in my situation, I was one morning accosted by an old merchant who had professed a great friendship for me, and informed that he had a proposal to make me. He soon unfolded his idea: it was that I should go to Rio de Janeiro for a year or two, and act as his mercantile correspondent; and he supported his proposition by offering me just thrice the salary which I then received. He would give me a week to think of it, he said, and then we parted.

I need not tell you that this proposition was the subject of the most anxious consideration to me throughout the week, for the idea of leaving Annie nearly unmanned me and paralyzed my resolution. The dear girl saw the struggle in my breast, and understood perfectly that she was the obstacle in the way. She besought me not to refuse—that, great as her distress would be to part with me, it would distress her still more to reflect that she embarrassed my movements and clogged my advances toward prosperity; and she added that I need not be uneasy about them at home, for they were now very comfortable. Mrs. Claston urged the very same views.

It was not until Annie and myself were alone, that leaning her lovely head upon my shoulder, she cried, and said she would remain "mine in life and death." I recollected these words afterwards.

Well, not to lengthen out my story, at the end of the

week I accepted the offer of my friend Mr. Aiken; and having made every arrangement with the house where I had been employed, I sailed in a month.

I went on shipboard one night; and thus remained with Annie and her mother all the evening. I recall that evening now perfectly; and especially the crimson sunset flooding the trees of the square yonder, from whose summits crowns of gold seemed gradually lifted by the fingers of the night. Mrs. Claston was a little indisposed, and I took leave of her in her chamber—receiving with tears almost that blessing which she gave me, laying her thin white hand on my head, as I kneeled beside her. The storms of many years have beaten upon my brow, and changed to gray my raven hair, or swept it away, but still the touch of that pale thin hand of the pure lady is on my brow, and I kneel before her once more on that night of parting.

Annie and myself lingered long in the little parlor I need not say; and the golden crowns all disappeared from the fringed summits of the elms before we parted. It was not "in one blind cry of passion and of pain"—but it went near to unman me. Those caresses and endearments which are the language of lovers, and have therefore been derided by the cold and stupid world which does not know that God has given them to His creatures to express the depth of pure and holy love—those faltering words and tearful pressures of the hand which say so much, were a thousand times ended and renewed; and then the end came.

Annie wrung her hands, and like a fearful child followed me to the door. It was nearly dark, and I must go. I turned to take leave of her again—but throwing a handkerchief over her head, which made her countenance resemble a Madonna's weeping, she drew me toward the corner, some steps distant only as you see, there to bid me farewell.

I had there first met with her—there she had seen me, too, for the first time. As our eyes now met in a long, long look, the whole past rose up again, and condensed itself into a moment—a moment crammed with love and happiness, the recollection of which threw a glory almost over the canopy of night.

And there at the old corner we parted—a long embrace; smiles breaking through tears in the eyes of a man and a woman—that was the spectacle which the friendly stars beheld.

Annie went back, crying, and I continued my way to the wharf and embarked. When I opened my eyes the sun was rising over the Atlantic. But I saw nothing but the figure of the maiden—I felt nothing but the sweet agony, the bitter pleasure of that parting.

It is well that I looked back instead of forward: but let me proceed in sequence.

# CHAPTER V.

## THE RETURN.

I WAS reading, the other day, a book which has been much spoken of in Europe—the story of a poor, lost girl, from the dark gulf of whose nature, full of woful depravity and misery eating into her heart like a cankerworm, a flower of innocent love springs up, and purifies her, smoothing her dying pillow. I thought at first that the work was a fiction; but it was too strange.

Only the thoughtless and unobservant will consider what I have said a paradox. We do not get at *fact* anywhere, because it wraps itself in the triple folds of self-esteem, reserve, and fear; and thus, seeing only the outside of life, some persons think that it is new, prosaic, and commonplace, and that all the tragedies are attributable solely to the vivid imagination of dramatists and romancers.

I know family histories which I would not dare to relate in their naked, simple details, though the scene were laid in another land and the names changed, for the majority of my listeners would declare me crazy. I know histories of individuals which I could verify step by step, incident by incident, from yellow and moth-

eaten letters and papers, which histories the world
would no more believe, than they would the existence of
devils in a man of this century. They would rather say
that I forged the papers, than credit what would make
their hair stand on end. But I am wandering from my
story, which is not quite so terrible as some others, my
dear friend, though, at the time, it seemed to me that
woful tragedy and despair had touched its climax.

I remained in Rio de Janeiro for three years; and at
the end of that time set sail homeward, with the satis-
factory feeling that I possessed what was amply sufficient
to enable Annie and myself to commence house-keeping.
My delight, as I approached the friendly shores of my
native land, was even increased by the fact that I had
not received one line from home for more than a year;
and while the explanation of this lay simply in the fact
that the ocean mails were very irregular, I had often felt
a sort of foreboding, such as most persons experience
when they love deeply. At such times we fear that such
an immensity of happiness as we dream of can not be
unmixed, even if it exist: the heart doubts, however
powerfully the mind reasons against these doubts; and
we wait, in trembling suspense, the sight of the familiar
shores, the old mansion, the beloved face.

Thus, while I experienced the most exquisite delight
as I saw the well-known rows of buildings and discerned
many familiar forms upon the wharf, I waited with
anxious expectation for the moment when I should recognize a building more familiar still, a face more dear
to me than all the world.

Ten minutes after entering the hotel, and after throwing merely a passing glance at my brown face and long, black mustache in the mirror, I was at the door of the little wooden house yonder. Everything was just as I had left it—the honeysuckle blossomed on the porch, as it did on that evening in June when I parted with Annie; a pigeon or two circled in the golden atmosphere, or lit upon the roof; even the curtain at the window of the little parlor, from behind which Annie watched with tender eyes, as I left her every evening, was still there; the trees, lastly, of the beautiful square rustled in the warm breath of the summer evening, and on their imperial summits the same crowns of gold were slowly lifted by the dusky fingers of the twilight. Every object, every ray, every shadow, every odor—there was nothing that did not speak eloquently of Annie; and leaning for an instant against one of the white pillars, I placed a hand upon my heart to still its throbbing. I look back now on the figure of myself, standing there on the very threshold of my fate, and almost feel again what I felt soon after.

A strange servant came to the door. Was Mrs. Claston or Miss Annie at home? — Sir? Was Mrs. Claston at home? I repeated; if so, tell her that a friend had come to see her. The reply was that Mrs. Claston did not live there, but she would see. The maid went and told her master, who came at once and invited me in. I entered the little parlor, and, for a moment, thought the beating of my heart would alarm the host. He did not seem to observe my agitation, however—he was a fat, good-humored old gentleman, not given to imaginative exertions—but in a polite and smiling fashion invited me to be seated.

I sat down ; and again my eyes made the circuit of the apartment, whose mantel-piece, cornice, wainscoting, and curtain, brought vividly back the old days with Annie. With Annie !—yes, with Annie !  I was losing time—and I turned to my host.

The information which he conveyed to me, was briefly as follows :  Mrs. Claston had been dead for a year, and he had understood that her daughter had gone to live with an aunt at the other end of the city, whose name he had heard but did not remember.  Was Mrs. Claston a friend of mine ?  He was extremely sorry to have uttered what seemed to distress me so much.

And, seeing me almost unmanned by the distressing intelligence he communicated, the kind old gentleman bustled out and returned with some wine, which he forced upon me.  I touched the glass only to my lips, and, thanking him, rose to go.  He suddenly called me back as my foot touched the threshold, and said that he now remembered the name of the lady with whom Mrs. Claston's daughter went to live—Mrs. Peters.  I thanked him again and took my departure, leaving, with slow steps and a heavy heart, that house in which I had been so happy.  I had thus lost one most dear to me : that blessing, as I knelt by her, was to be an eternal one, never to be renewed ; beyond the stars of the bright evening, the white face shone with the glories of heaven. The kind, pure lady was gone, but she had left me a priceless consolation in Annie. As I thought of the girl, my heart throbbed and my cheek glowed—from death I returned to life.

I went to a shop and asked for a directory; I had known the man, but he did not recognize me, with my hair crisped by the tropical sun, my cheeks burned of a deep brown, and my lips covered with a long, black mustache. I easily found the address of Mrs. Peters, and thanking the man, who said I was very welcome, and I thought gazed curiously at my foreign dress, I walked rapidly away.

I preferred walking, as the exertion was some relief to my overburdened feelings—feelings oscillating like a pendulum, uneasily, between gloom and delight, between hope and fear.

## CHAPTER VI.

### A WOMAN,

I HAD gone two or three squares, and was crossing the street, when a carriage, drawn by two splendid horses, with a driver and footman in livery, passed rapidly before me; and as the brilliant equipage flashed on, enveloping my person in a cloud of dust, I distinctly perceived, framed as it were in the velvet-edged opening, the face of Annie.

I stood gazing after the carriage, which disappeared around a corner, with an expression upon my countenance, I am sure, of perfect stupefaction. Then I had found the person I was hastening to meet and clasp to my bosom with a hundred kisses. I had found the Annie of old days, of the humble dwelling, of the timid and modest existence, returning as it were, beneath the shadow of the old elms which threw their wide arms above the humble roof—this Annie of my heart and my dreams, I had found in the splendidly dressed woman, glittering with jewels and satin and lace, and darting onward like a meteor in the downy velvet of a splendid chariot, which scattered dust upon *me* as I stood, within two paces, unrecognized.

I was not seen, it is true; but had I been seen, would I have been recognized? I was simply a sunburnt stranger—a pedestrian who looked at a fine carriage as it passed. Had the world turned from east to west, or was I insane or dreaming?

Then the face of Annie, as she passed, rose before me again; I thought she looked pale beneath the load of flowers above her brow—she looked sad in the midst of this splendor. What did it mean?

There was an easy solution. I should doubtless know all from Mrs. Peters, whose carriage she probably used. I had heard of this lady, the sister of Annie's father, long a widow—and, as well as I could remember, not much had been uttered in her praise. Well, we would see. And I set forward rapidly again toward the house.

I found it at last. It was a very handsome residence, the front door approached by marble steps, with an ornamental iron railing. I ascended and knocked.

A servant appeared, and I bade him carry my card to his mistress, and say that I desired to see her.

I was shown into a magnificent parlor, in which everything was overpoweringly splendid and arranged with the primmest elegance; and in ten minutes a rustling of silk upon the stairway preluded the entrance of Mrs. Peters.

She entered, and inclined her head stiffly. She was a woman of about fifty, with hard, cold features, an icy gray eye, and the heavy double chin indicated a tendency towards good living.

"You wished to see me, sir?" she said, coldly, subsiding into a seat, and holding the tip of my card, as if she would be glad to toss it, as one does a worthless piece of pasteboard, into the fire-place. "Pray, to what am I indebted for the honor of your call?"

I saw in an instant this woman had distinctly made up her mind to oppose and overcome me, and I had plainly nothing to expect from her but coldness, perhaps insult.

"I came, madam," I replied calmly, "to see a friend of mine."

"Ah, sir!" she said, in the same tone of coldness.

"I refer to Miss Annie Claston, who is a very dear friend."

"Of *yours*, sir?"

And barbed with the deadliest hauteur, her insult struck me full in front; but I only grew colder, in spite of the beating of my heart.

"Of mine, madam," I said, calmly. "It may possibly astonish you, that I, a poor stranger—though not, I perceive, a complete stranger even to yourself—that I should speak of Miss Claston as I do. But what I have said is simply the truth, and it is quite impossible for me all at once to adopt an air of ceremony in speaking of one—I may as well say—so dear to me. You can not be ignorant of the relations existing between myself and your niece—you must understand——"

"I understand nothing, sir!" she said, contracting her brows with sudden and haughty anger, "and I desire that you will not further confide to me your private affairs!"

I rose from my seat and bowed, a movement which the lady imitated, in a manner which indicated dismissal.

"I am sorry to have offended Mrs. Peters," I said,

with a flushed cheek, "but I have at least the satisfaction, in leaving her, to know that I have not uttered a single word which could be construed into an impropriety. I have simply said that Miss Claston occupies a position toward myself which it is impossible for you to be ignorant of."

"And I have replied, sir," said the lady, flushing like myself with indignant fire, "I have replied, sir, that I understand nothing."

"Is it possible that Annie has not told you?" I said, coldly.

"Will you be good enough to terminate this interview, sir?"

And trembling with anger and disdain, the lady deliberately tossed my card into the fire-place.

"I shall certainly do so at once, madam," I said, with the most ceremonious bow. "I am not naturally fond of insults, which you seem to take pleasure in inflicting upon an unoffending gentleman."

My coldness, and the shadow of disdain in my voice, must have profoundly enraged her; for, advancing a step, with flashing eyes, the folds of her great chin swelling and her lips quivering, she said:

"I do not regard you as a gentleman—I know you perfectly well, sir; and I see in you only the individual who attempted to take advantage of the unsuspecting innocence of my niece, in order to inherit my property! I do mean to insult you, sir! If Annie had married you, she might have starved and died in a gutter, before I would have given her a mouthful! You need not put on that air of a great lord, sir!" cried the furious woman; "that is what she would have come to, had you been successful in persuading her to follow your beggarly fortunes! You practised dishonorably upon her feelings, and inveigled her into your toils, and it was a year before I could do away the effect of your arts. But I succeeded, sir; I got the better of you. She confessed that you had tricked and deceived her—said that she would never again think of you, sir! And I now inform you, for your satisfaction, that my niece has been for six months the wife of Mr. Lackland."

Had a thunderbolt fallen upon my bare brow, it could scarcely have produced a more terrible effect upon me than did these words. I staggered, and raised my hand to my eyes, before which a cloud of the color of blood seemed to pass, from whose folds horrible faces peered at me, and pointed to me with long, bony fingers and diabolical laughter. I gasped for breath; my bosom seemed weighed down with a huge load, and gigantic fingers seemed to compress my choking throat, and inject my temples with burning floods.

In the midst of this terrible phantasmagoria—when I was still oscillating upon my feet—I saw indistinctly the face of the woman who had struck me to the heart; and her countenance wore an expression of hateful triumph, for she profoundly detested me and enjoyed my agony.

But she was nothing to me now at all. I did not look at her again. I did not utter another word, but, putting on my hat, went away, feeling cold, though the day was warm.

I remember stopping at the crossing where I had seen the carriage pass, and smiling at my foolish fancy, that this fine lady with the nodding plumes had any connection with *my* Annie—that she resembled her. I would go to the hotel and change my dusty garments, and before the golden crowns rose from the summits of the trees, would clasp to my heart the pure and faithful girl and her dear mother, and mine.

I hastened on, and wondered if the passers by suspected my happiness : poor creatures !

Before the hotel some Italians were playing on hand-organs, and a crowd was laughing at the antics of some dancing dogs. I had time to look at them, and sitting down, I commenced thrumming with my fingers and gazing with smiles and delight at the merry dogs.

Five minutes afterwards a sort of cloud swept before my eyes, I heard a loud exclamation, and some servants ran to me and lifted me from the pavement, upon which I had fallen senseless.

For three months I was prostrated by brain fever, accompanied by delirium, which brought me to the brink of the grave.

# CHAPTER VII.

### THE OLD HOUSE.

ONCE, when I was travelling in Italy, I met, between Naples and Salerno, a woman who walked
wearily along the highway and, indeed, seemed scarcely
able to get out of the track of my horses. She was old
and thin, and I offered her a seat in my vehicle, which
she accepted with a sort of wonder.

I asked her where she was going, and she told me her
history. Her husband, sister, father, and three children,
had died, within ten days of each other, a month before,
and she was going to Salerno, to try and get employment.

She related all this without agitation, and scarcely
sighing. I asked her how she had been able to forget so
soon—for, you know, I am a curious student of human
nature. The woman looked at me simply, and said, in
her calm voice : "God consoled me. My loss was a
blessing."

"I understand," I said ; "but these pious impressions
might have been made upon your mind without this immense misfortune."

I shall not soon forget her reply.

"Signor," she said, looking at me calmly, "on the blue days we play, and sing, and keep the carnival. It is only when the sirocco burns from the south that we feel who gives us the flowering laurels and the cool breezes of the sea."

The woman's answer touched the chord of memory, and I felt that we had gone through a similar ordeal.

I rose from my sick bed entirely changed, and I trust that my life, since that time, though not so useful as it might have been, has not been without benefit to my species. The sirocco had burnt into my very soul, and I bowed my head and submitted without groaning, after a while—and now wait for the hour when the grass, if not the laurels, will whisper over me.

I converted my small savings into a letter of credit, and went abroad—travelling for five years through Europe and the East. I saw a great deal of human nature, I think; for I mixed with peasants and nobles— the high and the low, the rich and the poor—coming, for all my pains, to the final and most rational conclusion, that humanity is much the same in every land—that Giovanni laughs or groans under much the same influences as John; that a knot of ribbon and a festival pleases Lisette in Paris, as it does Betty in the country here—that it's all the same old story.

I was beginning to count the florins in my purse now, when, one day, a packet with a red seal was brought me, by a servant of my friend the consul's, and I had the pleasure of being informed, by Israel Jones, attorney-

at-law, etc., etc., of my native county, that I was sole
legatee of my respectable uncle, deceased, who had
always quarrelled with me, and that the estate was esti-
mated to be worth from seventy-five to one hundred
thousand dollars. I was glad to hear it, and as I had
seen enough of Europe, I thought I would return home,
or to what had once been a sort of home to me—to the
spot where I had been, for a brief season, wholly, completely, supremely happy. The song says truly, that
"'tis home where the heart is"; and I was just as
strongly drawn toward the old place, and figure, as
when I sat in the counting-house at Rio de Janeiro, and
sent my heart across the seas to Annie, praying for me
in another land.

Do you know why I loved her? We are considering,
let us say, a mere series of events, and, therefore, we may
philosophize. My unabated love, then, for this woman,
in whom I had implicitly trusted, and who had broken
my heart, sprung from the fact, that, as a living person,
she was completely dead to me. As far as I was concerned she did not exist—she was mouldered to dust,
beneath a piece of sward, the grass waved over her. It
was the Annie of my youth—for when I returned I was
already growing old—the Annie of former years that I
loved. Since the momentary glance which I had caught,
on that evening as she passed onward in her carriage, I
had never laid my eyes on her; and I did not wish to see
her. All was broken between us—she was nothing to
me, I nothing to her; we went different ways—I and
Mrs. Lackland.

My Annie was not Mrs. Lackland. She was the ever splendid and gracious vision of my youthful dreams and hopes—the pure, faithful maiden, with the kind, frank eyes, holding no trace of guile. *My* Annie never could have yielded to the threats of a base and degraded woman, and broken an honest heart which was wrapped up in her—ruined a man who cared nothing for life without her love. Mrs. Lackland lived in a splendid house—my Annie in the humble cottage beneath the elms. Mrs. Lackland rode in an elegant carriage, and wore satins, and jewels, and birds of paradise—my Annie walked, and was clad in a little blue dress and chip hat. Mrs. Lackland was a false woman, pining in magnificent misery—the Annie of my memory and my heart was an angel, with an angel's purity and happiness in her azure eyes. But I will not continue this dissection of my heart—I will proceed with my story, which draws to an end.

The five years of my second absence had worked greater changes even than the three years formerly—or as great. Every familiar face seemed to have disappeared from the scene—even the faces of those who had wounded me most cruelly; and I walked alone, not even encountering enemies—only strangers.

Lackland the elder had completely failed in business, two years before, and I soon heard had wholly impoverished Mrs. Peters, who sank under the blow, and died, soon afterwards, of apoplexy.

Young Lackland had become the slave of intemperance —had treated his wife with notorious cruelty, and, finally, the father and son, with the wife of the latter, had disap-

peared, no one knew where.    Thus every face was gone—
I had not even a successful rival to welcome me.    I went
to the little house, and found a new tenant, who stared
at me, and evidently thought me a suspicious character,
when I looked around the walls of the little parlor and
sighed wearily.

I asked the name of the owner of the house, and, on
the next morning, purchased it.    Three months afterwards, I occupied the house myself.

I will not pause to speak of the bitter pleasure which I
experienced in this house, where those golden days of the
past had flown on, brilliant and serene, like a morning of
June, in the light of eyes now dim or dead to me.    For
long hours I sat in the little parlor, where I had so often
sat with Annie, dreaming of the past, and breaking my
heart with her image.    There she had stood, resting her
white hand on the old mantel-piece, and looking at me,
with eyes moist with tenderness, when I rose to go ; yonder she had sat, by the little table, with the light upon
her hair, the white collar around her snowy neck, her
fingers busily sewing in the long evenings, as I sat beside
her ; finally, there was the window, and the curtain,
which she thrust aside, to follow me with her kind, tender eyes.    I will not further dwell upon those hours of
agony and delight, of joy and anguish.    One morning I
knelt down on the spot where she had stood so often,
covered my face with my hands, and, crying like a child,
prayed and sobbed ; and rose, finally, and went away.

I returned to Europe, and remained abroad for ten
years this time—a wanderer in many lands.    As before, I

occupied myself with that eternal, endless study—humanity. At the end of the ten years I came back again, led by a presentiment that something connected with my past was to happen to me. I was not mistaken, as you will perceive when I have briefly related what occurred soon after my arrival.

Briefly, I say; for upon this I dwell even less than upon other scenes; and my history draws to its close.

# CHAPTER VIII.

### AT THE CORNER.

I CAME back, then, and found that the home of my early manhood was stranger and more unfamiliar to me than the desert, Damascus, Rome, or the furthest bounds of the East. "Here a god did dwell," as says the Latin poet; but his fane was desolate, and the contrast made the familiar scenes more strange than an untrodden wilderness. But the old house remained—because it was mine. While I live it will stand, as it did nearly half a century ago.

This house and the corner where I had first met with the woman who had ruined me, were the only landmarks by which I recognized the locality. As my object was to live in the dead days, rather than the living, I secured the apartments which I now occupy, and had thus before my eyes, constantly, the two objects.

The neighbors talked for a month about the foreigner who lived so secluded, and then they gave up talking, because they could discover nothing. All that they found out was, my habit of walking about after nightfall —and, after awhile, this habit failed, too, to excite curiosity. I went on dreaming and promenading.

One night I had walked to the other end of the city—had returned nearly to my apartments—and was passing the corner yonder, when a woman with a baby in her arms touched my sleeve, and in a stifled voice asked charity. I was wrapped in my cloak, wore a wide, drooping hat, and stood with my back to the gas-light. The light thus fell upon the face of the woman—it was Annie!

I stretched out one hand, and leaned thus upon the cold iron of the lamp-post, for a deadly faintness invaded my frame and arrested my blood.

She was wretchedly clad, her face was as thin and pale as a ghost's, and her broken words were still further broken by a hacking cough. She said that she was suffering from hunger, and that her child would die unless I aided her—"For the love of God, sir!"

She held down her head as she spoke, and cried in silence, and this silence was broken by myself.

I strangled a groan and a sob, which tore its way through my breast, and said :

"Have you no husband?"

As I spoke, she raised her head quickly, with a wild light in her hollow eyes, and gazed at me with a look of startled surprise—almost terror—which I shall never forget.

"Yes!" I groaned. "I see you recognize me. I am George!"

She turned as pale as death, and tottered. I caught her in my arms, or she would have fallen to the ground.

"No! do not! do not!" she cried, wildly. "I am

not worthy to lean upon your arm! Let me kneel to you, and ask you to forgive me, for I am miserable and heart-broken. But it was not my fault. They told me that you were unfaithful!—that you were dead! And my aunt forced me to marry the father of my child! Oh, no! no! Let me go away—I will receive nothing from you. I can die now that I have told you, George! God has led me here to give me one consolation before I die. It was not my fault! I struggled long! No letters came from you, and in a weak hour I yielded! Let me go—I am happy now, and can die more peacefully! Good-by!"

As she spoke thus, sobbing and shedding floods of tears, she withdrew herself from me and turned to go. But the agitation of the meeting in her prostrated condition was too much for her, and her weak steps wandered. She would have fallen upon the pavement, had I not received her form in my arms. This time she had fainted.

I forced open the door of the house there at the corner, and laid the cold form upon a couch, in the midst of a startled group assembled around the evening fire. A few words, however, explained all; and very soon Annie revived, and was assisted to a chamber by the kind and compassionate ladies of the house.

In that chamber she died. With her last breath she explained all, and begged my forgiveness. The diabolical plot, concocted by the woman Peters and Lackland, was revealed in all its hideous deformity. They had endeavored at first to tempt the girl by rich presents and by representation of my poverty. Then, finding this unavailing, they stated that I was married to another. Finding that the girl did not believe this, a letter was forged, announcing my death. This was so adroitly done, that Annie had been convinced. That I was unfaithful, she never would believe ; but she was forced to give credence to the story that I had fallen a victim to the fevers of the tropics. When she was still prostrated by this intelligence, Mrs. Peters, to whose house she had gone on the death of her mother, commenced a systematic attack upon her. She resisted for a whole year ; and then, worn out, despairing, more dead than alive, went like a phantom to the altar and yielded herself up. Mrs. Peters was rewarded for her exertions, and the girl was the wife of Lackland.

He possessed a body—the heart and soul were paralyzed or dead. They gave her splendid dresses—she received them passively. They endeavored to cheer her spirits— she gazed blankly at them, with eyes fixed far away, as on that evening when she had passed me in her carriage —a phantom covered with satin and jewels.

Then had come the failure of the elder Lackland—the intemperance of her husband—the ruin of the family. Since that time she had been carried from city to city by her drunken and tyrannical husband—abused, ill-treated, struck more than once; and then, this man had been killed in a drunken brawl, leaving her worn down by ill usage and sickness, with an infant at her breast.

She had struggled against her misery for a little space —then had come to understand that the seeds of death were in her frame ; and she had bent her steps toward the scene of her brief happiness and after misery, to lie down and die upon the threshold of her early home, or on the grave of her mother.   She had reached the place without money, and exhausted by her journey, during which the exposure had aggravated her complaint, and, for the first time, had begged assistance from a stranger.

That stranger was myself.

You know now, from this brief relation, the whole current of this woful life, in which a poor girl was betrayed and brought to the grave, by a base and inhuman woman, swayed only by avarice, and a coward, who was guilty of forgery to effect his purpose.   She told me everything in those last moments, when all was again clear between us—when no cloud obscured the past—when, faint and pale, like a white flower of autumn, she slowly faded and went from me.

It was the thin, white hand of my Annie which I held now in my own, and covered with tears and kisses, praying, as I did so, with agonized supplications, that God in His mercy would preserve her life, and bless me with the privilege of consoling and comforting one whom I loved still, as no woman ever was loved.

But it was unavailing.   She slowly sank—the gentle, gradual undulation of her slender form became fainter—with her hand in mine, and her dreamy eyes fixed to the last upon my own, she went away from me ; having to console her the conviction that my love was greater even than before, and that I would be a father to her child.

And past that corner, where I had first met her, young, smiling, with the light upon her hair—past that corner she now went again, with nodding plumes; but, oh! such sable plumes, which waved mysteriously toward another land! There, I pray God, that I may join her; that we once more be united—forever united, where the light upon her hair is the light of heaven. There, the two hearts, so cruelly severed upon earth, will never again be separated, and hand in hand we shall live and love eternally—for God is love.

# CHAPTER IX.

### CONCLUSION.

MY story is done, good friend. I have related it calmly—with no sobs, no tears, as you see.

Why should I? I do not look back shuddering and moaning; because, from that dim region, a figure rises stretching toward me the softest and tenderest hands, smiling upon me with the kindest and most loving eyes— consoling, and soothing, and whispering to me of fairer scenes in another existence.

I think I am happy. You consider me sad sometimes, when I am only tranquil. The dim look in my eyes, which you often refer to with the solicitude of a friend, does not spring from sorrowful recollections—for I am thinking of Annie. All the grief and passion has disappeared—tranquillity and kindness remain. I enjoy many things—I do not keep away from my species. Dives invites me to dinner, and I go; and when Mrs. Grundy sends me word that a few friends will assemble at her residence on Thursday next, I put on a white waistcoat, and go up and fulfil my social duty, by talking to all the elderly ladies, and exchanging views with Mrs. Grundy upon the events and personages of the day, upon which occasions I generally hear a good deal to amuse me. As a contrast to this "high life," I entertain myself, as you know, with Lazarus, who is certainly a low fellow, I must admit; but he interests me. I have told you that I sometimes call at Miss Tabitha's, who certainly is an extraordinary likeness of a former friend of mine, long since dead—Mrs. Peters.

As I retire, after one of these little evenings at Miss Tabitha's, I am apt to murmur to myself, "forgive us our trespasses, as we forgive those who trespass against us."

To prove to you that I am not the sad, miserable old misanthrope and disappointed individual the world may think me—to show you that I am still pleased with the simplest things—I will add that even the sight of my little school-friend, the one with the blue dress, who passes my window every morning, touches and pleases me.

Her name is Annie Lackland.

The child lives with the family at the corner yonder; and when I make a friendly call upon these excellent people, she calls me "Uncle George." I have a fine young relative, about eighteen, who is studying for the bar, and the rogue has already fallen desperately in love with the little maiden of fifteen. Well—the match will not be imprudent, as my whole property will go at my death to the young people.

What a fine evening it is! My story has filled the afternoon, and the golden crowns are slowly rising from the summits of the elms, which glitter in the sunset. The little mansion basks in the warm light—and look at

that pigeon which has lit upon the portico, embowered
in the fragrant honey-suckle !

The street is filling with the merriest children—they
dance, and laugh and play in front of the old house,
which smiles upon them—the fountain in the square is
tossing up a cloud of cooling foam—and look! down
there ! do you see ?   There is Annie at the corner !

# THE WEDDING AT DULUTH.

I HAVE been at "Duluth" for a month, now, watching the movements of a little feminine humming-bird. Her name is Fanny. She has been the pet of her old bachelor cousin ever since she tottered about, and said "tuzzen" when she addressed me; and the very first person who ran to meet me when I walked up from the old wharf on the river through the elm-skirted avenue to "Duluth," was my young humming-bird, now seventeen. She hastened on before everybody in the beautiful summer evening, and when the family had greeted me, took quiet possession of me; drawing a cricket to my side on the old shaded portico, and leaning her head with its bright auburn curls against my shoulder, intent, she declared, upon "a good talk." She was really fascinating at that moment, with the crimson of sunset lighting up her red cheeks, and lips all smiles; and Duluth and all was bright with home and welcome.

273

I soon found that Fanny was, or appeared to be, amusing herself with two young friends of hers of the opposite sex; and I have varied my tranquil perusal of Montaigne and other favorites, on an old " rustic seat " in the shade of an ash on the lawn, by musing upon the little comedy I see playing before me. I like such diversions for I am a little—a very little—alone in the world. I am not unhappy ; for if life is not all roses, smiles, and sunshine, neither is it all gloom and vanity and vexation of spirit in my eyes. I keep my sympathies too fresh for that, and take too much interest in the happiness of those I love.

I am putting down my notes from day to day. Fanny has negatived the Montaigne and rustic-seat programme almost completely. What a little witch she is ! She is certainly a beauty, and constantly suggests a resemblance to a rosebud. Her cheeks are red, her lips are red—the very little ears, peeping out from her ringlets, are rosy. She has very large blue eyes, bright at one moment and then as soft as velvet. And she is all the time laughing, teasing people, and running about like a child. *Mem.* her feet are small, clad in morocco slippers, with large pink rosettes, and secured by black bands crossed over the instep. Her name is not Fanny Warren, and she is not the daughter of my good Cousin Henry Warren, proprietor of "Duluth." She is Fanny Kincade, a connection, and is on a long visit.

Fanny came out to my seat this morning, and evidently designed conversation. So I closed my book, smiled, made room for her, and said :

"Well, my child, what have you done with Mr. Middleton?"

Mr. Thomas Middleton being an elegant young gentleman from the city of B——, who has now been two or three weeks at "Duluth" endeavoring to capture our little bird, whom he met in town during the winter.

Fanny's reply to my question was vivacious, but not to the point.

"You are just the same ridiculous, absurd, darling old thing that you always were," said the maiden, "and I do believe you are growing *bald!*"

"What in the world has that to do with—— "

"You are growing old and smart!" exclaimed Fanny. "All bald people are smart. But, oh! how glad I am to see you! Now, give me an account of yourself, you dear old cousin—tell me everything; tell me—— "

"No, I thank you, madam," I responded, "I prefer hearing first all about yourself. But, no; you are growing up, and will not confide in me as you did once."

"Growing up? I am not growing up for you! I never will. What shall I confide?"

"Your love affairs, of course."

Fanny shook her head.

"I haven't any love affairs, cousin. It's terrible, but I haven't!"

I shook my head in turn.

"That is impossible, Fanny. Have I no eyes? I have been at Duluth long enough to see that Mr. Tom Middleton and my favorite Harry Warren are crazy about you."

At the name of Harry Warren Fanny blushed a little, but immediately replied with a laugh :

"How absurd for me to think of Harry as—in that way ! Why, he's my brother."

"He is no relation to you—or very distant."

"Well, near or far, relation or not, Harry cares nothing for me, and I care not for him. I never lay eyes on him—he's down at that horrid old sawmill all day long—and so let us talk about something else, cousin !"

"Willingly; but we are not to have the opportunity. Here comes Mr. Middleton."

I did not take notice whether Fanny was pleased or otherwise with the interruption; I was absorbed in contemplation of the approaching visitor. Mr. Tom Middleton was a handsome young gentleman, though his face might have been considered a little effeminate. This fact, however, did not assort ill with the rest of his appearance. He was a most elegant youth. His hands were white and soft, his feet were small and cased in the tightest and most delicate French boots; he held a kid glove in one hand, and dangled a light whalebone cane in the other ; his necktie was a wonder, his hair was curled —he was an Adonis half-natural, half-fashioned by the best city tailor.

The young gentleman's countenance was illumined by a gentle smile as he approached. He fixed his eyes with modest ardor upon Fanny ; and with a polite bow, inquired in reference to my health this morning.

I looked at Fanny. She was blushing a little, as when I uttered the name of Harry Warren. Which was it ?

II.

I do not know which it is. When I ask Fanny she simply responds that I am the most ridiculous and absurd of all the old cousins that ever existed, and that it is neither.

This, I am convinced, is a fib; and, with all her fine and excellent traits, Miss Fanny is not above this reprehensible and immoral method of defending herself. Indeed, I begin to think my little pet is developing an immense genius for flirting. She has a way of looking over her shoulder while she is singing at the piano, and directing the most languishing glances at tender portions of the song toward her admirer, Mr. Middleton, as he leans in a graceful attitude upon the instrument beside her; and, last night, I saw the young witch standing on the portico in the moonlight, gazing down, pulling a rose apart leaf by leaf, and listening with an air of modest confusion to Mr. Tom Middleton.

When the maiden was about to dart off to bed, I stopped her for a moment in the passage, and drew her aside.

"Did he—propose?" I whispered.

Fanny placed her lips close to my ear—pursed up her mouth—whispered "No——o—o!" and bursting into a ringing laugh, ran off to bed. I imitated her, except that I did not run, and shaking my head, found myself muttering:

"Woman, woman!—and girls especially—who can understand you! Not I!"

### III.

I begin to fancy that I have the clue to Fanny's
"views and intentions." I think she has made up her
mind to become Mrs. —— Tom Middleton.

Before narrating the events of this evening, however—
which events have brought me to the conclusion in question—I will first say that Fanny has, in the most shame-
less manner, acknowledged that she told me a flat fib in
reference to the scene upon the moonlit portico. She
made her confession in the most penitent way; declared
that she was ashamed of herself : but she had forgotten,
she said, that it was her dear, ridiculous old cousin who
asked the question ; she never had concealed anything
from me—and—yes—Mr. Middleton *had* been good
enough to express his sentiments—and—she believed he
*had* asked her—if she would not——

There the young lady began to blush ; then she
burst out laughing, and leaning her head upon my
shoulder, looked up at me with her roguish, wicked eyes,
and said in a whisper:

"I said——'No !'"

"It was not 'no' that you said," I replied, "I observed the young gentleman when he came in ; he was
sad, but not hopeless ; and this morning at breakfast he
ate, as usual, the whole wing of a bird !"

"I do declare you are *too* bad !" was Miss Fanny's
vivacious rejoinder ; "you are always laughing at Mr.
Middleton, and making fun of him ; and I do believe—
yes ! I do—that you are trying to make me prefer—somebody else !"

"Harry? Well, I should."

"And I do not."

"You do not like his big hands perhaps; and he has no cane or kid gloves."

"Absurd! But Mr. Middleton *is* the most agreeable—you know he is."

"And therefore you said *No!* It was not that abrupt monosyllable that you uttered, my dear—was it now?"

"Well—that is ——" said Miss Fanny dubiously. "Well—I did not mean that I used the *exact word*. Perhaps —— "

I began to laugh in so satirical a way that Fanny boxed me, then kissed me to make amends, and then asked me if I would not like to accompany her and everybody to the sawmill—the dam was nearly washed away, and they were working very hard to save it.

I at once put on my hat. Harry, I knew, would be foremost among the workmen; there was positive danger, I well knew; and as the youth was a great favorite with me, I hastened with my Cousin Warren, Mr. Middleton, and Fanny toward the scene.

This sawmill has been, since the war, my cousin's main resource. His estate is large, and once enabled him to live in the greatest comfort and even in luxury; but with the high prices of labor now, and the successive failure of the crops for some years, it would have been difficult, without the sawmill, to "make both ends meet" at Duluth. It was formerly used only as a convenience on the estate; but of late, when the demand for lumber has been active and the price high, it has been looked to as a source of profit, and, indeed, as I have said, has proved the main pecuniary resource of the family. It has been managed entirely by Harry, who is just twenty-one, and I don't think I have ever known a finer fellow. He is tall, stalwart, with short, shaggy chestnut hair, frank hazel eyes, full of honesty and determination too, and is silent, hardworking, and earnest. The most marked trait in Harry is a cool independence. He enters a room with a firm, composed, and stalwart tread, looks everybody straight in the eyes, smiles slightly, sits down and opens a book, and all with an air which I like extremely; the air of a man who works hard, has come in to rest, has nothing on his conscience, is pleased in a quiet way with everything—and would like to have his supper and go to bed! Sometimes I see Harry looking out from beneath the wide straw hat which covers his shaggy chestnut curls and sunburned forehead at Fanny. But you read little in his glance. I know him to be in love with her, but he has never spoken a word of love to her, I am very sure.

A short walk brought us to the sawmill, and the scene which met our view was worth the walk.

## IV.

All the preceding day and throughout the night a torrent of rain had fallen, and a small stream, which was dammed up by a rude dyke, and so furnished water-power to turn the mill-wheel, was rushing on in the wildest and most furious manner that can be imagined.

When we approached the spot where half a dozen of

the hired hands were working with Harry to save the dam, the stream was roaring in a hoarse and most threatening style. Instead of decreasing, the freshet seemed gathering greater strength with every passing moment. The surges lashed the fabric at the dam, which shook and seemed about to give way. At one point now, and then at another a part was torn away; the waters gushed through the gap, tearing it wider and deeper, and it required the utmost exertions of the men, laboring with pick and axe, up to their waists in the water, to hold the torrent at bay and save the dam.

Harry was "in command" of the squad, and you could easily see that it was his natural place, and that the rough workmen looked to him as the natural master. His costume was not of the drawing-room description. He was up to his middle in the water, axe in hand, and had on neither coat, waistcoat, nor hat. His arms were naked to the shoulder, and the water had been dashed over him until his face and hair were drenched. Tall, muscular, cool, directing everything, and filling up every breach in the dam as rapidly as it was made, Harry was the genius of the scene and the master of all around him—to the very water, it seemed.

Twice he was swept from his feet and disappeared beneath the current; once a timber struck him, and the lookers on uttered a terrified scream. An hour passed in this conflict, and then the dam was saved. The water had begun to fall, and the young man came out and walked up the bank to the spot where everybody was standing. I glanced from the wet and dirty youth to the elegant Tom Middleton. The contrast was certainly striking. Harry was a brawny athlete, sunburned, with shaggy locks, coatless, bare armed, his pantaloons and boots full of water. Mr. Middleton was irreproachably dressed; his boots shone, his shirt-bosom sparkled with a diamond, he wore kid gloves, and his hat was smooth and glossy. Harry came up, and as I was nearest, said:

"Well, cousin, the dam is all right."

He then looked about for his hat and coat, put them on, and informing us that he was going to get some dry clothes as he was wet, walked toward the house—a tall young giant, moving with a long swinging stride.

Fanny had not said a word to him. Did he notice that fact or look at his rival Mr. Middleton? I do not know. But something has followed this scene; and this I am about to relate.

Fanny and Mr. Middleton walked out upon the lawn in the beautiful moonlight after tea, and the rest of the family sat on the porch conversing.

"I am going to Colorado," said Harry, who was smoking.

"To Colorado!" I exclaimed.

"Yes, cousin. I have a position upon a new railroad offered me, and I think I shall accept it; in fact, I have made up my mind."

This was said coolly, but there was the least perceptible alteration in the youth's voice.

"The truth is, I'm rusting here doing nothing. I have no career, and can not help anybody. I shall be well paid on the railroad, and can send home plenty of money, and live the life I like besides."

A step was heard on the grass, and I saw the white dress of Fanny in the moonlight. I looked at her and saw that she was blushing—as to Mr. Middleton, he looked the picture of happiness.

"I don't believe a word of it," exclaimed Fanny, with a little tremor in her voice. "The idea of your going to Colorado! I should like to know what you would do in Colorado?"

"I should be transit man on a railroad," said Harry with extreme composure.

Fanny tried to laugh, but did not succeed.

"You know nothing in the world about railroads."

"That is true," returned Harry with his immovable coolness; "but I have no doubt I shall soon learn."

"And—and—you really do think of going so far from —us all—and by yourself."

This time Fanny was certainly moved. The small hand resting confidingly upon Mr. Middleton's arm was agitated by a nervous tremor. The strangest smile came to Harry's face—a rather bitter smile—but his voice was perfectly composed when he spoke.

"I ought to be able to go by myself and take care of myself; and intend to travel alone, unless I can get Mr. Middleton to go with me."

The elegant Tom Middleton smiled in a gay manner, and said:

"No, I thank you! I'm not in the engineering line. I think I prefer Duluth to Colorado."

"You are right," said Harry quietly, "it is a much more agreeable place, I have no doubt, to those who like it."

With which words he rose, said he was tired, and went to his chamber, whither his mother followed him.

V.

Fanny and Mr. Middleton had taken their seats at the other end of the portico. My Cousin Warren had followed Mrs. Warren to Harry's room. I found myself *de trop* and retired within also. When, an hour afterwards, the bell rang for family prayer, Fanny and Mr. Middleton came into the drawing-room, and a glance at his face convinced me more than ever that he had "made his arrangements" with Fanny, and induced her to promise him her hand. She was blushing and avoided my eye. When she retired she did not look at me. Mr. Middleton was what the novel writers call "radiant."

This result of things has profoundly depressed me. Who would have believed it! So my little humming-bird has flitted by the tall, stalwart sapling Harry, to light upon the Middleton flower! Poor, poor Harry! I know that he loves her, and he is going with the conviction that she is to marry his rival! Human life is a sad, a very sad affair. Poor Harry!

VI.

I don't think human life is such a sad affair after all, and when I next assume the tone of the author of the book of Ecclesiastes, I shall think my secretions deranged.

The last lines written in this record of my days at Duluth referred to scenes which took place one month ago. On the morning after the announcement by Harry

Warren of his intention to go to Colorado, I heard Fanny say to him in a low voice as she passed him upon the stairs, "I want to see you—come out after breakfast to the rustic seat;" and after breakfast duly the young people were observed side by side, by the present historian, on his own favorite seat, of which he was thus deprived.

I state frankly that I availed myself of my position in the drawing-room, where I was reading behind one of the lace curtains, to look at the pair, and to try and discover the nature of their interview. This, I regret to say, I found impossible. My eyes begin to suffer from age, and the spectacles now made strike me as wretchedly inferior. In an hour Fanny and Harry rose, and the expression of his face was certainly more agitated than I had ever seen it before. As to Fanny she was blushing deeply, and was unmistakably pouting, as though something had occurred which was far from being to her taste.

When I tried to intercept her as she came in—Harry having left her at the portico to go and attend to some of his farm avocations—she slipped by me, would not hear my voice, and disappeared in her chamber, the door of which she closed with a bang. I forgot to say that during the interview upon the rustic seat, Mr. Middleton had been seated at the piano, upon which he was a really excellent performer, and amused himself playing a bar here and there from one of Fanny's operas. He smiled, I observed, in a confidential manner to himself, and seemed to have no uneasiness on the subject of the interview between Fanny and Harry. Had not his rival declared that he was going away—and ——

Fanny has just run in and thrown her arms around my neck, and burst into tears, and laughed, and cried again, and then laughed again—and departed.

Was there ever such a little witch? And she thought I knew nothing about it! I knew all about it. I listened, I eavesdropped, I acted on the sly, and behaved generally in a most dishonorable and highly improper manner. It was last night that I was guilty of the proceeding here denounced, and as after all I am not so much ashamed of it, I shall tell how it happened.

Harry had made every preparation to go to Colorado to-day, and we were all in a very gloomy state of mind about it—Fanny, I think, the gloomiest of all. She would tell me nothing; had lost all her confidence, and remained so much of her time in her chamber that it was almost discourtesy to Mr. Middleton.

Last night occurred the *dénoûment*. It was about ten, and I woke from a prolonged nap on my old rustic seat to hear voices near me.

"You must not go," said the voice of Fanny trembling.

"I must."

This voice was Harry's.

"It is perfectly absurd—you are going away—you say because, because——"

" Because I love you," came in deep, strong tones, and love you so much that I would rather die than stay here and see you marry another person."

"I have no intention—to do so."

The voice fluttered.

"Fanny !"

This time it was Harry Warren's voice that trembled.

"What made you take such a foolish fancy ?"—there was a little quiet attempt at a laugh here—"I'll die an old maid before I'll marry the person you mean! And oh, Harry! Harry! what a goose I must be, and a foolish little flirt, to have everybody, yes everybody, even my dear old cousin (that was me) think me so deceitful! I only told Mr. Middleton—or, rather did *not* tell him—that—I wouldn't!"

I chuckled quietly. These two negatives charmed me!

Fanny's voice had sunk to a bashful murmur; then it died away.

"My dear, dear Fanny!"—I never heard a man's voice express such tenderness—"you have made me very happy! Make me happier still. Tell me not to go to Colorado!"

They had moved away, and I saw nothing, and heard no more. Yes I did. I heard a kiss, and a sob, which appeared to be suppressed in some measure, from the fact that the young lady's face was leaning upon Harry's breast.

There is no doubt of the result of the interview. Fanny has just announced with blushes, laughter, and tears, as I have described, that she is engaged to Harry; and as she has no relative but an old aunt, who is devoted to her, the marriage may be regarded as already a *fait accompli*.

It has taken place. Mr. Tom Middleton was not present, having departed from "Duluth" long since, with irate general observations on the character of "flirts." I think he did Fanny injustice. She only looked fascinating, and "didn't tell him that she wouldn't!"

The wedding at Duluth was a charming affair, and Fanny looked exquisite leaning upon the arm of her handsome and stalwart Harry, who is not going to Colorado. He will do better—that is to say, take the management of the old Kincade estate, which is going to rack and ruin, and transform it by his energy and brain into a home of wealth and comfort for Fanny.

I never saw my little humming-bird look prettier than when she stood by Harry, blushing and smiling under her white bridal veil and wreath. This morning they left us on their little tour, and I felt the arms of Fanny around my neck with a pang at my heart. The very sunshine seemed to go away with her.